MW00945717

To Grace,
Brave the

STORM!

A SALT NOVEL

DANIELLE ELLISON

Entangled Publishing, LLC
2614 South Timberline Road
Suite 109
Fort Collins, CO 80525
Visit our website at www.entangledpublishing.com.

Ember is an imprint of Entangled Publishing, LLC.

Edited by Stacy Cantor Abrams and Alycia Tornetta
Cover design by Jenny Adams Perinovic

Ebook ISBN 978-1-63375-073-9
Print ISBN 978-1-50231-467-3

Manufactured in the United States of America

First Edition September 2014

For Traci Inzitari, who has a magical soul and a selfless heart.

Chapter One

Three days ago I went to hell.

Well, not technically hell. I went to De'Intero, the place between hell and earth that looked more like it was from a low-budget B-rated film. Yesterday, I took my public vows to be an Enforcer, along with my boyfriend and my best friend. Today, Ric, Carter, and I are card-carrying members of the C.E.A.S.E Squad, trained witches who serve and protect non-magical humans from demon attacks. Well, they're not really cards so much as gold triangle badges. Even though a card would be cool. Like a modern-day realistic Ghostbuster. "Who you gonna call?" Penelope Grey, Enforcer.

Today's a new day. First day as an official Enforcer. And how am I spending it? Running.

And the demon chasing me hates it. That's part of why I enjoy it so much.

I scan the area as I move, looking for the easiest way to maneuver it away from the crowds. It's busy in Clarendon today—Sunday brunch will do that—so I've got to get the little devil away from everything with a pulse. Except me. I glance over my shoulder to make sure the bugger is following me. It is, its eyes flashing demon-green in the Non body it's possessed. I still hate when demons take over Non forms.

Sweat drips down my arms. It's freaking hot out here—the summer is atrocious. I pick up speed, leading it away from the street and toward a park off the main road. But even from far away I can see how packed it is. There isn't a lot of cover out here and none of the Nons can see me. The park won't work. I change direction toward a dead-end street. Beggers can't be choosy.

I mutter the barrier spells as I run, and smile to myself as I feel the magic pour out of me. I adore this feeling, the energy as the magic channels from me and out into the world. I spent most of my life not having magic on my own unless I was near someone in my family or, more recently, had Carter to pull it from. But that was before my little soiree in De'Intero. Now, I'm a freaking genie. I see it, say it, wish it, and sometimes even feel it, and *boom*—magic. It's pretty freaking cool.

Freezing in the center of the street, the demon jerks to a halt feet from me. Its beady green eyes focus on me, shifting between brown and green in the Non skin. Brown eyes mean the Non is still alive in there.

"Witch," the demon hisses. "Have you given up so

easily?"

I shrug. The power practically oozes from my fingertips. At least, in my head it does. "I thought that you might reconsider your stance on trying to kill me."

"Why would I do that? I know who you are."

I try not to cock my jaw in annoyance. Three days ago I was nothing more than a normal witch (mostly), and now they've all heard about me. The girl who made the demons disappear. I was in De'Interno, about to die during a demonic Fight Club face-off, when Carter kissed me, and *bam*—hundreds of demons gone.

"Then you should be even more interested in reconsidering, since I'm a badass." But it won't. Not now that it has found me. I motion my fingers in the air. "Go ahead, then. Wow me with your witty, insulting last words so they may remain with me forever."

The demon laughs, that familiar white noise sound, and licks its lips. "You really do smell like they all say."

It hisses and charges toward me. Before, I'd run or I'd fight. I can fight—really well, I might add—but thanks to my new Hulk-like magic, I don't have to do anything like that anymore. I get to use magic. I flick my wrist, and the demon freezes in the air, the sound of it gasping for breath fills the space.

I *tsk* and cross my arms. "And here, I thought you'd be more original."

I let the images fill up my brain of the demon exploding, but then I remember the Non. I need to save him if I can. I alter the picture so the demon is forced out of the Non's body. The Non rests on the ground while the demon explodes. I picture the Non recovering, breathing, living another day. I really don't know what I can do yet with the void, not really, but if my increased power means more Nons are spared, I'll take it.

I open my eyes and push the images out. "*Virtute angeli ad infernum unde venistis*," I whisper, even though I don't need to do that any more, either. It makes it feel more like I'm in control of what happens.

The magic from the void tingles through my toes and every cell in body before it shoots out of me toward the demon. I inhale sharply. I'm still not used to that feeling. With the essence, normally, we pull the magic from the elements and manipulate it to our will. It never actually becomes part of a witch. But this, the void, the source of magic for demons, seems to claim every piece of my body from within before it rushes out.

The screams from the demon piece the air, and then everything I saw in my head is happening to the demon. The Non falls to the ground as the demon shudders back into its original form, scaly with light gray and red eyes. Another snarl slips from its lips and it looks pretty angry with me right before it explodes into demon bits.

The magic from the void flows back into me and I stumble. If there's one thing I've learned in the last few days: the void is relentless. Whatever it wants, wherever it comes from—within me or outside of me—is more powerful than I ever seem to expect. The magic seems to settle into me, sort of like my stomach feels after eating too much pie.

"Penelope," Carter yells, running up toward me out of breath. He looks around me, eyes switching between the demon goo and the Non on the ground. "I was waiting."

I was supposed to meet him at the edge of the park. "I

had to choose an alternative course of action," I say as I pull out my phone and dial 911 for the Non. "I couldn't go to the park. Too many people."

Carter looks toward the Non on the ground as the emergency responder on the other end of the line asks me questions, and I give her only an address before I hang up. Carter starts walking away from the Non and I follow. As much as it sucks, we can't stay to see if he survives. We can't risk being questioned by Nons.

"I don't like you using the void on your own."

I sigh. Carter doesn't approve, but it's magic. Magic that I can control. "I didn't have a choice."

"You could've come to me like you were supposed to."

I have magic. How can I not use it? "There were Nons around."

"The whole area was under a cloaking spell."

"It's fine," I snap.

"It's not fine, Pen. You don't know anything about that magic. Until we can get some sort of information, I don't think you should use it," Carter says as we walk back toward the park across the street. I bite my lip. He's concerned about this sudden magical ability and what happened when we made the demons disappear in De'Intero. I am, too. I got magic right after we did that. Part of me should wonder too, that I should be cautious, but I also have magic—and that's the only thing I've ever wanted. I have to use it. That's the part he doesn't understand. Finally, for the first time, I matter on my own.

"Do you not want me to have magic at all?" I ask. The sound of sirens fills the distance, and I scan the streets to try to find them. Eight minutes to arrive. Not bad, medics.

He pulls my face back to make me look at him. And it's pretty easy to stay focused on his green eyes and dark hair and the little bit of scruff that's starting to grow along his jawline. "That's not what this is. I support you."

The first time I met Carter I had no idea he'd become so connected, so important to me. It's because of him, and the magic he'd ignited, that I even became an Enforcer. Before, I had no magic on my own. Then, we met and the magic I thought I'd lost bubbled in my stomach and freaked out when we were together. Somehow he made me have my own magic. It wasn't until we learned it was because we were both half-demons, and that he had something I didn't. I'd lost my essence to a demon, and he had both the essence and the void. His void, since he didn't need it, filled my empty spaces so I had magic. It's all very poetic, really.

But ever since we were downstairs, the magic is always on alert inside me. Even at his touch it remains this steady unsettling stream, like somehow, it doesn't need him to respond to me. Like maybe the magic really is mine, and not borrowed from him. I can't pretend it's not a dream come true.

"I don't want you to get hurt," he says, wrapping his arms around my waist. My body folds in closer to his. Layers of clothing separate us, but through them I can feel the heat of his body against mine, all tingles and light. My stomach jumbles with the familiar sensation of being close to him, and he presses his lips against the curve of my neck. "We can't risk anyone finding out anything about De'Interno or us."

"They won't," I respond, forcing myself to speak under the strain of my voice.

Whether I turn to him or he turns to me doesn't matter.

It doesn't even matter that we're in public, or that we've killed a demon, saved a Non, or that everything is at stake. We have each other.

In a heartbeat, his lips are on mine. My body is on fire as warmth seeps through our clothes. As hands trail on my back, on my neck, on my hips—on anywhere he can touch me. My hand trails up his shirt and come to rest on his chest. Me connected to him, and him to me, the way our bodies sing together, it's like we're one. He pulls me tighter against him, and chills trickle down my body. There's never enough of kissing this boy.

His mouth trails away from mine, and his hot breath is on my ear. "Please be careful," he whispers, sending another chill over me.

I smile and press a soft kiss to his lips. "I'm always careful."

He laughs against my skin, so close that the rumble of him trembles through me. I move to allow some space between us.

"What?" I ask.

Carter shakes his head. "It's cute that you think that."

I push him away, and he grabs my waist to keep me there. As if I was really going anywhere. "Shut up. I'm practically Scruff McGruff."

He wrinkles his nose, and it's adorable. "The crime prevention cartoon dog?"

"Exactly." I smile, and he gets this mischievous look in his eyes, the one that says he's ready for another kiss. I lean in as my phone beeps. Ric and Maple found a demon's nest. "Back to work."

Chapter Two

CARTER

Penelope may be resourceful, but I'm William Carter Prescott. I've spent my life working to understand one thing: demons. I grew up knowing I was a halfling and hanging around demons in hope of finding my demon-mom. Every time I looked for her, I told myself I wouldn't find her, that she was really dead, and at some point I started to believe it. Then, she showed up as one of the leaders. It's been a lot to process over the last few days.

The point is, I haven't spent that much time searching, hunting, and killing without learning a thing or two about demons.

"This is it?" Pen asks.

I look around the abandoned buildings, just outside the

borders of town. "No doubt."

Fact one: demons like abandoned buildings. The Nons that tend to hang out in those parts of town are usually strung out or have nothing to lose. Easy prey. Which also means easy to find, if you know where to look. It's no surprise that Maple and Ric stumbled onto this spot, and a whole nest of demons during patrol.

Nothing gets me energized like a demon nest. Already I can feel the itch in my hand.

Fact two: demon nests are rare. Or they used to be. Demons, until recently, never hung out in pairs. They were solo artists, which made them easier to kill but harder to track. Now, they're leaving trails all over the place, getting sloppy.

Fact three: when demons are in a group, then they're probably planning something huge.

"What's wrong? Are you still upset about earlier?" Pen whispers.

I look at her face, eyes open and round and cheeks flushed. I'm still upset about earlier, yes, because it's not smart to use the void when we don't know even the basics about it. But she's not going to like hearing that. Mostly because Penelope is predictable in her unpredictability. I can count on her to act now and ask later, which is why I can be upset about the magic all I want and it won't do anything. Not until she's ready.

The stubbornness is part of why I love her. Usually.

"We can talk about it later," I say.

She starts to protest, but Ric gives the signal across the street. I motion to Pen, and she nods. The element of surprise is on our side right now. Demons are pretty stupid when they're comfortable. They get sloppy, miss the signs that we're on their trail, and never seem to be ready to fight. But when they're smart they're strong, cunning, and unpredictable, if not a little too prideful.

Maple moves around the building, setting up the cloaking spell so no one can stumble on the mess that's about to happen. The strong smell of sulfur blows my way in the summer breeze, and I'm ready. As much as I enjoy being an Enforcer, protecting the Nons and all that, the reason I do this is for the demons. I want to rid this world of every single one of them.

They turned my mom. They led her astray. They nearly killed Pen and me. They're the reason halflings have to live in hiding, that I have to pretend that William Carter Prescott is happy serving as a Triad, smiling. It's what I do, what I have to do in order to survive as a halfling, to stay a secret, and that's all because of demons.

It's only fair that I return the favor by ending as many as I can.

Once the protection spell is up, Maple nods. Pen touches my shoulder. "Ready?" she asks.

"I was born ready."

We watch as Ric and Maple race into the building, salt guns armed and pointing. My finger twitches against the hilt of my knives, and I check the holster of my gun to make sure it's there. The battle between demons and witches is simple—destroy them before they destroy us.

Even if the Triad is more focused on maintaining harmony and defense instead of offense, the truth of our survival is to kill or be killed. I choose to kill. Why should they be the ones making the first move, when we witches are more than capable?

Pen jumps up before I'm ready and runs toward the building. I clear my mind of all thoughts and chase after her.

Demons are on us as soon as we enter. Ric and Maple must have tipped off our arrival, and normally, it'd bug me that we lost the element of surprise. Pen is ahead of me, taking on two of her own demons, Maple next to her. I knock a mustard-colored demon to the ground. Another one jumps on my back. I'd take them down faster, but I'm in the mood to at least pretend like it's a challenge.

The demon tries to knock me to the ground and scratches its talons into my neck, but I have the advantage. I throw myself backward into the wall and the demon hisses against the brick. I step away and then pound myself back into the wall. Each time I do it, the demon makes a sound and it brings me some satisfaction. After a few more hits against the wall, the demon seems to be dead weight, so I yank the knife from my pocket, thrust it into the demon and mutter the incantation. The demon explodes into goo. I wipe away some of its guts from my hair. *Job well done.*

The mustard demon is back on its feet, and it charges at me like a bull. I kick it in the stomach, and mutter an incantation that sends it flying across the room. That can't be all the fight this thing has. Ric yells my name from somewhere deeper in the building, so I toss a handful of salt on the demon and send him back to hell before running toward Ric's voice.

The sound of chaos lingers through the hall. A girl screams, and I burst through an open door, hoping that it's not Penelope. I'm on the ground as soon as the door opens, demon snarling in my face. I push it away from me as its claws find my arms. Drool drips on my face. The demon's green eyes are bright against its black scales, and the blackness reminds me of Kriegen. My mom. Her demon form was black like that. Black like her soul, apparently. The way she planned to turn me and Pen into demons, like her. She wanted to kill Penelope, to rip the magic from her soul with an ancient black dagger. She didn't even care about me except for how she could use me.

Pushing the demon away, I manage to flip it off me. It only lands a few inches away, but that's all I need. I get to my gun before the demon is back to its feet, and I release a salt pellet into its heart. The demon screams, and I yell the incantation before it explodes.

It takes a second for the surrounds to settle while I catch my breath. My eyes search the room for Pen. I see Ric first—he's in front of me, taking on three demons at once. Maple's in the other corner of the room tossing salt on another demon. A demon screams a high-pitched cry, and I jerk around at the sound. Pen's to my left in the back of the room, standing on a table. Below her, three demons are on their knees, and a forth is a lump on the ground.

I can't look away from her.

The way she stands there and they sit in submission around her. Pen seems to be staring at them, waiting. I take a step toward her, but then they all explode in unison. Her lips didn't even move. She's using the void again. She's glad she has it, but each time she uses it I feel like she's risking herself. Risking us. Risking me.

Her eyes catch mine from across the room, and her smile fades. Yes, I am pissed. And I'm worried. I'm feeling more than I can figure out how to explain because of this demon magic.

I can't believe she's doing this right now with Ric and Maple around. Ric knows about De'Intero and that she's a halfling, but no one has any clue about the void except the two of us. Even if Ric is her best friend, there are some things that are too dangerous to share. Her having the void is one of them. It's reckless — and I'm all for her being brave, but there's a difference between courage and stupidity.

God, I sound like my dad.

She's next to me in a second, blond hair falling out of its ponytail. "I'm going to give Ric a hand."

I grab her arm. "Say the words out loud, Pen. *Out loud.*"

She responds with a slight nod, then she's on the other side of the room. I run off to help Maple, who's suddenly surrounded by more demons. A demon kicks her from behind, her gun slides across the room and she turns her back on the crowd of demons to take down her attacker. Where are they all coming from? I charge at them from behind and shoot the salt gun on their backs. Two fall down before the others realize I'm right there. Maple yells the incantation, and a bunch of them explode.

I toss my gun to Maple, and wordlessly, she goes to work. I don't need a gun. I slide the knife from my pocket. Two more demons run toward me. Bring it on.

Chapter Three

A few hours later, Carter stares at me from across the table in the Enforcer Unit of the Nucleus House. He's been giving me his angry eyes for an hour now. I've been avoiding the gaze—and him kicking my shin to get my attention. I don't want to talk about what happened earlier, or the way he scolded me. He doesn't understand what the magic is like, or how it feels to be helpful after years of uselessness.

When he tosses a pencil at me, I finally look up from my papers. "What?" I snap.

His eyebrows crease into an annoyed look. I mimic it. "What was that earlier?"

"Instinct," I say, as if that's all the answer he needs. Because really, it is. This is my magic, my life, and I should be able to use it how I please.

Carter shakes his head. He looks like more his dad when he has his angry expression. "Twice in one day."

He says it like I'm unaware that I used magic. Of course I'm aware. I'm the one who did it. The void is too powerful to just let me sit back and do nothing. He can't possibly understand that, which is why I haven't said anything about it. "It's fine."

"It's not fine. If they find out…it's not just you they'd be after," he leans in and lowers his voice. "I'm not saying don't use magic, but cool it. At least until we have more information."

Yes, it was risky—using the void in front of Ric. No one knows we even went to De'Interno except for Carter's dad and Connie, and even they weren't told the whole story. We'd be lab rats somewhere if we told them we'd made a bunch of demons disappear.

"Stop worrying so much. You'll get wrinkles," I say, trying to lighten the mood. We're not going to agree about this. I said the wrong thing. His green eyes seem to darken in anger.

"Can't you take anything seriously?"

I scoff, and cross my arms. "I do take this seriously. Can't you let it go for a single minute and stop worrying?"

"No," he snaps, a little too loudly and another Enforcer looks over at us. He realizes the extra attention and leans back in his chair. "I can't. I don't like messing with things I don't understand. Someone needs to be worried about it."

I don't have anything to say to that. I sit here, quietly staring at him until he shakes his head and focuses on his paperwork as if it's the most interesting thing on the planet.

In the silence, Ric's laugh resonates through the room, and then he covers his mouth when Maple shushes him. I watch them talking back and forth in a whisper.

I'm glad all that's worked out. When they were first paired, it was sure to be a disaster. Maple wanted a partner she could marry, and Ric, being gay, was not that person. I'm glad that they connect because it makes it all easier. The first few days of their partnership was rough, but now, I think they're going to be a great team. Considering they'll probably be partners for life, it's a good thing. The bond between paired Enforcers is a strong one.

When we perform the ceremony, we swear loyalty through a blood oath to our cause in protecting the Nons and to our partner as long that lasts as we wear Enforcer triangles. Blood oaths can't be broken, not unless you want to face some major consequences. I'm not sure exactly what will happen, but it's not good. No one's ever really breaking them, and if they are, then they aren't talking about it. Enforcers are part of a whole when they're paired. Most people don't recover from losing their other half.

And now I get why Carter's so angry. He's scared. For me and for himself. A halfling witch who can access the void? I doubt the Triad would be understanding of that. He would lose me if the wrong people found out what we were, what we did, and what I can do with the void.

"I'm sorry," I whisper. Carter looks back at me, eyes wide and softer than before. "I'll be more careful."

He sends me a smile, but it doesn't stretch across his face. We're not in the clear, not a resolution to this mystery of my magic, but it's something.

I sign my name to the bottom of my report and walk it

toward the filing stack. When I turn, Taylor Plum is behind me. Her dark brown hair is smooth around her face. It looks cute.

"Penelope," she says, throwing her arms around. Taylor Plum is, apparently, a hugger. I doubt her badass Enforcer sister Shira has that quality.

"Taylor," I say, backing away slowly, my stomach churning. It's the magic, the void, but I wonder if I'll get used to it. "What's with the hug?"

She shrugs. "I'm in a good mood. The Statics got to come to the Nucleus House today for a meeting. I never get to come inside."

Another downfall of being a Static, a witch without magic. When Statics are eighteen, they're exiled from the community. No contact with any witches, which includes family. No WNN, Witches' News Network. No meetings. No Triad. Nothing. They're cut off our community, but some Statics stay connected with each other. Like a support group.

"Why are you here?"

Her eyes light up, making the brown look more like the color of honey. "The Observance. The Statics get to have a whole segment at the party. Today's the first meeting."

The Observance celebrates the biggest historical event in the witch community—the creation of the Triad and the Council. It's supposed to represent the future by honoring the past. Basically, it's the fourth of July—a symbol of importance, but a big excuse for a party with fancy dresses.

I smile at her excitement, but secretly, I'm glad I'm not one of them. Before Carter, I worried about exposure every day, but now, I'm secure in my position as an Enforcer, and even more importantly, as a witch. The void gives me that.

"Good luck with that," I say.

She starts to turn away when Carter walks up. Taylor's eyes get wider as she looks at him. "William Prescott?"

Carter turns on. It's crazy to watch, like one of those animated dolls that respond to movement. His name spoken as, 'William Prescott', is a trigger that turns him into someone else. A soldier reporting for duty.

"How are you today?" he asks Taylor.

She blushes. Literally blushes. And squeaks. If I was a smaller person, I'd be jealous. But then I'd not be with he-who-makes-all-women-swoon.

"Fine," Taylor says. She pulls me into a hug again and whispers in my ear. "He's so hot. I can't believe you're with him." And then she jerks away and rushes out the door.

Carter raises an eyebrow. "What was that about?"

That was the typical response, I think, but I shrug instead and don't even try to hide my smile. "She said she wants to borrow you for a night. She'll pick you up at seven and bring you back in one piece. Hopefully."

Carter blinks, but he's smiling. "Oh good. I needed a break from my girlfriend. Do you think she likes to make-out on street corners with crowds around?"

"If she knows what's good for her," I say, and I intentionally find his hand. His smile fades from one of amusement, to the one that's mine. The one that says he loves me. Whatever anger from earlier isn't totally gone, but at least it's on hold. That's good enough for now.

Hand in mine, we walk away from the desk. "But really, what was that?" Carter asks.

"She's excited to plan for the Observance. I guess the Triad is letting Statics participate."

Silence falls between us. His hand is still in mine, but now he's rigid. It's because I mentioned the Triad. Carter has issues with them, but mostly with his dad. I can't blame him. They do things that I don't agree with, either. Any time we talk about this he extinguishes, like tossing water on a fire.

"Hey," I start.

Carter shrugs, trying to be normal.

"We should go see Poncho," he says.

We need to give him the black dagger, see what he can find out about it. We've been holding onto the dagger since we left De'Intero. It's the thing that killed Kriegen, the same weapon I saw her use to release a witch's magic, and the one she wanted to use on me. We're not sure what it is, but we both know it's important.

We grab our bags off the table and Ric and Maple stop laughing as we approach. I look at Ric's paper. It's still empty. "I see you're being productive."

"I work better under pressure," he says.

Maple smiles. "He's distracting. Did he tell you about the waiter from the French place?"

"Ah yes, Pierre." The one and only hot Frenchman who Ric wanted to date for months. We went to that place so often that I still can't smell Ratatouille without the urge to hurl. It worked out when he got the date, but of course Pierre from Lyon ended up being Paul from Richmond.

"He's got the best dating mishaps," Maple says.

I smile. "You should ask him about Brian, and John, and Riley."

Ric flips me off. I stick out my tongue. In my head, it felt effective.

"Real mature," Ric says.

"Whatever, I'm awesome."

Carter shakes his head.

"Are they always like this?" Maple asks.

"You haven't known us long enough yet, but yes," Ric says.

"It's how we show love," I add.

I look back at Carter, who nods toward the door. Right. Poncho. "See you both at dinner?" Gran insisted they be there for Pop's retirement dinner. Inviting my friends over is the closest thing she will get to a party.

"Will there be pie?" Ric asks.

"Is the sky blue?"

"Sometimes it's gray," Maple adds.

I don't even have a response to that. Way to ruin my metaphor. "See you both later," I say.

The library doors squeaks open when we push through them. My feet clack on the marble ground and echo through the space. Hyde the cat sits at the circulation desk next to Poncho and hisses when he sees me. Seak, the library's other cat, curls against my feet. Hyde's disdain is the only way, aside from the color of his ID tag, I can tell the two cats apart.

Poncho looks up at us through his dark slanted eyes as we enter. They look like slits on his extra-round face. "Miss Grey, Mr. Prescott—I didn't expect you today." There's a slight smile on his face, slight enough that I can see the endearing gap in his teeth.

"We have a situation we need to discuss with you," I say.

"Privately," Carter adds. Even though there are only like three people in here. It's never that busy.

Poncho nods slowly, his gray-blue spiked hair not even moving. "I see." He looks between us and then places a little sign on the information desk.

WILL RETURN. DO NOT TAKE ANY BOOKS WITHOUT PERMISSION.

The implied "or else" is practically written in blood.

"My office." And then he leads us down the hallway, Hyde and Seak following behind him. Carter and I exchange a look before following. As we walk, I notice the singular sock with the red stripe, the other one on someone else's foot. I still don't fully understand how Vassago has the mate, but one day I will ask.

Poncho's office is dark, filled with candles, a fireplace, and leather chairs. It's drafty. The walls are lined with books—lots of books because they're aren't enough outside, you know, in the actual library—and papers that he's stuck up all over the place. The books don't seem to be in any certain order and some are in Latin, some in English, and some in whatever the demonic code is. Varying shapes and sizes of skulls align the walls.

"What kind of animals are those?" I ask, pointing to a skull with two horns where the cheeks are.

"I don't think they are animals. At least not from this world."

I blink. "Demon animals? Demons?"

Carter shrugs. "I doubt he's collecting dog skeletons."

This office officially gives me the heebie-jeebies.

"What are we here to discuss?" Poncho asks, sitting in

his chair. Hyde and Seak jump on the desktop.

I toss my bag on the chair and watch Carter as he searches his for the dagger. "We have this." Poncho's eyes widen as Carter holds it out to him. "We need to know what it does."

Poncho's hand lingers above, but doesn't move to touch the dagger. The black hilt and blade shimmer in the light of his lamp. The blade has some dried demon guts stuck to it and the handle is engraved with five symbols, but right now they're caked with dirt from where we buried it three days ago when we got back from De'Interno. We knew if we had it we could get caught. It was too important to let the Triad get it, so we kept it buried.

"Where did you get this?"

"Kriegen had it," Carter said. His voice is completely stable when he speaks, but I look at him anyway. I know he has strong feelings about his mom, even if he doesn't say them out loud.

"I saw her use it on the witch in the woods and then we used it to kill her in De'Intero."

Poncho *hmms*. "In the woods, the redhead?" I nod. "This is what she used to separate the witch from her essence."

"Yep, and then she released it into the atmosphere. Kriegen said she didn't need it, but it's still strange." Demons want our essence. It's why they hunt witches, and when they take our essence, our source of magic, we die. It's what happened to my parents. A witch can't survive without an essence. It's sort of like bone marrow. I'm the only one who's ever survived, because the demon didn't take all of my essence, and I had the void. Lucky me.

The only time a demon doesn't want a witch's essence

is if the demon used to be a witch, like Kriegen. Witches who undergo the transformation, the change from witches to demons, have more power than demons that are born or created from Nons.

"May I?" Poncho asks, pointing to the dagger. Carter nods and I watch the delicate way Poncho removes the dagger from Carter's hands. He dusts off some of the dirt and traces the weird circular symbols on the hilt.

"What is it?" Carter asks.

Poncho shakes his head, which is surprising. He knows everything. It's sort of what he does. Have we been sucked into the Twilight Zone? "These symbols go back to the beginning. They were the markings of Taliel and Lucifer, part of the secret language the demons created."

This dagger goes all the way back to the beginning of our creation, then. Taliel was the other angel who fell with Lucifer, one of his closest companions. We knew it was important, but this? Wow.

"I can keep it safe and do some research for you. Each of these symbols has a meaning. It will require a few days' time," Poncho says.

Carter looks at me for an answer. I believe in Poncho. Even if he has a few secrets that don't make sense to me yet, I feel I can trust him. "No problem," I say.

If it means we get some more answers, then I'm up for anything.

Chapter Four

CARTER

I can't help but look at Pen. Sure, I always like looking at her. At the curve of her neck and the way her hair falls against her spine. The way her blue eyes always seem to darken when she's up to something, or sparkle when she's happy, which are nearly interchangeable. At the curve of her breasts and her hips and the way every single part of her short frame is perfect. Even that freckle on the back of her neck that she probably doesn't know is there. But there's something about her that seems unfamiliar now.

I watch her reflection in the mirror as she twists her wet blond hair into a bun. For the last few days she's got this *thing*. She's more confident. I can see it when she stands, when she speaks, and definitely when we're using magic.

Almost like having the void, even if it may not be good, makes her feel like she's more.

I hate that she feels like she needs magic to be the best. That's part of the problem with our society—the Triad has placed so much weight and power on a witch's status and the rights you have versus when you're a Static or—God forbid—a halfling.

Penelope's an amazing Enforcer, and she could kick my ass even without magic. That's definitely part of what makes her stand out from others. Better. It's not the magic, or how she looks, and it never has been. Not for me.

"What?" she asks, a nervous smile reflecting back at me.

I shrug. "Thinking."

Her eyes narrow the way they do when she's worried. It's cute. "About what?"

I feel myself smile at the look on her face. "You."

She turns and leans against the dresser, her eyes on me. "If this about today, I'll be more careful. I hate fighting with you. I got carried away, that's all. It's…." she pauses and inhales. "I can't explain what its like. It's like when we use magic together, only a thousand times more."

"Addicting?"

She shrugs. "A little, but in a good way. Like somehow this is who I was always meant to be."

I don't like that thought or the look on her face. Just because we're halflings it doesn't mean that we're meant to do anything with void magic.

"No, that's not right, either." She waves off the thought. "I haven't found the right words yet. Maybe there aren't any. Like being with you."

I can see the sincerity carved into her face, but that

doesn't mean I like being compared with demon magic. But, if being with me is like what I feel when I'm with her, then I get it. There's something freeing and terrifying all at once. Debilitating and invigorating. Words I'd never imagined I'd use for another person.

"I don't want to lose you," I say. And the fact is, if anyone finds out, I could. I'm not sure what I'm more afraid of: the Triad finding out that she can access it and exiling her forever, or what my dad would say and do under the guise of protecting me. If there's one thing I know more than anything, even more than demons, it's that nothing matters more to Victor Prescott than me.

Prescott men protect themselves above all others.

Or rather the Prescott name, which I have the lucky misfortune of bearing.

Penelope sits down beside me on her bed. "Where'd you go?"

I shake my head, then look at her, raise an eyebrow, and smile. "You don't want to know where I went."

"What if I do?" Her cheeks get a little rosy—I love that I can do that to her. Making her blush is one of the highlights of my day. That and the way she can practically purr under my lips when we kiss. And the feel of her skin on mine. Really, everything. Even when she pisses me off because she risks herself like she does. Maybe especially then.

"Do you think you can handle it?" I ask her.

She nods and sits up straighter next to me. "I'm braver than I look."

I lean in closer to her so my mouth is a breath from her ear. She inhales when I speak. "I went here," I say, and I press my lips in that spot under her ear. "And here." I kiss her cheek. "And here," I kiss her jaw and run my hand over her stomach. My fingers touch the skin under her shirt. "And here," I say, kissing her neck. She's practically on fire under my touch as my fingers trace a line up to her belly button.

"And—" I move to kiss her but she turns her mouth to me first. Her hands press against my back, pulling me in closer to her as her tongue slides into my mouth. Then, there isn't any thinking. My fingers are all over her skin and she seems to curve into my touch. Every time her body responds that way, it makes me feel invincible. Like I can do anything and we can be anything and together, unstoppable.

"Why is this door closed?"

Pen and I separate and launch up from the bed. Connie, Penelope's sister, stands in the doorway, eyes filled with laughter. Penelope throws a pillow at Connie, and I look down at the floor and count to ten. *One, two, three…*

"You should knock," Penelope snaps.

A fast breeze swishes past my head and then back again, a soft thud landing on the bed. A pillow. "You shouldn't have the door closed. You know the rules. What if I was Gran?"

Pen scoffs. "As if you don't break the rules every day."

Nine. Ten.

Maybe I'll go to twenty.

"True, but at least I was always sneaky. You're pretty obvious," she says. *Eighteen.* "Ric and Maple are downstairs. That's why I volunteered to come up here for you. You're welcome."

I look up to see Pen cross her arms. Connie's in the doorway staring between us, smile on her lips. She looks like Penelope does when she's gotten her way. No one says anything for a minute. This is awkward.

"Thanks, Connie," I say, and flash her the Prescott smile. One of confidence and assurance that my dad taught me was part of the Prescott name, part of being in charge. Immediately, her whole face changes, and I'm a little surprised that worked on her. It's never done anything with Pen. "We were coming down."

Connie *mmhmms* and leaves us. Pen throws the pillow at the side of my face. "What?"

"Was that necessary?"

"It's just a smile." Even though I know it's not 'just' anything except one more attribute that my dad has instilled in me that I hate, but use anyway. I'm doomed, I guess.

"Don't fake-Prescott-all-is-well-trust-me smile to my sister. Got it?"

I hold my hands up defense. "It worked, didn't it?"

Pen grabs my hand and pulls me toward the door. "Let's go. It's party time."

Maple and Ric have dominated the conversation for the last twenty minutes, and we have barely eaten yet. Connie hangs on their words, but Pen doesn't say anything, which is odd. No one else seems to notice anything. Maybe I'm paranoid.

"It makes me hopeful for our future when you are the next generation," Frank Warren, Penelope's grandpa, says. "We're in good hands. Good hands, indeed."

I push the noodles around with my fork. Ric whispers to Connie and she laughs, covering her mouth with her hand.

"How does it feel to be retired, Mr. Warren?" Maple asks, her eyes wide. "Fifty-five years is a long time."

"Too long," Deborah Warren, Pen's grandma, adds. I watch as Frank takes her hand. Everyone's eyes seem to go there, to the two of them holding hands. No one in my life has been married as long as them. I've only known them a short time, but they definitely seem like a force to reckoned with.

Frank takes a sip of his water. "It's only been a day, so it's hard to say for sure, I reckon it will be a good change. More time with my granddaughters." He looks for a second too long at Penelope. "Right, Penelope?"

She looks up from her plate, confused for a second. Maybe she wasn't paying attention. "Right—yes. Yes. It will be good, Pop." She smiles pretty big at him, but it almost looks fake to me. I would know.

After dinner, Ric stops me, motioning toward Pen with his head. "What's wrong with her?"

My heart speed races for a second. It's always a strange feeling when someone else points out what you already noticed. To be sure I poke his thoughts more. "You think something's wrong?"

"You don't?" Ric says.

I glance toward Penelope and she's sitting on the couch, seemingly staring into space. Everyone's talking around her but she's not saying anything. She's never *not* talking. So, yes, I have noticed. What I don't know is why.

"She seemed so happy this afternoon, happier than she has ever since…" He points down and whistles. Yeah, I'm aware. "Do you think it's because of Maple? Am I being neglectful? Maybe I should hang out with Penelope more."

"I'm sure it's not that," I say.

I keep my eyes on Pen as Ric keeps talking about being

a bad best friend. She's smiling, but she looks tired. Really tired. And something else that I can't place that wasn't there earlier. Or maybe it was there, and I didn't see it underneath the confidence she was projecting. I should've seen it.

"I mean, I could go out with her. Even though we both have other people doesn't mean I don't need her around."

I rest my hand on his shoulder. "Dude, stop. It was a long day. I'm sure she's tired."

Ric nods slowly, but I can tell that he thinks it's more than that. "Yeah, that would make sense."

Ric goes and sits next to Pen and Maple. Deborah passes a present to Frank, and I join them. I strap on my smile too, and slide my hand into Pen's. She looks at me, her eyes soft, and then back to her family. She does seem off. When did that happen? I replay the day in my head, and I can't pinpoint when it started. She's seemed so much like herself all day.

"This is from Carter," Connie says, passing her grandpa my retirement gift.

"Thank you, son," Frank says, his old shaky hands tearing off the paper.

The rest of the evening, I keep one hand in Penelope's in case she needs it there.

Chapter Five

First thing the next morning, Connie is waiting outside my door, her foot propped against the wall and phone in hand, probably playing that game she loves so much. I watch her for a second. She looks like mom more and more with her big eyes and curls. She's got on boots that make her taller than me, which I swear she does so she looks like the older sister. My family has spent so much time protecting the secret about my magic that sometimes it feels like she is the older sister. The one giving advice, keeping the other safe, sacrificing happiness. No more. Now that I have magic, I can do it like I was always supposed to.

"You're actually awake," I say. It's after six, early for both of us, but I have to report to work in an hour.

Connie shrugs, her blond curls bouncing off her shoulder, and slides her phone into her pocket. "It's for waffles," she says with a smile.

"Not for me?"

"You mean you're coming too? Fine." She smiles, and then starts down the stairs. After I got back from De'Interno, we made a promise that we'd have breakfast once a week. Just the two of us. With everything going on—with Carter, patrol, Connie's Enforcer examinations, and then school starting again—sister time is important.

Outside, the summer air is crisp and still cool. The sun peeks through the trees and cars are already piling up in the streets to start the morning commute. We walk down the sidewalk toward this diner that's been here for ages.

"Are you feeling better today?" Connie asks.

Starting with Pop's party two days ago, I felt like I was in a fog. I barely remember much past kissing Carter in my room. Today, though, I feel good. I *am* good. I can't explain the change.

"Absolutely. Like a new person," I say. I realize I do. I feel energized and in tune. So much so that I could stop and feel my own heart pumping life through my veins. I could maybe even fly. Or not really, but I'd be willing to try. "Are you ready for the Enforcer examinations?"

Connie stuffs her phone into her pocket and almost makes a face. "Yeah, I'm ready."

Then, she's quiet, as if I said the wrong thing. The silence is awkward for a good four seconds. Far too long for me. "What kind of waffles are you going to get? I'm thinking Nutella."

"Banana walnut," Connie says back.

"Good choice," I say.

"Have you ever wondered what you'd be if you weren't an Enforcer?" Connie says suddenly. I steal a glance toward her while we walk, trying to read her face. There's nothing noticeable there, nothing that seems nervous or worried.

"Why? Do you?" I ask. She shrugs, then pulls her curls back into a ponytail. She's avoiding. Obviously she has. I touch her arm.

"It doesn't matter," she says, her voice flat.

"You can tell me anything."

Connie scoffs, and her eyes shoot toward mine. "Like you tell me everything?"

Touché. I am keeping a secret from her right now about the void, and I hate it. I almost tell her right then, but I see Carter's face. The way he always looks at me after I've used magic, the fights we have about it, the way he doesn't understand, the worry. I don't want to see Connie carry that. I want to protect her from this.

"I tell you things that are important," I say. She looks at me with disbelief, and I push away the part that feels guilty for keeping my secrets. She doesn't respond, so I sigh. "No, I haven't. This is what I've always wanted, and I'm living it. I found Carter, and my friends, and purpose."

I look at my sister but her eyes are distant. "What would you do if you weren't an Enforcer?"

Her brown eyes widen and focus on mine, a lightness to them. "I'd marry for money in a minute."

I blink for a second, and then I laugh. She's quoting *Breakfast at Tiffany's,* the scene with Holly and Paul. That's our movie. It was one mom used to watch with me before, and now we watch it. Mom loved Audrey Hepburn. "I guess it's pretty lucky neither of us is rich, huh?"

She chuckles. "I love that movie."

"Me too," I say. But that doesn't change the question. "Seriously, what would you do?"

Connie shrugs again, which is becoming her default that means 'I don't want to tell you.' "I haven't really thought about it. I'm nervous, I guess."

I wish I could say that it's fine to want another path, that she can be whatever she chooses, and that Gran would be thrilled if she was. That she's a free, wild bird that doesn't have to be in a cage. I don't say that, though, because I'm selfish and I wish she wanted this, too. To be like me, and Pop, and our parents. To serve and protect and fight.

But then she pushes past me into the diner, and neither of us mentions anything else about it for the rest of breakfast.

• • •

I am definitely a new person today. I'm Batman. *Try to get me, suckers!*

I duck a shot of magic from a demon. They don't usually fight this way, but whitey here is determined to knock me out. *Good luck, good sir.*

Having magic is kick-ass.

Seriously.

Another shot of magic barely misses my ear, but I somehow maneuver my body to avoid it. It feels like that scene in the Matrix when the bullets zoom by, but Neo freezes them all in that way only really awesome people can do. It's that. Only instead of bullets, it's magic, and instead of freezing them I can toss on some salt and blast them away with my mind.

I focus on the void and let the coolness of the magic fill me up, and then I blast it toward the demon. It falls back, trapped against the iron I created by the power of my mind.

I don't know how I lived without my own magic. Literally and figuratively.

The demon hisses at me but it can't move. It struggles against the barrier that I've created from nothing. I stand, watching it, and the demon tries to escape my hold, but it slings back like a rubber band. Its struggle against my magic is surprisingly sweet. I glance around, but Ric and Maple are on the other side of the woods, and I can only see Ric because of his red shirt between the trees. I smile a little and then say the incantation out loud, only because I don't want anyone to notice I can expel a demon without talking. Not after my conversation with Carter two days ago. *"Virtute Angeli ad infernum unde venistis."*

Without a pause, the demon explodes into goo.

Yeah, I lied. This is cooler than the Matrix.

"You good?" Carter says as he runs toward me. His cheeks are flushed and he's covered in some demon guts. We're both breathing hard, like air is rare and we're about to suffocate. His chest heaves under his ripped shirt. He's never looked hotter, and I nod with a smile. Like, a psycho-killer-clown smile. At least that's how it feels, but I can't contain whatever this is. Another side effect of the void?

I play it off like it's not a big deal. I try to, anyway.

And then I kiss him. Straight up take him off-guard and thrust myself into the space between us. My lips are hungry against his, and it takes him a few seconds to respond to me. But when he does, it's with his whole body. Hands in my hair, on my skin, everywhere they can be. Someone yells in the background, and when I pull away my head is spinning with him. Carter's staring at me, half-cocked grin on his face.

"More of that later," he says.

The sun is setting around us, but I can make out Maple's shadow through some trees not too far away. Ric and Maple are taking down a couple more demons. They don't usually put two pairs in one area, but there were a lot of incident reports today so Ric and Maple joined us. They secured the very large perimeter from Nons so they wouldn't see us kill demons or use magic, and now we're a double helping from the can of magical whoop ass. I watch across the way as the demons they're fighting burst into nothing.

Ric and Maple high five as they walk toward me and Carter, who, ever on alert, scans the woods for more demons. Demons are like a "come kick our ass" beacon to him. I'm almost positive he still hunts them in his spare time, even though I pretend he's not been doing it more and more over the last week. Hunting and killing. I keep telling myself that he'll mention it when he's ready.

"We are awesome," Maple says.

"They should give us all a wall of honor," Ric adds.

"And tiaras made of chocolate," she offers.

"That's my girl."

I laugh as they bump hips. The warmth of the void is subsiding, yet there's a shift from strong and good, powerful, to bloated like a balloon. Full, as if I could pop at any moment.

"Let's get out of here," Carter says, leading the rest of us out of the woods. He takes my hand as we walk, and the void stirs up again at his touch. He whispers in my ear. "We have unfinished business."

"Are you going to be part of the Enforcer bit for the Observance? The meeting is next week. One month until the biggest party of the century," Maple says.

The woods turn into the parking lot at the mall, and pretty soon we're all moving opposite directions to our cars. My stomach growls. I'm ready for some lunch, after we file our official Enforcer report. Maybe Chinese. I look toward Ric and Maple. "Do I really have a choice, or are you asking nicely?"

"Nicely," Ric says. He looks at Carter. "We'll put on a group number."

I can tell from the scowl on Carter's face that it's the last thing he wants to do. Which is good for me, because that means we can get out of it. "See you later," I say.

Maple waves, and as Carter and I turn to leave them, Taylor Plum plows into us. She looks a mess. Her dress is dirty—and is that the same dress she was wearing last time I saw her? Her hair is long waves all over her face, pointing in different directions. Her eyes are wide when she stares at us, but it's almost like she's not even looking at us.

"Sorry, Taylor," I say.

Taylor sputters, and then takes off in a dash down the parking lot. We all stand still, trying to figure out what happened.

"She's usually so excited," I say, stare after her. Taylor's already lost in the cars.

"Yeah, she's normally a doll." Ric asks.

Then, there's a scream. All four of us exchange a quick look, then move at a run toward the sound. It's the same way Taylor went. Carter shouts out a glamor to cloak us as we move, and faster than I imagine, we're somewhere in the sea of cars.

A body is on the ground, and I expect it to be Taylor. But, when I look, it's some Non. Taylor is in the corner huddled by the back tire of a large pick-up truck, terror on her face, tears streaming down it. I inch toward her and sparks fly from her hands, causing a lamppost behind us to crash to the ground. Taylor screams when it happens, her eyes wild.

"She did magic," Ric yells.

That's not possible. Statics can't do magic, but we all saw it. Taylor is shaking and sobbing. Maple bends over the Non and shakes her head. Dead. A Static killed a Non.

"Are you sure she's Static?" Carter asks.

"Positive," Ric and I say at the same time.

Yet somehow she has magic. I step toward Taylor and lean down. Carter pulls at my shoulder, but he won't sway me. I get how jarring it is to have magic when you haven't before—it's what happened to me when I met Carter. If she did this with magic, then I can help her. I hold out a hand to her, and Taylor's wide brown eyes look at me.

"Taylor, you can trust me. You have magic now?" I ask.

Taylor nods slowly. Her lip trembles as she talks. "It was only a spark or two earlier but I-I can't control it. I feel like it's tearing me apart," she says. Her hand finds a place on her arm, and her skin is bleeding. When I look closer I can see why. It almost looks like she's been scratching at her own arm.

"Did it just happen?"

She shakes her head. "No, two days ago. Right after I saw you."

I steal a look up at Carter. Five days ago we made all

those demons disappear, and I got my own magic, with the void. Then I see Taylor in the Nucleus House and now she has magic? That can't be a coincidence. I reach my hand out closer to Taylor. If she takes it then we can figure out a way to help her. Taylor studies my hand, but doesn't reach for it.

"You're safe with us," I say.

Taylor hesitates, but then her hand is in mine and I'm pulling her to her feet when her eyes give the briefest flash of this really, really dark green in her eyes. I feel it in that instance, an explosion inside me, and then her magic zaps me, sending me flying across the parking lot. All I can feel when it travels through my body is a numbing sensation. It seems to mingle with my magic and make everything swirl and spin. Vaguely, I see the others go to my defense.

Ric races toward her, then he's sprawled across to the back of the lot. My head spins. Carter moves toward me, yelling my name, and then I can't see him. Taylor tosses him down like a ragdoll. I'm on my feet in time to see Maple lunge for Taylor. Taylor is faster and Maple screams and she's slung across the parking lot—further and with more force than I can imagine—along with what looks like something bright and fizzy, electric almost. I hear the thud of her body smashing against the side of a parked semi in the back of the lot. I stand, cradling my head, because this is not normal.

It's not the act of throwing Maple or the fact that Taylor Plum has magic, but it's the thing I saw with the magic. The fuzzy bright light. No one has light like that. Ever. Even a witch with who has had powers all his or her life. Somehow, I saw it flow through her body. Was I the only one who saw it?

Taylor is sobbing, screaming at the top of her lungs. I can feel the power, too, tearing and bouncing and prying at the edges of me. It wants out. It's a burning ice under my skin, and I can totally understand why she feels like the way she does. Does it hurt her or is she scared? I should go help her, but I don't like that she has magic. Not when I had to do so much to just get a spark of it. She doesn't deserve it. She can't even control it. I could take it away again and then—

"Penelope," a voice says.

A figure stands before me, familiar. It's fuzzy at first, then it leans in closer to my view—it's the mauve-colored demon. The one that helped Carter and me escape De'Intero. We wouldn't be alive without it. Its eyes are on me, darting between Taylor and me. It hisses at Taylor, who starts screaming louder, and then hits her with some sort of magic that sends the Static—*former* Static—running beyond the cloaking barrier.

That was counterproductive. Now there's some girl on the loose who has no idea how to use magic. We have to tell someone. Her Enforcer sister, and the Council. Maybe even the Triad. They'll need to be told.

The mauve demon's eyes are on me. "I wouldn't do that."

I cock an eyebrow toward the demon. "Do what?"

"Tell people about this. It's happening because of you," the mauve demon says, its eyes darkening. "What were you feeling when you were looking at that girl? Not quite yourself?"

"What? Nothing." But I was angry. How did the demon know what I was thinking? Or that I was feeling unusual? Why was I angry? I shake the thought away. "What's because of me?"

Carter stands slowly, and then freezes when he sees the demon. The mauve demon looks between us, but I nod toward Ric. Carter goes to his side. I watch him from the corner of my eye, but Ric's not getting up. Is he dead? I push down my panic as the magic seizes me. The mauve demon stands, silent, and I wonder what its thinking. How is it here? It must know something else.

"Tell me."

The demon doesn't respond at first, but Carter gives me a nod that Ric's not dead. I exhale, and square my focus on the demon as Carter moves from Ric to Maple. The mauve demon looks me up and down, and then nods. Her eyes dart toward Carter as he steps closer to where Maple lies on the ground.

"Magic is a balance, and any tipping of the scale can destroy it all," Mauve says.

I've heard that before. Read it, in fact. The day I got back from De'Intero, that line was written in an open book on Poncho Alistair's desk in the library. The words are a message. Obviously an important message or this demon wouldn't be saying it. The same reason Poncho wouldn't have purposely left them out for me to see. "What does that mean?"

But something in my bones tells me I already know the answer. The demon doesn't say anything else.

"She's not breathing!"

I spin around to look and Maple's still sprawled out on the ground. All four of our phones chime the high note, low note, high note of the WNN. The demon glances among us all at the sound, and then as quickly as it comes, it flickers away. So much for being helpful.

"Call someone, Penelope," Carter yells.

I pull out my phone and run to Ric's side. Before I make

the call, I glance at the screen.

STATIC HAS POWER UNEXPLAINED MAGICAL BURST WHILE DRIVING HER KIDS TO CAMP: FOUR KILLED.

It's not only Taylor.

I ignore the message and call the Council. While I wait for someone to answer, my brain races to figure out how this happened, and what exactly it means. If the mauve demon says it's because of me, then why? What did we really do down there?

Ric coughs and I take his hand, but he doesn't squeeze it. His eyes flicker open, searching mine frantically. At least he's alive. That's what matters. He's alive.

A voice comes on the line asking me what I'm reporting. "Static attacked with magic—two Enforcers are injured."

I tell them my location and they say they're coming. When I hang up, the phone has more messages. One, two, three more incidents of Statics with magic.

Crap on a stick.

Then Ric screams. I cover my ears and he's sitting straight up, screaming. After a second he stops and falls back to the concrete. I look over at Carter.

What's happening right now?

But from the look on his face I can tell he's as freaked out as I am.

Chapter Six

Pen sits next to me in one of the uncomfortable plastic chairs. She turns her salt vial necklace over and over in her fingers. The waiting is the worst part, and there's nothing I can say to her to make it better.

"When are we going to hear?" she asks. Her nose crinkles up and her eyes get wider as she scrolls through the WNN alerts on her phone with her other hand. I want her to stop looking at that thing.

"Soon," I say, even though I have no idea.

Pen shakes her head. "There have been seventeen occurrences since we got to the hospital." An hour ago. "What's happening to the Statics?" Her voice gets lower. "What did we do in De'Intero?"

What had we done? We were going to die there, and she'd taken my hand so we could share magic. I couldn't die without kissing her one last time. The rest of what happened was beyond either of us.

"Statics have magic. They have no idea how to use it. How many Statics are going to get it now—everyone? Only some?" Pen asks. Her phone dings the tone of the WNN updates—high note, low note, high note—and this time she ignores it, sliding the phone into her pocket. "This is huge, Carter."

That's an understatement. Statics aren't supposed to have magic. Witches are born with magic or they aren't. No one had ever been an exception until I met Pen. Since her essence was stolen as a kid, she shouldn't have magic, either. But she does. Now she has even more thanks to the void. That can't be a coincidence. The mauve demon said magic was a balance. If what we did in De'Intero upset that balance, we need to restore it before anyone, especially the Triad, finds out we're involved.

"We'll figure it out," I say. I pull her close to me and I kiss the top of her head. If this is linked to us like the mauve demon said, then there has to be a reason. Luckily, I'm good at puzzles. I get them. They're like chess. A strategy, a method. You have to look at the whole board, see the whole picture before you can build it. One rule my dad made sure I memorized: know the moves you want to make before you make them.

Prescott men are always prepared to do whatever necessary to win.

Someone says Pen's name and we both look up. Connie stands in the doorway, and she is out of my arms and into her sister's in a second. "What's happening?" Connie asks, her voice uneasy.

Pen stands beside her, and even though she says reassuring things to her sister, I can see through the mask. I can see through it because I wear the same one. The one that says, "I'm in charge and I can handle it." Pen wears it almost better than I do, and I've been in training since I was a kid.

Prescott men must never show weakness.

I hate that my mind goes to my dad's voice. To his demand that I be exactly what he expects to me be—and that I always listen to him. How the hell does that happen? Sometimes it feels like I'm destined to be the other thing I hate. That despite the choices I make for myself, I'll end up exactly like him.

Pen and Connie move back toward the chairs, and a movement behind them catches my eye. A long white beard, like the demon Vassago—the demon of lost things. I take a step toward the hall but there's no smell of sulfur in the air to alert me that a demon's near.

I'm losing it.

I hate hospitals. They always smell too clean. Nothing is this clean, or this white.

The last of my coffee drips from a machine.

That's another reason I hate hospitals: the coffee tastes horrible.

My phone dings. A text from Pen.

Your dad is here.

Dad? I press a lid on the coffee and bolt back up the

elevator. Victor Prescott doesn't go the hospital out of the kindness of his heart. I know the way he works, the way the Triad works, better than that. If he's here then he's not here alone and he's on official business. If Statics are getting magic somehow, then he's here to do damage control.

Prescott men must never appear out of control. We are aware and involved in every situation.

As soon as the elevator doors open, I see the three of them standing near Pen and Connie. Pen's hands move around while she talks, a tell that she's nervous. Rafe Ezrati is talking to her, but I'm still too far to hear what they're discussing.

Sabrina Stone glances over her shoulder as I approach. When I was younger, I used to think she was the prettiest girl in the world with perfectly straight red hair and marble skin. I was this ten-year-old kid crushing on her. I know better now. There's a viper under that sparkle.

"William, I wasn't aware you were here," Dad says, looking over Sabrina's shoulder to me. I feel all the tension rise to my shoulders. I hate 'William' and that's why he does it. 'Carter' is an act of rebellion, and Victor Prescott doesn't approve of rebellion. I move to stand by Penelope, and Dad looks between us. I can't handle him today.

"Where else would I be?" I snap. Just seeing him here makes my blood boil. "I'm surprised to see you here at all."

Dad stares at me. "Two of our own were injured today. It's our duty to ensure they are well."

I scoff. Those badges are the only reason the Triad is here at all. "Because you care so much about them," I mutter clear enough so Dad can hear me. His jaw stiffens with disapproval. I feel Pen's eyes on me, but I ignore it. I don't like her seeing this side of me, but the man irritates me. His smug righteousness, his lies, and the facade that he tries to pass off as genuine. "I understand if you have more pressing matters."

Sabrina steps forward. She and Rafe always seem to be fighting Dad's battles for him. "We do need to ensure that our Enforcers are in a stable position."

Dad keeps looking between me and Penelope and I have no idea why.

"We're here to find out what happened out there. Miss Grey was explaining to us what occurred with the Static," Rafe adds. His eyes are softer when he looks at me. He's always been my favorite, of the three. He used to change my diapers, which is sort of weird to think about now.

"And there was no foul play?" Dad asks, eyes on me.

"Aside from a *Static* with *magic*?" Pen snaps. The Triad, Connie, and I all look at her and she stands. She's fearless. "No. None. Taylor Plum is still out there, confused and alone."

Rafe nods at her. "You make a valid point, Miss Grey. Many of the Statics are out there alone, afraid, and we should go see to them properly."

I meet my Dad's gaze as he leaves with the Triad. I don't like the look in his eye, the suspicion that's only there because I told him what happened last week after De'Interno. Most of what happened, anyway. I had to in order to explain it to keep the Triad from asking too many questions that day. That look makes me feel like he's not saying everything he knows. Or worse, plotting his next move. He's always one step ahead, always working his own agenda.

I hope I don't regret trusting Victor Prescott last week.

Chapter Seven

PENELOPE

After the Triad leaves, Carter is tense. He barely talks—which is fine because Connie does enough for all of us—but he seems distracted. I take his hand, but leave him alone otherwise. He's not like me. He'll want to think through whatever's going on, instead of word vomiting it out for the whole world to see.

Maple's family came an hour ago and the Lins sit on the other side of the waiting room, whispering in Chinese. I look over at the Lins, and Maple's sister sends me a soft smile, but no one else looks my way. How is she now? When they brought her in, she wasn't breathing on her own. I can still see her lying there, eyes closed, blood on the ground...

"Ric Norris." Carter, Connie, and I jump up in unison.

The balding doctor with thick-rimmed glasses walks in our direction. "You're his partner?" This whole floor of the hospital is the magical level. To the Nons, it's a regular floor with nothing exciting, but only witches come here. All the doctors who work on this floor are witches. Another way we stay cloaked in the Non world.

"Family friends," I say. But Carter steps forward.

"William Prescott, and you are?"

"I'm Dr. McGervey," he says.

Carter holds out his hand, and the doctor takes it. I stare between them and watch as Carter uses his name to get something else done that they'd never let us do normally. "Mrs. Norris is on a flight in from Seattle. It will be another hour, at least, and we're really the only people here for him."

Dr. McGervey nods slowly and flips open Ric's file. Apparently his Prescott charm works on everyone. There's nothing readable from the stony expression on his face. "Once he was stabilized, we were able to do a CT scan. He suffered a mild concussion, and we had to do emergency surgery on a ruptured spleen. He has a few broken ribs and some bruising, but he should recover fully. He'll have to take it easy for a couple weeks."

Ric doesn't do that. Rest and relaxation are not in his vocabulary.

"Can we see him?" Connie asks. Her voice is practically dancing with excitement. Ric is my best friend, but he's like a brother to her. He's always been around us, eating dinner with us, scolding boys who looked at Connie too long. Ric is family for both of us.

"One at a time," he says.

"And what about Maple—Che Lin?" I ask, looking

toward the family on the other side of the room. Dr. McGervey follows my gaze, then lowers his voice.

"She's still in surgery, as far as I'm aware."

"Thank you," Carter says. "Your service is impeccable."

As soon as the doctor walks away, Connie throws her hands around my neck. I stand there as she hugs me, and close my eyes. What a relief. I could've lost Ric today. I could've lost someone else who I love.

"You can go to him first," I tell Connie.

She looks surprised and shakes her head. "He's your best friend, he'll need to see you."

As much as I want to go, the ground feels shaky. Carter's hand rests on my back without me saying anything else. "I need a second," I say. "Go, please. I don't want him to think he's here all alone."

Connie nods and heads down the hall to find Ric. Carter's hand rubs against my back and I turn to face him. Ric could've died. I could've lost my best friend and it would've all been my fault. A week ago, I was so determined to save Carter from the demons I thought took him that I caused people to die. Statics have magic now and have killed people. Their blood is on my hands, and I'm horrible for being thankful that it's not Ric's.

"He's all right," Carter says, pulling me into his arms. He holds me against his chest, and I breath in the familiar scent of him. It's crazy how much of my life Carter has become. Sometimes I feel like I didn't have anything good before him, and that's a scary and strange feeling. I'm only seventeen. How can I need someone so badly?

Carter's phone buzzes in his pocket. He pulls it out between us and makes a face. Probably his father. "Take it,"

I say.

He looks conflicted, but says, "I'll be right back."

While he's gone, I sit again and fiddle with my salt necklace so my fingers and brain have a distraction from this whole mess. I scroll through my phone and stare blankly at the seventy alerts. All of them related to Statics. How do I stop this?

A blond woman with an oddly disproportionate body and a large red hat lowers herself into the chair beside me. She smiles at me, but I can't focus on anything but that hat. She could seriously injure someone with it. I slide my phone back in my pocket—I can't read any more of this—and stare out into the space of the hallway. The woman clears her throat and rests her hand on my forearm.

"I'm Lindley Arthur. I notice you're an Enforcer," she says, eyes moving to the gold triangles on my shirt. Right. I'm still in uniform. I nod toward her and she clasps her hands together. "Quite a lot of ruckus going on these last couple days. My friend said her second cousin manifested yesterday." Taylor Plum said it was two days for her, too, but she was the first report. How is spreading around our area so quickly?

"I love your hat," I say, changing the subject.

"I am quite fond of it," Lindley Arthur says with a smile. "Anyway, we are all hoping that the Triad has a plan in place for all of this. Is there any clue about which Statics are going to get magic? Or why? Or when?" Her voice drops into a whisper. "As one myself, I'm quite interested in obtaining some magic."

There's no response to that. Magic isn't acquired—you have it or you don't. At least, that's how it used to be. Now?

Who knows. She's staring at me like I have some secret answer to change her life. What does she expect me to say? I have no answers to any of this. "Well," I start.

Right on cue, Carter appears with his million-dollar smile that's oh-so better than mine. "Hello, Mrs. Arthur," Carter says. The woman turns to look at him and he rests a hand on her shoulder. She practically melts because he can do that to people. Even fifty-year old women. "I'm William Prescott—"

She nods, huge smile on her face. "Victor's boy. Your father has a dangerous situation on his hands, young man. I sure hope he can handle it."

He gets this reaction a lot from the women. I'd be a little offended if I didn't completely understand it.

"These are dangerous times even before the Statics, Mrs. Arthur. I can assure you that my father and the Triad will make the best of an unusual situation. You know what his number one priority is?"

"The Nons," she whispers. Her eyes are serious and glassy. I hadn't even thought about how much danger the Nons are in.

Carter shakes his head. "You. The Statics. He told me personally that someone such as yourself—best-selling author of some most beloved children books—is required to be under the protection of the Triad, in case the magic comes your way as well."

I blink. How does he know that she's a 'beloved' author'? Surely he hasn't memorized every single person around.

Lindley Arthur gasps. "He said that?"

"Directly to me a moment ago," Carter says. He's such a good liar. Or is he lying? He did have a phone call. "The

Enforcers have a meeting to discuss all this. But I promise that once we have information, we will share it with everyone in the community."

"Even Statics?"

Carter smiles that Prescott winning smile. "Especially Statics. Until then, let's focus on more exciting things. Like the Observance. You'll be attending the party, won't you?"

Of course she will. Everyone, witch and Static, come. It's the one time we're given an exception to the separation in our community, even if it is for show. Lindley Arthur's face lights up. "I wouldn't miss it."

"Excuse me, Mrs. Arthur, but we have to attend to some official business," he says. Carter grabs my hand and pulls me from my seat.

"You're going to make a great leader, Mr. Prescott." Lindley Arthur calls as Carter and I leave the lobby. He doesn't look back toward her, but by the way he squeezes my hand tighter, it's the worst thing she could ever say to him. Ever. Not just the idea of leading of the Triad, but calling him 'Mr. Prescott.'

We're down the hall across from Ric's room before he lets go of my hand. I explore his face. "You all right?"

"Yeah," he says. "Never better."

I scoff. "You're a horrible liar."

He flashes that smile. The public one, not the real one. "I'm a great liar. I'm a Prescott."

"Well, I can tell when you're lying so you're not that good," I say. He smile fades and looks at me with those green eyes. With eyes like that, I'm not sure how I didn't know he was a demon. "You're good at it."

"What?"

I sit next to him and inhale. He's not going to like this speech, but as his loving girlfriend it's my duty to tell him what he doesn't like to hear. "You could lead the Triad. You would be a better leader than your dad."

"I don't want it," he snaps. I take his hand quickly, before he can pull it away. I need him to hear me out.

"Yeah, but you could do it better. You're already twice the man he is. And you're great with people," Carter finally meets my gaze. I keep talking since I have his attention. "Leading people, convincing them that everything will be work out, keeping them all calm, even joyful. You do it for me every day. You care about people, not their social status."

A silence spreads between us, but I can tell he's thinking from the way his cute little eyebrows furrow together. "There are too many things I hate about the Triad."

There are things I hate about the Triad, too. The way they force some into marriage, test us all for Enforcer duty, and keep the Statics away from the witches, like they have some disease we could all catch. The way they focus on purebloods, don't equip witches to protect themselves without Enforcers, and what they would do if they knew we were halflings is deplorable. Since he's got more direct access to them, I'm sure Carter has more on his list than I'm aware of.

"Maybe you could change some of those things," I say. I lean into him. "I'm not saying you have to do it and I will stand by you whatever you choose. But if you change the way our whole society works, then that could be a great thing." I almost see it as I talk. A better way for Enforcers to get hired. Stopping those arranged marriages, a removal of emphasis on status in the community, a re-integration and acceptance of Statics. All of it could be better.

He pulls his hand away. "I don't want to talk about this right now."

I sigh and lean back in the chair. "Please think about that before you write it all off."

He looks at me, surprise and anger flitting across his face, but nods.

Connie bounces out of Ric's room. Her face is bright, which is a good sign.

"He's making jokes, so I guess he's almost normal," Connie says. She tilts her head to the door. "You ready now?"

I nod, but jokes aren't an indication of normal. More like a hiding place. "Stay out here in case his mom shows up?" I ask. Carter nods my way and I leave him and my sister to go see Ric.

Ric doesn't look so good. His face is really pale and his eyes are bloodshot, but he smiles slightly when he sees me. I refuse to look upset or guilty or anything but positive right now. "Hey, buddy."

"Buddy?" he repeats.

I shrug. "Would you prefer hot stuff?"

"You're not my type," he says.

"I won't be offended." I force a smile and sit next to his bed.

"Don't look at me that way," he says, his eyes on me. "I'm not dead."

"You could be." The words are barely a whisper. Saying

it is all too real, and if he'd died then it'd be on me. Ric squeezes my hand.

"I'm *not*. Any word on Maple?"

I shake my head. Silence fills the small room, and I wonder if he feels as vulnerable as he looks.

"So, this Static stuff is crazy. Any idea what's happening?"

"Not yet. The Triad is working on it." The words are supposed to be some kind of comfort, but they aren't. "Your mom should be here soon. Your dad called me twice."

"Nothing like an injury to reunite a family." The bitterness is not missed on me. I get how he feels about his dad. Not only the anger that he's gone, but the sadness, too. "I have a bad feeling…"

I shake my head. "Don't. Don't focus on that."

Ric's eyes are a little glassy. He cannot cry right now. I can't handle that.

"Not for me, for Maple. It's strange but it's almost like I can feel how hard she's fighting. Maybe it's part of the pairing ceremony, of the magic and the vows, but they definitely never tell us about that being a thing," he says. His voice is like a whisper.

I lock my jaw, and try to be positive. To be strong. He needs me, and I have to be the one he can depend on right now. "The Triad is going to figure this out. The Statics will be fixed. The doctors will save Maple. You'll heal. Everything is going to be fine."

But even as I say it, I don't fully have faith that all of those things can work out, even if I want them, too.

Chapter Eight

CARTER

The next morning, the WNN announces a mandatory Enforcer meeting. Dad must have figured out what to say. Probably some new plan for a cover-up. They can't keep it quiet now—it's too late for that—but they'll want to keep all of this as calm as possible.

"Cutting it close, William," Dad says when I come into the kitchen.

I look at my watch. Two minutes until ten. "I was trying to miss seeing you completely. Next time I'll be better," I say.

Dad smirks across the table. Sometimes I really hate him.

Lucy, the current housekeeper, brings the food in. I watch her scurry around the room and steal a glance at Dad.

Even though he doesn't talk, I can see him critiquing her movements. He does this with all of the Statics he hires. The help, he calls them, which is more insulting than calling them all Statics. Most of them have a two-month turnaround. No one wants to stay in the Prescott manor. Not even me.

"Thank you," I say to Lucy. She nods at me. They're always so surprised when I thank them. God knows that Dad doesn't. I take a fork from the table, and look at my plate, filled with some kind of omelet.

Dad takes a knife to his sausage. "Do you have thoughts on the situation with the Statics?"

I groan. I hate when Dad tries to make me feel involved. It's his job to fix the problems, not mine. "No," I snap. Aside from telling him what the mauve demon said, I have nothing. Yet. I'm not going to trust a demon until I have hard facts. I'm not telling Victor Prescott anything else about Pen and me.

Dad takes a sip of his water, eyes on me from across the room. "You tend to have a thought about everything, so I figured this would be the same."

It's not like I have anything solid. I only have a feeling. "I feel that the whole thing is convenient."

"Convenient?"

I stare at him. Last week I had to trust in my dad, even though I don't. I had to pretend like I could. This time, I can't do that. Not yet. There's really no one I can talk about this with except Penelope. When we have answers, then we'll share them. Until then, I'm playing with my cards close to the chest.

"Demons always want something," I say. He stares at me from across the table. I hate the way he looks at me like that.

"What? Say whatever it is."

"I was thinking that you looked like your mother today."

I drop my fork on the plate with a clash. "Why would you bring her up?" My voice is rougher than usual. But talking about Mom is too fresh. It was only a week ago when I learned she was really a demon. Only a week since she tried to turn us over to her side. I'm not ready to talk about her. Especially with him. He was the reason she chose demons and left me.

"Because you do," he says. "I was thinking that you're going to make a fine leader in the Triad." I shake my head. There it is. The not-so-subtle hint that my life has a purpose. "I would do anything for you. You're my number one priority, even above this position."

"Are you trying to make a heartfelt moment? Because you're not so good at them."

"William."

"Carter, Dad, Carter. Stop trying to force it."

"Your name is William."

I stand at the table and my chair makes a scratching sound against the floor. "No, it's not. And none of this is about me—it's about you." It all comes out in one big rush. Once I start, it's hard to shut off. "I don't want this. That's you. Your whole problem is that I'm your number one priority. It should be this community, not me, not this secret." His face changes immediately from stoic to harsh lines of disappointment and warning. The look he wears when he's trying to remind people that he's in charge and they're about to cross a line. Good. I'm going to jump over that damn line and never look back.

"I'm a halfling, Dad." I say the words slowly and

purposefully. He doesn't want to face the truth and that's on him. My mom was already pregnant with me when she became a demon. Dad found out and kept her locked away until I was born, and then he sent her out. He told me that I was a halfling when I was nine, and he has always used it as a warning. *Stay in line, William, or everyone will know. Statics are exiled from our community. Halflings shouldn't exist.* Me not existing, him losing his power, those are his biggest fears. The latter more than the former. I'm a piece of his game, a pawn, and he needs me around to win. "You need to accept that."

Dad's face falls. *Good.* Anything I can do to show him how much I don't want to be here, that I don't have to live my life as his, I will do it.

I toss my napkin from my lap onto my plate. He opens his mouth to speak, but I leave. I don't want to stay to listen to any of his crap.

• • •

There's an itch in my hand that's only satisfied by blood. It's always like this when I feel like I'm losing control. It's my escape. But today, I need to fight it. To not be that person who needs to kill demons for sanity. I need something else to focus on, so I drive.

I don't have a direction when I get in the car. It's probably for the best, since it's a Saturday in Washington, D.C., and traffic sucks because no one here can drive. I turn the music up and head toward Interstate 495. I only have an hour before our meeting, but it's a short break. At least on I-495 I can go fast. Mostly. Sixty miles per hour doesn't really satiate the need for speed.

Why did he have to mention my mom? Why?

My mom is dead.

I spent years looking for her, following clues about where she could be, and then I find her and she's a demon. Now she's dust.

My mom chose that as her ending. She chose being one of those as her life. She wanted this more than being with me. I can't forgive her for that. What was so bad about me that she couldn't stay?

Him.

Victor Prescott. He was the bad thing. He's always the problem.

I hate him.

My phone rings and even though it's Penelope I don't answer it. I need a minute. I'm allowed to be angry. I'm trying to stay strong for her, encouraging and in contour. But I can't be that right now. Not right now. I need a minute.

I don't answer and she sends me a text.

Maple didn't make it.

Shit.

When I look up toward the road, I swear I drive past what looks like Vassago with a long white beard walking on the side of the road, but I look back in the rearview mirror, and there's nothing there.

Chapter Nine

Carter sits next to me at the meeting. Rafe informs the others about Maple's passing, funeral, and offers a moment of silence. Her funeral's tomorrow. Rafe and Sabrina switch places.

"In less than twenty-four hours, there have been thirty-four instances with registered Statics," she says. She stands on a dais in front of us all, and I have to admit that she looks regal. "There is no common denominators, aside from their status, no expectation of when or whom or why."

"Four hundred and seventy-nine registered Statics in our region have yet to manifest," Rafe Ezrati adds. "We must determine an effective course of action to control the Statics."

It's in my head, but I feel like their eyes are on me when

they speak.

Victor Prescott stands. When he does it's like the room shifts. Everyone was paying attention before, but now they're all hyper-focused. "Let us remind you that it is important that Non protective measures be kept intact during this time. We implore you to study the new material we added to the *Witches News Network Daily*."

I look over at Carter, at the stiff line of his jaw, and as much as he hopes for a different future, I really can see him leading. It's part of him, in some way, and we both know how hard it is to hide and deny a part of yourself. Even the parts you don't want.

"We believe every Static is susceptible to this," Victor says. "There does not seem to be a reason or pattern among them—as it is affecting every age group—so we must be on alert with all."

Someone in the back of the room stands, a guy, judging by the deep timbre of his voice. "You make it sound like it's a disease. It's magic."

Some murmurs flood the room, but they stop when Rafe puts up his hand. "All Statics are temporarily unstable. If you see a Static acting oddly, report it. Use your skills to keep those around you safe. You are trained Enforcers, taught to be prepared in any circumstance. We need you now."

Thinking about the Triad and watching them in action are two totally contrasting experiences. In my head, they're always wrong. Always smoothing things over with smiles. But in reality, they're beacons. Sabrina and Rafe aren't as demanding as Victor, but they might as well be the Justice League. Or the Avengers. I'd hate to be on their bad side.

There's another comment from the back of the room.

I missed it and tune in toward the end. Straining my neck to see who's talking only reveals the top of a man's balding head. "What if we evacuate Statics? Or Nons?"

Sabina Stone shakes her head, not even considering the question. "Evacuation is not a solution. This phenomenon could be spread worldwide. Why the Statics have magic, or how it spread, has yet to be determined, but it is clearly dangerous. Che Lin has already died. Do not let her death be in vain, but instead, rally together in this moment. Remember that the magic is uncontrollable for them without proper training."

"So, what's the solution then?" another Enforcer asks. No one chooses to admit it, but everyone is scared. Victor rises again, and Carter tenses beside me. He must see something in his father's grim expression that I don't.

"The other regions are taking preventative measures, should this spread any further. Our goal is to contain this issue until we're able to reverse it," Victor pauses. "There is a spell that dates back many centuries and will allow us to not only contain the magic, but keep track of the Statics who have manifested. It is called a marking."

Murmurs spread through the crowd. I glance at Carter. "What is that?" I whisper.

His jaw is clenched but he shakes his head. I look back toward Victor, who holds a hand up to the Enforcers again. "We are evaluating the best way to use this spell. We'll be contacting a few of you individually after the services tomorrow for Miss Lin. Until then, be on alert. If we all work as one, we can protect our people. The best and brightest witches are on this. We thank you for your service."

My phone beeps from my pocket, and I pull it out. Poncho is summoning me to the library. Maybe he's found information about the dagger.

I look around the room for Carter. He's talking to Jordan Stark, but when he sees me waving he nods at me, a smile spreading across his face. The rest of our world may be a mess, but at least we're still good. That's pretty big, considering everything.

"Poncho," I say, as he comes over to me.

Carter and I head toward the library without another word.

When we get upstairs, Poncho is sitting behind his desk with the cats. He perks up when we come in. "That was fast," he says.

"We were downstairs," Carter says, stepping toward Poncho at the desk. "What's going on?"

Poncho puts up a finger, and leads us around to the other side of the library. I hate going into the stacks. It's strange to be scared of a library, but they are endless, dimly-light tunnels. We stop in the middle of some row, and Poncho pulls a book of the shelf.

"What is this?" I ask, taking the book.

He stares at me. "The dagger led me to this book. Page 140."

On the page, there's a picture of a ritual and in the drawing what looks light pours from the person's fingers and hands. Under the picture it reads

IMAGE OF RYANE KAHN, 1314, AS DEPICTED BY AN
EYEWITNESS.

"What is this?"

Poncho looks between us. "Destiny led you to each other. Your purpose and this dagger are connected."

Poncho loves to talk of destiny, but I haven't even had lunch yet.

"How?" Carter asks.

Poncho reaches out and turns the page. A similar picture.

IMAGE OF SARAH VANE, 1414, AS DEPICTED BY AN EYEWITNESS.

He turns the page again.

1514.

1614.

I don't need to see anymore.

"These images occur every one hundred years, as far as records show, and the time is upon us for a repeat performance," he says.

This year.

"But what is it?" I ask again.

Poncho looks square at me. "Magic, Miss Grey. Magic that is stronger than any other."

"And it's connected to the dagger?"

"What is the magic?" Carter asks.

Poncho looks between us again. "It's both good and bad and neither. It is the greatest."

More riddles. I hate riddles. "Which is what, exactly?"

"It's coming. The time is upon us all," Poncho whispers, and the goosebumps form on my arm.

"For what?" I ask again.

"The gift will be known soon," he says. There's a moment where he's quiet, and then Poncho looks at me again. "Matters of the heart are poisonous." He said that to me right after I got back from De'Intero. What does it mean?

And what's the gift? Before I can ask, he walks away and leaves us in the stacks.

Carter stares at me. "What does that mean?"

"I have no idea."

But it can't be good.

. . .

Carter drops me off at home, but we linger outside his car a little longer. There are only a couple of lights still on in the house. Gran's probably been waiting up for me. The WNN alert beeps and I stare at my phone.

"I don't even want to look anymore," Carter says.

I don't check, either, since it's probably another Static incident. Thousands of Statics exist worldwide, hundreds in our area alone, and if all of them manifest magic, this could never end. "What if we really did this?"

Carter takes my hand. "Then we'll figure it out. We'll undo it or whatever we need to do."

"And if we can't?"

He doesn't respond. I need him to say that we can, that I'm being too negative, that there's always a way. I need him to lie. But I know he won't.

"Can't we tell someone? Your dad—"

"Not my dad," he snaps. His face contorts in a way that makes me wish I hadn't suggested it. "I don't want him involved in this. Let's deal with it ourselves. We can figure it out."

"Will we?" I challenge.

"Yes," he says without hesitation. "Believe me."

"I do," I say. But really, I don't. It feels bigger than even

I can handle. Than we can handle.

Carter looks at me, his eyes piercing green, and I know he sees my doubt. There's no way it's not written all over my face. He brings a hand to my cheek.

"You're not a good liar, either," he says, a grin on his lips.

"Maybe you know me better," I say back, echoing our conversation from yesterday.

"I do. So, please, let's try this my way, and if it doesn't work then we can try anything you want." His eyes are so serious, so pleading, that I agree and nod against his palm. He guides my face closer to his and presses his lips to mine. His kiss holds the same fervor of desperation and desire that I saw in his eyes. We get lost in it, relish it, and let it consume us. This kiss, these moments, feel priceless and fragile in the wake of everything. As if, at any moment, we could fumble and lose each other. I won't let that happen.

When we part, he rests his forehead against mine. Neither of us say anything else—we don't have to. This, that, says everything.

"You should go in," Carter says, and I sigh.

"Yes," I say. "See you tomorrow."

I'm at the door to my house when Carter drives away. Then, I smell sulfur—a demon. Very near. I turn around to look. Nothing.

My brain kicks into Enforcer mode. Aside from the smell, there are no flickering lights, which means the demon has been here longer than me. New arrivals make the lights flicker from the power surge. A pull gnaws at my stomach, and I move around the front yard. It's too dark to notice if there's any dust around, the trail a demon leaves from possession. Gran has the house warded, so I'm not worried about a demon inside.

It's definitely here, though. I can smell that tart, rotten egg smell. With BO like that, it's no wonder they aren't friendlier.

Around the back of the house, a hand grabs me. I ram my elbow into whoever it is and feel the scales of a demon. I pull the demon toward me, swipe my foot across its leg, and guide the demon over my hip. In a quick movement, I roll the demon off and over my body with all the force I have. It slams into the ground, and I rip the salt off my chain.

"Penelope, don't."

When I look, really look, it's the mauve demon. I squeeze its neck tighter. "What the hell?"

"Can you get that salt out of my face please?" it says. I move it closer instead. The demon snarls. "You are a hard girl to track down sometimes."

"Really? Because you sure seem to find me pretty easily," I snap. I don't move my grasp or the salt. One wrong move and I will toast this thing. "What do you want?"

The demon looks past the salt and into my eyes, the green of its eyes unnatural. "To talk about your Static mystery."

"I don't really hang out with demons."

"My name is Lia, and you should listen to me."

I lower the salt and release the demon. Lia rubs her neck as she stands, and I hope that wasn't the wrong decision. But so far, Lia is the only one who claims knowledge about the Statics and I'm interested in whatever she knows. "This isn't really the best time or place for that," I say.

"A few hours from now then?"

I nod. "I'll meet you in the park."

Lia flickers away from me, and I flee into my house, hoping I made the right decision.

Chapter Ten

CARTER

I can't sleep. Poncho's weird prophecy shit is on replay, but Dad's recent comments about Mom haunt me the most. I had one moment with her for my whole life. I hate that. I hate that Dad lied to me about her. I hate what he's trying to turn me into. I toss the covers off, put on a hoodie, and go.

It's way after midnight before I get out of the house. The streets are quiet through our neighborhood of Georgetown, except for a couple of bars. I need a clue. There has to be a demon with information about what happened to the Statics. Or at least a demon who can tell me why Kriegen wanted us. I'm not sure what I'm looking for with the demons. Not yet. I guess I'm hoping one of them will accidentally be useful.

For the rest of the night, I don't have a name.

I don't have gold triangles.

I don't have anything except demons. Lots of demons.

And an itch in my hand that can only be calmed with the blade in my belt.

. . .

Lights flicker off in the apartment above the street, as I pound a demon's head back against a brick wall. I hope it hurts. Just like the last four I've killed tonight. Not killed, but ridded the world of. "Last chance."

"Let me go," the demon hisses in my face.

I don't even respond to it. I shove the salted iron dagger into its heart and say the words in a whisper. *"Virtute angeli ad infernum unde venistis."* Then, it's guts.

This is the only thing that makes sense to me. Tracking demons, looking for answers, destroying. I hate them all. Living with the fact that their magic and blood runs through my veins, sometimes I hate myself, too.

Another demon jumps me from behind. I should've suspected there were more in this location. Ever since Kriegen, they've been working in groups more and more. Its nails dig into my skin, and I force it to the ground. It hisses through sharp fangs. I can't reach the salt in my pocket, but I don't need it. I punch it in the face.

Claws and fingers dig at my shoulders. Its legs kick and teeth show as I drive my fist into its face. Again and again. I stick the point of the dagger into its neck, and a howl so loud fills the street. I don't stop. Goo-like blood seeps from the spot on its neck. All I have to do is say the words and end it. But I want it to suffer. Like I am, like I have.

And then I'm going to destroy it.

Destroy it like they all did my mom.

Like she tried to kill Pen.

Like the Static killed Maple.

Like my dad tries to kill who I really am by making me someone else. Making me him.

The demon cries out again, gasps in breaths of air. Demon blood is all over my hands and a gaping wound is across its neck. I did that. I should feel bad, but I don't. It deserves this. Its eyes widen and glisten, hands close around my arm. I whisper the words. "*Virtute angeli ad infernum unde venistis.*"

And then it's gone, except for the remains of its flesh. I expect to feel better. I don't. Somehow it makes me want more.

I mutter another spell to get rid of the blood on my hands, and then a scream echoes through the air.

That was not a demon. It was a girl.

My instincts go on high alert, and I run toward the sound.

I'm standing in a parking garage as another scream fills the air. Someone is in trouble. The pavement of the garage angles up, and I follow it. Halfway to the top, a sound echoes down toward me. Demon laughter and the sudden pungent smell of demons drift toward me. They must have a Non.

"Hey kid," someone yells from behind. I turn, ready to end get rid of another vermin. The skin it possesses is thin, practically falling off, a sign that this poor guy has been possessed for too long. It comes toward me, and I take it down with a swipe of my foot. Pretty lame. I expect at least a bit of fight.

"Tell me about the Statics," I yell.

The demon doesn't answer. My blade rests against his throat. There's no saving the Non he's wearing anymore. It makes me want to end the demon more. To slash its throat.

It would be so easy to slide this iron a little deeper.

"Don't kill him," a familiar voice commands. "Good help is hard to find and it's a busy time of year to be searching for replacements."

I don't release the demon, but I look up. Vassago stands before me, looking the same as usual with his disgusting white beard flecked with bits of food, graying, dirty clothes and one sock. What is this? Vassago wouldn't have taken a Non. He's not that kind of demon, surprisingly. He's the demon of lost things, a guide, not a murderer.

"Where's the Non?"

"There is not one here," he says softly. He looks at the demon under my blade. "You seem troubled, Mr. Prescott."

"I'm not," I say.

"Then release my goon, please." Vassago says calmly, looking from the demon to me. I stare at Vassago, and his eyes are intent on me. "It will solve nothing," he says.

I look back at the demon, and it doesn't fight me. I ignore the urge to end it and lower my blade. He scrambles away from me, and I glance back at Vassago. "If you don't have a Non, why was there screaming?"

Vassago raises an eyebrow. "How about a match, Mr. Prescott?"

I look past Vassago toward a little table set up with Scrabble. "Are you serious?"

"I anticipated your arrival. Come." He turns away without me and walks toward the table. This is ridiculous.

I cross my arms. "I don't really feel like playing Scrabble."

"What do you seek then?"

"Answers."

Vassago gives me a nod. He moves to sit at the table in the middle of an empty parking space, waiting for me. I stand there for long, silent seconds. I don't want to play Scrabble.

"A quick one," Vassago says, "since you are already here and it is set up."

I am here, and obviously Vassago went through some trouble to make that happen. Why would he do that? Has he been keeping tabs on me? I sit next to him on the opposite side of the table and glance at the board. It's surprisingly pristine for a demon that burrows through the trash and keeps a collection of crumbs in his beard.

The whole thing reminds me of being a kid. Dad and I used to played chess. The first time I sat down to play with my dad, I was six. He is always white because he likes to make the first move. Back then, his approval was the only thing I longed for. It was before I knew better. That first day when he explained the rules of chess me, he said the most important thing to know about chess—and every other game—is to have a strategy.

Every move has a counter move if you are able to see it.

"Choose wisely," Vassago says, passing me a sack of letters. I get an 'M' and he gets a 'J,' so Vassago goes first. Almost immediately he puts down CENT. It's only six points.

"Really?" I ask. "Six points?"

"It's what I have," he says. "Do not underestimate. The end result can be stronger with a slow start."

I reach in for my letters.

L C Y X G A E

I stare at the pieces, and then see the word LEGACY and put it on the board. Sixteen points, since Y is a double letter score. I don't have a strategy in Scrabble aside from winning.

Vassago makes a noise at my move. "Interesting choice."

"All I do is draw the letters from the bag," I say.

"Or are meant to draw these particular ones?" Vassago asks. "It is your job to make the words, after all. Perhaps destiny is at play as well."

I have no clue what that means. I watch him while he puts his own tiles on the board. What have I gotten myself into? Is he going to make everything have a higher meaning? The letters I draw from this bag are just letters. That's all.

"I don't really accept that crap," I say. Destiny, fate, all of it is an excuse.

Vassago spells out CHECK and then I add MATE and it makes him laugh. He plays REMAIN and I play MANY. He must find the whole thing amusing because he's laughing and muttering and smiling.

"I also enjoy chess," Vassago says randomly.

I was thinking about that a second ago. I raise an eyebrow. "My dad taught me, but it's been awhile since we played." Years, really. I can't even remember the last time I could be in his presence without hating him. Which meant avoiding him at all costs.

Vassago nods, putting down a 'G' onto the board. If anyone had told me I'd be playing Scrabble with a demon in the middle of the night in a parking garage, I would have never believed them. Vassago's hand flits over the board, freezes, and then he looks at me. "Do you remember the incident with the red balloon?"

Red balloon? For a second I don't, then he touches my leg with his foot, and it all comes rushing back toward me.

I was three or four and Dad and I were in the park. There was a festival with balloons—mine was red—I wanted blue. I wasn't aware I had the void, but the magic changed it to blue. My dad was so angry with me that he popped it. I cried and he told me to stop crying. "This is not how Prescott men act," he'd said.

"Your move," Vassago says. I look at the board. DAGGER.

I stare at him. What the hell just happened? "I'd forgotten that moment."

"Your move," Vassago repeats. I shake my head and look at my letters. I really only have one option, so I play KING.

"Ah yes, the King's safety is crucial," Vassago says randomly, looking at the board. I look back up at Vassago's goons, standing frozen, and then meet his gaze. "Your father is also aware of that rule."

"Why are you bringing him up again?" I watch him, waiting for Vassago to pick the rest of his letters.

"He is the reason you are out killing innocents, is he not?"

I scoff. "Demons aren't innocent."

Vassago draws another letter. "Some are. You are. Penelope is."

My jaw tenses. "We're not the same as them." He can't even try to compare us.

With a curt nod, Vassago leans over the board. "Perhaps not yourself, but she is the same. Her magic comes from us now."

I lean closer toward the table, mimicking Vassago. "How do you know about all that? What am I doing here?"

Vassago licks his finger and then holds it in the air, muttering words I can't make out. "A storm is coming. And a cold front, I expect."

"Cold? It's August."

Then he looks at the board and lays down the rest of his pieces. I stare at the board. His new word says

MAUVE

Chapter Eleven

"Took you long enough," Lia says. We're standing in the middle of an empty park at two in the morning, and she's complaining as if my tardiness is the most inconvenient part of this.

"Yeah, well, human."

Lia *hmms*, eyes on me, and I notice for the first time that her eyes are blue. Very blue. I've never seen a demon with blue eyes, only green, and it makes Lia seem almost human.

"Why are we here?"

"I have information for you, and I think you'll be even more inclined to think about it considering your current predicament." The demon's lips snarl.

I cross my arms. This demon is tuning into the wrong

news channel. "I don't have a predicament."

"You do," Lia says, looking me over. "It hasn't occurred yet—not beyond the whole 'giving all the Statics magic' thing."

"Right. You think I did that."

"I know you did," she says. She doesn't look back at me, but I see her chest move as she sighs. A demon with an attitude. Great. "Magic is a balance, and any tipping of the scale can destroy it all."

That quote again. It's becoming one of those earworm songs that I hate, but gets stuck in my head all the time. "What does that mean?"

"It's a fact," Lia snaps, jumping off the railing and moving toward me. I try not to gag as the sulfur smell fills my immediate breathing space. "You need me, and I need you. You are the tipping point on the scale. You changed things when you made the demons disappear, because you used both sides at once. The void and the essence."

"Is this a re-run? You told me that part, thanks."

She's close enough now that I can see the dark black skin under her scales. "Magic isn't supposed to be wielded that way. It's one or the other. Someone who can access both sides? Dangerous. For both sides."

"I don't have the essence," I say. Kriegen made that perfectly clear to me before. I only have a little jolt of my family's magic, not enough to power up on my own. They filled up the rest of the essence to let me have power. Like a supercharged battery.

"Yet, before you met your halfling, you used it."

"Only with someone in my family."

Lia shrugs. Demons. They're always so cocky.

"You're pretty annoying. You demons only like to say half of whatever you're trying to say. Humans like sentences."

Lia's standing next to me now, and I move to the side, not because I'm scared, but because I don't like what she's saying. It can't get any better from here. Not with that blue steel look of determination on her face "Sentences, right." She pauses. "I've learned your story, Penelope Grey, and all about the demon who took your essence—you survived, because he didn't take it all." She moves around me toward the other side of the park, and despite my better judgment, I follow.

Lia stops at a streetlamp and peels off a sticker, then she says, "It's like that. A sticker that's been on a surface for a few years. When you take it off, the outline still remains. It becomes part of what was."

"Did you plant that there for this demonstration?" I ask.

"Your essence is still part of you, Penelope, even if there's not enough for it work on its own. You've been using the void since you met your halfling loverboy, and after that encounter last week, there's no question that it liked what it saw, and I'm assuming that it's staying."

I scrunch up my nose. Magic is a balance, and before I used the overflow of the void that Carter had and didn't use. And now the void likes me? Destiny sure likes making crap confusing.

"You're dangerous when you use the void, especially with the halfling," she says.

I scoff. "He does have a name."

She doesn't pay attention to that. "Even as you tinker with it now, you're opening the crack, and it will only be a matter of time before you can access the void regularly.

Until it moves from liking you to becoming part of you. The void isn't the same as the essence—it's more alive. It's more innate."

I raise an eyebrow. I do like the void. It's easy and natural, like it's always supposed to have been part of me.

"I have power with Carter," I say.

She snorts. I think. It's hard to tell what the sound is actually supposed to be. "You have a glimpse with him. The magic you've used already is only a sliver of the potential. The void will do what it desires with you, and you need to be ready."

If what Lia is saying is true, then the dam was sealed and now that it's been cracked, I can take whatever I need to from it. Will it really try to overpower me? And what does that have to do with the Statics?

"You said you would give me information about the Statics. This isn't information."

"I am helping you, you daft girl," Lia crosses her arms. "When demons take a witch's essence, it's absorbed. It becomes part of a demon, but it changes the magic that already exists inside a demon and becomes tainted. All those demons in De'Intero you killed? You also pushed out their magic. Released it. The magic couldn't return to the source it came from because it was tainted."

The magic couldn't go home. "So, where did it go?"

"All magic needs a host."

The gleam in her eye

Suddenly, it all makes sense. "The Static witches."

She nods. "Those with ability but not with power. At least not until now."

"Why are you telling me this?"

"You have a responsibility to magic now. You alone. The fact that you can access it makes you a target. Don't you feel it calling to you?"

I don't answer that, even though I always feel it. It's always trying to come out, ready to be used.

"You can trust me," she says.

"I doubt that," I say. Trusting her is the opposite of everything I've been taught. Everything I've learned. "You should go."

Lia nods. "I'll leave, but this isn't over. You need me."

She flickers out and leaves me standing alone on the sidewalk of the park.

Chapter Twelve

I stare over all the words on the board. These don't feel random. I reach for the bag, Vassago grabs my elbow.

"The questions that are coming, I have already answered for you." He says. His eyes take on a light white color for a second, the same look they've had before when he was delivering a prophecy.

"I don't have any questions," besides what he's talking about.

Vassago drops my arm and taps the table. "I said the ones that are coming. The ones the change will bring. She will be marked, and the time will be upon us."

Whoa."She? Who is she?" I look at the word MAUVE.

He doesn't look away from me. "Remember the balloon."

"The red balloon?" What the hell is happening right now?

He grows quiet and after some awkward silence, I look back at the board, unsure of what move to make. It's my turn, right? I've lost track now.

"You need another letter," he says calmly.

I take another from the bag and stare at everything in front of me. Letters that don't fit on the board yet. Clues that I don't understand. Answers to questions I haven't asked.

"It's unnatural for things to become what they were not intended to be," Vassago says in the silence. I look at him again. "Other times what they are intended is not what they must become. Keep in mind the words I told you before." He motions toward the board. "Your move still."

What he told me. The only other time we talked was… "In the bar?" I ask. He gave us the prophecy or vision or whatever name it has. *There is one who seeks the same as you and one who hides the truth from you. Only when the two meet shall the lost be found.* I make my move because he taps the board. "I thought we dealt with that. It was about my mom, and Pen's family secret. Is there more?"

Vassago grins. "There is always more, Mr. Prescott."

I cross my arms as he studies the board. "You're really unhelpful."

A hand flutters to his heart. "I service to the lost, and you are lost, but she is more lost than you. I found you because I find the lost. This is my duty. Your duty is to protect your partner at any cost." His eyes narrow in on me. "Especially when your partner is also the girl you love."

I groan. "Stop talking in riddles. I don't understand what you're saying to me."

Vassago doesn't even blink. "Serve, assist, and guide. This is our purpose." Then, in a quick movement, he points to the board. "Your turn still."

I throw the letters I have on the board and spell DEMON. Vassago rubs his hands together. "A good chess strategy suggests that when you develop your pieces, you make moves that threaten. Moves that can come as unexpected."

"We're not playing chess," I say.

"Aren't we?" he responds.

Quickly, he places down his tiles. The word "cent" has been changed. Now it says

OBSERVANCE

I point to the Scrabble board. "What is all this, Vassago?"

"Have you noticed how Scrabble is like chess? It's strategic, and much like life in that you must think two moves ahead of your opponent. I like a good challenge, and you do as well, or you wouldn't be out here in the middle of the night."

Middle of the night, right. Today has sucked. I came out to escape it all. I look at the board at all the words and then back at Vassago. "How did you have this whole set-up ready and waiting for me, Vassago?"

He sits up in the seat. "I knew you would come."

"How?"

"The change is upon us, and it was your destiny—and mine—to be here."

"Destiny, huh?" I look at the board and a few letters. "What if I had said I didn't want to play?"

Vassago smiles. "You are a Prescott. You were taught

never to back down from a challenge. That is part of your path. Some destinies are chosen for us. Others we choose. Others are left up to us to determine."

I put my last tiles on the board and write PEACE. "Which one is yours?"

Vassago looks at the board, and then at me. "That's still to be decided."

I glance at my phone. Three a.m. "I should probably get home."

He nods his head thoughtfully, eyes on the board. I stand up from the table, feeling more unsettled than I did before I left home. Vassago studies the board and then he smiles. He picks up a final few letters and places them down. He spells out QUEEN.

"I think I win with that," he says.

"Thanks for playing," I say, extending my hand.

Vassago looks at it for a moment before taking it. "A change is coming, Mr. Prescott. A storm is forming that will soon arrive. Every side will be playing soon, so prepare your moves."

I glance back at the board. OBSERVANCE is where my eyes go first, and then across the rest of the board. This game with Vassago and the conversation with Poncho from earlier must connect. Poncho mentioned a destiny, and Vassago has, too. Maybe destiny centers around the Observance?

He drops my hand. "Be sure you don't bring your Queen out too early. The King may be the goal, but the Queen is the most powerful."

• • •

It's nearly morning when I get home. Uncertainty has settled in my chest that I can't ignore. I grab a piece of paper and start writing down the words on the Scrabble board, before I forget. If the conversations and the words on the Scrabble board are one piece, then I should figure what he was trying to say.

CHECK. REMAIN. DAGGER. MAUVE.
OBSERVANCE. QUEEN.

I only have guesses here. 'Queen' could be Penelope, but why? Queen of what? Mauve is that demon. It's conveniently around lately and I can't ignore that. 'Observance' is obviously the party. 'Dagger'—is that the black one? It could be any dagger, I guess. I don't know what 'remain' is, or 'check.'

Vassago talked about chess a lot. In chess, check is when the other player's king is in danger. The threat must be stopped or the king needs to move. If the king can't be moved then it's a checkmate and that player loses. Vassago laughed when I changed check into checkmate.

If Pen's the queen then then who's the king? Or is Pen the king? She could be the king.

I'm too tired for this.

I leave the paper on my desk and head to bed. As soon as I'm there, the WNN dings. I have thirty-six missed notifications, all attacks on demons and Statics. But it's a message that makes me freeze. A message from the Council to Pen and me. We have a meeting with them after Maple's funeral.

Chapter Thirteen

During the funeral, Ric didn't say anything. He sat there, sandwiched among his mom, me, and Connie, staring, and when he managed to make eye contact, his eyes were empty. I could almost see the pain in them like a tangible thing.

"Don't miss me too much," Ric says softly, tossing his carry-on bag toward the ground. I see the grimace at the simple motion, even if he'll never admit it.

Mrs. Norris sees it too because her eyes widen with concern. "I'll get our tickets," she says, leaving Ric and me awkwardly standing out of place in our freshly-pressed funeral clothes. Maple's only been buried for hours and Ric is already leaving. The Triad said Ric should get away, that he needs time to recover from his injuries. Which is a fancy way of saying they need time to figure out if he should get a new partner. And who.

His mom agreed, and now that his dad is back from his honeymoon, it's a solution. One Ric is not thrilled about.

I slip my arms around Ric into a hug. He kisses my cheek, but that sad look is still in his eyes. I want to know what he's feeling, but I also don't. I can't imagine it at all. "Don't give your dad too hard of a time."

Ric groans. "I'm more worried about the step-diva. Can I call her my stepmom if she's only a few year older than us?"

"As long as you don't call her 'step-diva' to her face I'm sure it will be fine."

Ric looks over his shoulder toward his mom. She's only dropping him off to his dad's car, and then she's on another plane to wherever she has to go next. "Mom said it was a good chance to face some demons. I told her I do that every day, and she didn't laugh."

"At least your dad is still alive," I say. Ric sighs, but I don't regret saying it. I'd say it again because I want him to remember that. We've both lost enough people. "You have a second chance—I'd hate to see you miss out on it."

"I'm stuck in a house with him for the duration of this restcation. I won't miss anything." Ric pushes the bag up on his shoulder. "I'll call you."

"Boarding pass acquired. See you, Penelope," Mrs. Norris says. Ric steals another hug and then with a final glance back, he's gone. The high-low-high notes of the WNN chime. I expect another attack of some sort, but it's not. It's a reminder/repeat message about my meeting with the Triad in an hour.

Your attendance is mandatory.

I shove the phone into my pocket. It's not like I could forget.

. . .

The counsel chambers are empty. Nothing except the sound of the clock fills the empty waiting room. I close my eyes and take a breath. Deep, cleansing breaths and happy thoughts run through my head, but they can't stop this. Whatever this is. Somehow, it feels like all the things I've worked for are this close to being gone.

"We're going to be fine," Carter whispers in my ear. He squeezes my hand tightly until I look at him. He says it with so much conviction that I wish it was true.

The council summoned us two hours ago, and we've been sitting here. Waiting.

"They're looking for more details about Maple and Taylor Plum. It's nothing, Pen."

"How can you be sure?"

Carter takes my hand. "They're going to ask some questions. We'll answer them, and we'll leave. That's it." I start to protest but he puts a finger to my lips. "Whatever is going on, we'll get through this." He presses a quick kiss to my lips and I smile.

He's right. This is nothing more than a checkup. That's it. They said they'd be looking into the Static situation, so that has to be all this is. Some questions.

The door opens and Mrs. Bentham stands in front of us, her hair pulled back in its usual up-do and her cheeks pinched. Behind her is Ellore, stunning as ever. I haven't seen either of the councilwomen in the week since our partnering ceremony, but now neither of them are smiling.

"Miss Grey, Mr. Prescott, come with us," Mrs. Bentham says.

That's all. No 'hello' or smiles or 'good to see you'. This is so bad.

Carter takes my hand and we follow behind Ellore and Mrs. Bentham out the door. The Nucleus House is alive with people, and maybe it's in my head, but all of them look at us as we pass. Ellore and Mrs. Bentham lead us down a hallway back into the testing rooms for Enforcer Examinations.

"It has come to our attention that the two of you have committed an indiscretion. The council and the Triad frown upon these accusations."

"I thought this was about the Statics?" I say.

Carter squeezes my hand tighter, but I replay the attack in my head and wonder what the accusations could be. Could they know about De'Intero? "What exactly is our indiscretion?" I ask.

Ellore and Mrs. Bentham exchange a look. A cold one. Mrs. Bentham crosses her arms. "You cheated on the Enforcer Examinations."

They know.

How could they find out?

What else did they discover? Do they know about the Statics? That I didn't have magic on my own when I took it? My whole family could get into trouble…

Carter squeezes my hand like an anchor. "That's not even possible."

Mrs. Betham still doesn't say anything, but she looks at me, and there's a curiosity in her eyes.

Ellore says. "We're following procedure."

Mrs. Bentham continues, "It has been mentioned, and now that it has we simply cannot turn a blind eye. We are giving you an opportunity."

Carter glances at his cousin. "Ellore, is this for real?"

I can't say anything. My mind is racing, but unable to focus on anything. All my thoughts are fleeting, swirling like smoke.

Ellore nods. "Very real."

"We're giving you both a chance to prove to us that this accusation is wrong," Mrs. Bentham adds.

"It is wrong," Carter says. But I can't speak about it, because it's not. We did cheat—even if I'd never thought of it that way.

"Good," Mrs. Bentham interjects. "Then you have nothing to worry about. Mr. Prescott, with me. Miss Grey, with Ellore."

That snaps me out of it. "What?"

"We're going to re-test you both separately. With me." She points to the left.

I look at Carter over my shoulder, and beneath his calm exterior, I can see in his eyes that he's freaking out. Normally, I'd freak out, too. This is our future. But he doesn't know what Lia told me. The void is more than me pulling from him now. It wants me. I could be powerful with it. This could be the thing that saves me.

Ellore pulls me into a familiar white room. A simulation.

"Penelope," Ellore says, lowering her voice into a whisper. "I don't think you did anything. This is a precaution, a piece of the investigation into Miss Lin's death, that's all. We had an anonymous tip and it's our job to follow up."

I don't say anything. There's nothing to say. She's right. I can do this. A week ago, I'd be screwed, but now I have an advantage.

"This will start as soon as I leave and you'll have five minutes."

The room flashes a warning, but I'm ready. The void is ready, a steady pulsing. In a moment the white fades away from me and I'm standing in the middle of the National Mall. They put me in the middle of the action. It's a sunny day, tourists walking around and people playing Frisbee on the lawn. Everywhere I look there are people, which means I'm going to have to do whatever is happening without drawing unneeded attention.

And I have five minutes.

Last time I had a simulation during the Enforcer Examinations, I had to find the demon and a weapon to fight it. I bet this is similar. I'll have to find the demon myself—it's not going to attack me. And it's probably in Non form—since there are so many around.

I look to my left and right. One way leads up to the Capitol building, and the other toward the Washington Monument. It could be in any one of the Smithsonian museums or monuments for miles. I bet there are even more Nons inside, so that would be nearly impossible to find in five minutes.

No, it would be outside. I feel like it's outside.

How much time is left?

I should go and stop debating.

Eeny meeny miney mo—the Monument it is.

I pick up my pace and head toward the other side of the mall. The music from the carousel fills my ears, and I glance at it ahead. I used to like that thing. Before the demon, Azsis, killed my parents, I came here with them. Connie was a baby, but I remember my dad let me pick out my seat. I chose this white horse, but it was next to this really creepy blue and green seahorse and I cried. Dad stood in front of it the whole time and said he wouldn't let it hurt it me.

I push away the memory because this is so not the time for emotional instability. I doubt the Council or the Triad would allow that to be a reason for failure. What would happen to me if I fail? I don't even want to think about that.

As I get in front of the carousel, I smell sulfur. A crowd is gathered around the ride, kids waiting in line and old people watching. Crap. One of them is definitely a demon. I walk through them trying to figure out which. No weird eyes. No black sulfur dust in the ears. The demon can't be on the carousel because I'm sure that thing has iron on it. Maybe it's not even anywhere near me yet.

I take a few steps closer to the carousel and the scent gets stronger. There's a tug on my shirt and I jump. It's a kid, a girl with black curls.

"Do you have a quarter? I don't have enough money."

I reach in my pocket and pass it over. As soon our hands touch I look at the little girl, and she smiles. "Thank you," she says. But it's not right. Her eyes are bright green, tinged in red, and her smile isn't innocent. It's evil. Oh, boloney…

The little girl gets in line the carousel.

She can't get on it, right? It's iron. Demons don't do iron. But then she does. Crap. This is a test. A big test. She's not a real demon—she's a simulation. Maybe simulated demons can handle iron horses, or maybe this is a special case. But those eyes are unmistakably demon.

I jump on the carousel before it takes off and follow the little girl around to the seat of her choice. Once she's sitting, I sit near the assumed demon girl. The music starts and the whole foundation moves around and up and down. It makes me a little sick. What am I going to do?

I can't use magic against the demon with people watching, and there's no way I'd get the cloaking spell up in time to do both. Or be inconspicuous about it.

Think, Penelope, think.

I push the demon girl off the carousel once we're on the opposite side of the crowd. I wait for some angry mother to attack me, but nothing. The girl hisses at me, and in seconds the demon sheds the girl's skin. Now I'm face to face with a real-live pearl-colored demon.

It lunges at me and I move out of the way. Another lunge, another move. There's a light post behind me, so I stand closer to it. When the demon attacks again, I move quickly enough that I think it's caught. But it's not. These simulations are smarter than real demons. Or the whole iron thing doesn't work here, which, considering the carousel, makes sense.

I focus on the void. I try to see everything in my head—my magic bursting and filling me up. Killing this demon, guts all over the place. It's hard to access, like there's a wall between it and me. If I can't do this then we'll be separated, I'll be stripped of my badge, and my family. If they find out I can't do magic, then he's lost to me forever. My family is lost forever. I'm nothing.

I hate that. And I hate the demons for putting me here. And I hate that I can't change any of this.

Suddenly, the magic burns at my stomach. The sensation means the void is ready.

But I have to make this look convincing. I rip the salt-filled charm off my neck and toss the salt on the demon. It cries out in pain. A bell dings somewhere in the distance—a one-minute warning. It's now or never.

The magic is so strong that I feel like my skin is melting, exploding, and I have to get it out. I focus on the demon and yell the incantation for good measure.

"*Vitute angeli ad infernum unde venistis!*" The words are barely out when the magic comes pouring out of me. It feels endless and strong, and I see it coming from my fingertips, and it's so bright I have to squint.

The demon explodes in an instant. Translucent guts all over the place. It takes me a second to regain control of the magic, because it doesn't want to stop. Like it's stronger than me. I have to close my eyes and pull it back in. It makes my head pound, and I cry out in pain, falling to my knees.

Then I'm back in the white room.

Everything falls back into place within me, except my spinning head.

The door clicks open. Ellore is standing before me again, her eyes wide. "We don't…I've never…"

I look toward her, and her face is pale. She's never seen it before—the magic be literally shooting through my pores. Because it's not Essence. It's not normal. What happened?

Ellore pushes a finger to her ear, someone is talking to her through that thing. What are they saying? Her eyes get wide again when she looks at me. "Come with me," she says. Her voice shakes. I messed up. I totally messed up.

But how? It's never done that before.

I push away from the wall and look down at my shaky hands. And that's when I see it. On my left hand pinky finger, there's a small black dot, purplish.

I scrub at it, but the spot doesn't come off. It's not a spot on my fingernail, but under it. I'm pretty sure that only happens when you hurt yourself. Like the time I slammed my finger into a car door.

I'm positive that wasn't there before.

Chapter Fourteen

Penelope hasn't come out, and it's been an hour. I was in and out of my test in twenty minutes. I stand up again, look out the window, sit down. Where is she? What would they do to her?

An anonymous tip. Who would report us for this? And why? And more importantly, how does anyone know? None of this makes any sense.

"Carter," Ellore says my name and I jump up out of my seat. She's alone. No Pen.

"What's going on? Where's Pen?"

Ellore can barely look at me. Her hands are shaking. I've never seen her like this. I try to be patient, but I can't handle her not looking at me. "Something happened in her test."

The worst words ever said. "Where is she?"

"They're taking her."

I shake my head. Taking her…"What are you talking about? What happened?"

"I've never seen anything like it—"

"Like what?" And she looks at me, eyes wide and hands shaking. She holds them out in front of her, like she doesn't understand her own hands. And I get it immediately. It wasn't that Penelope didn't do magic, it was that she did. She used the void. I grab Ellore's shoulders. I need her to focus. "What happened, Ellore?"

"It came out from her fingertips—bright. So bright. I can't even explain it. I—"

Just like in De'Intero. Everything was so bright then, and if she did it in her re-testing then there's no telling who saw her. This is trouble. "Where is she?" I hear my heart pounding in my head. I have to find her. I have to stop whatever's about to happen. "Tell me. Please."

"The Triad voted." My dad. The Triad has approved our re-testing, and he's aware of our magic, that we're connected. Did he set us up? He wouldn't do that. Would he?

Ellore mutters. "They think it's safest if she's contained, until they can figure out what's going on. She's in transport, but they'll…"

I don't wait to let her finish that sentence. I run.

I burst into my dad's office, unscheduled and uninvited. Both things that he hates. "We need to talk."

Believe you are the most determined presence in the room

and others will accept it. You are a Prescott, after all.

Kenneth Slade and Sacra Lenore, two members of the council, both look in my direction. Their expressions say it all: how dare I burst in and demand time with the Triad leader? Kenneth raises an eyebrow at me. I don't give a damn about procedure. Not right now. Not while Pen is in trouble.

"Now," I add. I use my best Prescott tone. See Dad? I have been paying attention for almost eighteen years.

Victor Prescott crosses his arms, but doesn't even blink. His suit crinkles around his shoulders as he waves a hand in the air toward Kenneth and Sacra. Only that movement and they're already on their feet. Dad presses his lips into a tight line. "We'll resume this later."

As soon as the door closes behind them, I look at my dad and cross my arms to mimic his stance. "Stop this."

He leans back in his chair with a sigh. I hate when he is condescending. "Sit down, son."

I shake my head. "I'm not sitting down. Whatever's happening to Penelope—stop." I'm past the point of saying please. We're both aware of what I'm doing here. "She hasn't done anything to deserve any of this."

Dad raises an eyebrow, leaning back in his seat. The chair squeaks. "She cheated on her exams."

"You reported us?"

He holds his hands up. "I did not, but I should thank whoever did."

I slam my hands on his desk, and give him the finger in my head. He doesn't even flinch. "She didn't cheat."

"You gave her magic, William, and that's cheating. Even indirectly. She's told lie after lie. As have you."

"This isn't fair."

Victor Prescott straightens in his chair. I said the wrong word, and I can tell from the look on his face. 'Fair' isn't a word in our language. "You've spent most of your life ignoring my advice and instructions, but expecting fairness? That is not what I raised you to be."

I won't be anything he raised me to be. Always on alert, ready for action, stern but open, better. I won't pretend my way through life, or smile and agree. I want to live my own way and to be as far away from him as possible.

"Aren't you going to sit?" he asks.

I ignore him. "Let her go, Dad. She's not a threat to anything."

"Normally, I would agree—but now I have a mess. How do we explain today? What she did, that doesn't happen with *normal* witches." Witches pull the magic from the elements, we exist and use magic from nature. "That light? It's only seen when a witch is undergoing a transformation into a demon. When they've killed another witch and given up this side for evil. It's a sign of betrayal." Dad says. I bite my tongue, press down until I taste the iron. Dad notices, even if he doesn't acknowledge it. "There's only so much I can do," he adds.

I have to keep my cool, even though I feel it slipping away each moment I'm here and she's there. They can't think Penelope betrayed our kind. She'd never kill another witch or choose evil. That's not Penelope. "You can ignore it. You're the leader of the Triad."

"Ellore and the rest of the Triad saw the test, son. You said she had access to the void, but that?"

I lower myself into the seat. I shouldn't have told my dad anything about who Pen was. But I had to after De'Intero.

If he hadn't been on our side, no one on the Triad would've had more questions about why we missed testing and what happed in De'Intero. Questions that we wouldn't have been able to answer. We would've been found out immediately and never become Enforcers. I had to protect her, protect myself, and telling my dad was the only way to do that.

I sigh and look at my dad. Fine. "Containment? She hasn't done anything."

"She came between us."

I lean up toward my dad's desk. There it is—the blame that he so easily places on other people. "You came between us when you lied about mom."

"Ever since you met Miss Grey you've been wild. Demon hunting. Lying. Not to mention risking your life at De'Intero."

"I did all those things before Penelope, Dad."

"It has only gotten worse with her. Two people's secrets are harder to keep than one."

Arguing isn't changing this. I need to play this like my dad would. I need to play it to win. What would he do? He'd manipulate, convince, and wager. "You can convince them it was a mistake, a fluke, and erase it all."

"I could." He presses his lips into a line.

I nod toward him. My dad will never give up until he meets his goal. That's the way this power play works. "What do you want?"

A thin grin spreads onto his face. Even under his beard it looks sinister. Dad's brown eyes widen, and I've said the right thing. This is what he was anticipating, but this is the way he plays chess. Even though it's someone's life, it's the same thing to him.

"What I have always desired: your safety. You can have no doubt placed on you or on your status."

Status. I hold back a groan. "How do you propose that happens?"

Dad almost looks proud as he leans back in his chair. "I'll set things straight with Miss Grey. She'll be stripped of her badges, and she can't serve as an Enforcer." That's going to kill her, but it's better than the alternative. "As her partner, you'll be forced to step down as well."

There it is. He never liked me chasing the path of Enforcer anyway, compromise or not. "That's it?"

He holds up a hand. Yeah, that's never it. "You'll embrace your path. This," he points to his office, "is your destiny. You will train up for your future, leave behind the rest of your hobbies, and protect yourself. You're not a child anymore. This is your life. Our legacy."

He's had my whole future planned out since I was born. The Prescott name. The Prescott legacy. The Prescott smile. *Prescott men can never be wrong, or show weakness if they want to lead. They always lead.* I scoff. "That's really all that matters to you?"

Dad's eyes focus on mine, which isn't what he usually does. He's looking at me directly in the eye without the mask. Without the motive behind the words. "When it comes to keeping you safe, yes. You are the next leader of the Triad, and you must embrace that. I cannot have you wasting time around the city, so you'll be here. I will have your support on decisions in the community. You will embrace who you are, uphold the Prescott legacy."

I'm done talking about legacy. I can agree to all of that. I hold out my hand, but he doesn't take it.

"We will be forced to figure out a solution for Miss Grey."

"You can't contain her or exile her. If you do, the deal's off. Convince them of another way," I say. Dad stares back at me, silent and then nods.

"Sabrina and Rafe will not settle for letting her walk away from this unscathed."

"As long as she's safe." I hold my hand out to my father without hesitation. If me embracing the Prescott legacy means keeping Penelope safe, I will do it. I will do whatever it takes. "Now set her free."

"I have to talk to the others."

"Dad—"

"It will be a few hours, William. You can go to her until then. She's in level four." He doesn't have to tell me twice. I'm halfway out the door when he says, "I expect you to be home in time for dinner. Don't be late."

I don't respond as I leave. Mostly because I feel like I've sold my soul to the devil.

Chapter Fifteen

I hear everything Carter is saying, but it isn't sinking in. My brain doesn't want to accept it. Even after two hours of us talking about it through a containment window.

"I'm losing my badge," I repeat.

"Dad couldn't figure out a way for you to keep it—but he found one for me to keep you."

His words are intentional and they make my heart race. Normally, I'd let them linger on my soul and make a mark there, but right now, it's all a lot to process. Carter suddenly decided to trust his dad. They've been on the outs ever since he learned about Kriegen, when Victor Prescott said that all the secrets were for Carter's own good. I can't imagine what it took for him to go to his dad. For me. "Why did he agree?"

Carter looks away. "It doesn't matter."

"It does," I say.

His eyes are sharp on mine. "It's dealt with, Penelope."

Penelope. He only calls me that when it's serious. I won't push him, for now, but I doubt his father would go through all of this for me. Not without a cost. "Thank you."

"I'm sorry I couldn't save your badge too, but at least it isn't your life. Dad promised he wouldn't exile you," he says again.

I don't know if he's trying to convince himself or me. He's right, really. I'm alive and I get to stay with my family, with him. I can't say for sure what would happen if Victor hadn't agreed. Magic came out of my fingers. Anyone who saw that will question everything I do. My loyalties, my magic, me…

Being an Enforcer is what I worked my whole life for. What is my life without that?

"I told you not to use it anymore." Carter says. He means the magic. The void.

"What choice did I have? If I had no magic at all then it would've been worse. They would've punished us for cheating, and then we'd have to explain how. The answer to that isn't one they'd like." If I'd failed, been found out as a halfling, then my whole family would be punished for hiding me. They'd be tested for their magic, and we'd all be maintained. Killed. And if they found out about Carter, I doubt his dad could even protect him from that. This is what they do with halflings.

He shakes his head. "And look what's happened now."

We don't have the chance to talk about it anymore. The doors open and a few members of the council appear there. They all look at me, equal parts disgust and equal parts fear.

"The Triad is ready for you," they say. This is it. The end for me as an Enforcer, and who knows what else.

The walk to the Triad chambers is a surprisingly short one. The first time I came in here I expected an elaborate space similar the rest of the Nucleus House. It's not that. It's simple, with ten chairs for the council and three on a higher pedestal for the Triad. Everyone is already seated. Carter is stopped at the door, and I wish he was next to me.

"Miss Grey," Rafe Ezrati says. "It is with heavy hearts that we call you here. It's not every day that we are incorrect about one of our own."

There's a long pause and I want to speak, but I'm pretty sure that's on the "no-no" list. It's too late now for talking anyway, now that they've all been called here.

"The Triad and the council have discussed it, and we are granting you amnesty for your discretion." Sabina Stone says.

Discretion?

"The unorthodox ability you possess will not be shared beyond the confines of these walls. Everyone here is sworn to an unbreakable secrecy, but Miss Grey, your case is officially under investigation." He pauses. "We will discover why you have these unique abilities, and the purpose for them."

I glance at Carter. What does that mean? He looks as surprised as me.

"Until that is resolved, your standing as Enforcer is revoked," Victor Prescott adds.

With that word, Victor, Sabina, and Rafe all flick a hand in the air. The whole room is silent, and the badges emblazoned on my shirt disappear. I'm no longer an Enforcer.

"Until the investigation of your magic is cleared, you

should consider yourself on probation. You will be kept from magic until we decide otherwise," Sabrina says. The Triad waves their hands again, muttering words in Latin.

Kept from magic? My wrist burns and a long thin gold band appear around my wrists. I hold them up to watch as the band wraps around them, and then sinks into my skin. It burns, but only for a moment before it flashes gold and disappears. The outline is still visible. What was that?

"You've been marked," Victor starts.

That doesn't sound good. Isn't that what they were planning to do with the Statics?

Victor holds his head higher. "It allows for us to find you or call upon you, should we need your compliance. No one else will see it on you, and it will not interrupt your daily life. It will prevent you from access to the essence, the Nucleus House, the WNN—anything controlled magically—until our investigation has a result."

"I have vouched for you, per my son's insistance," Victor adds after a moment of awkward silence. I look toward Carter, grateful that he put himself on the line. But what did he have to give up in exchange? There's no way this is all out of the kindness of Victor's heart. "His trust in you and mine in him is allowing you to walk free until the investigation has been closed. Do not show that we have made an unwise decision."

I nod slightly toward him.

"You have thirty minutes to clear your belongings from the Nucleus House, then your probation begins," Rafe adds.

The three of them rise and disappear out of a door, followed by the council. While they all exit, my mind races. I'm being tracked like Vassago and the Do Not Expel demons, or DNE's, and my essence is blocked by this marking. I examine my wrist. I see the outline of it there, the gold ribbon, about half an inch thick. I've never heard of a witch being marked before.

"Do you see it?" I ask Carter when he moves beside me.

He takes my hands in his and looks closer, his fingers trailing over the spot where we saw it land. "Nothing." He drops my hands. "We should go get your stuff."

"You can get it later. There's one thing I want to do before I can't come here anymore," I say. Carter raises his eyebrow. "Poncho."

When we get to Poncho's office, Hyde and Seak the cats, are waiting outside of the door.

"You're strangely calm about all of this," Carter says as the door opens. The cats go in before we do. It's no wonder curiosity kills them.

I guess I am. "I can't explain why." I should be angry, but I'm not. It's almost like I've somehow known that this wasn't meant to be. But that's not right, because it was the only thing I ever wanted.

Whoa, past tense.

The only thing I want.

I still want it.

Don't I?

"I wonder if it's because of the magic ribbon?" I offer. Carter *hmms*, but he doesn't sound convinced.

Poncho is scribbling on some pages when we approach his desk. "Miss Grey, Mr. Prescott," Poncho says, turning in his chair. Hyde and Seak jump on the desktop. "Good afternoon."

He obviously hasn't yet heard that this is my last visit.

"Is it?" I ask. I watch his face to see if he gives anything away, but he doesn't. Poncho knows everything, and even if he's masquerading as a librarian instead of some kind of demon, he holds it close to the belt. He can't, or won't, tell me whatever he knows. Which is really annoying.

"Most absolutely. I have news for you, which you could qualify as good if it ends up being news you are pleased with." Poncho can never say a simple 'yes' or 'no.'

"I guess we'll see then," I say.

Poncho lays the dagger on the table. It's in the same condition as when we gave it to him, except there's no dirt or blood. The handle and blade are black with five symbols engraved on the handle. It's really pretty, if I can forget the fact that it's able to rip a witch or demon's magic from its body. That little thing has more power than I used to have. Or have now, thanks to the ban on all things Penelope.

"You found something." Carter says.

Poncho nods. "I've researched the dagger and the symbols." He points at one of the symbols on the handle. "This symbol means 'rebirth', which old demons liked to consider becoming new. This one," he points to another, "is 'recycle.'"

"Demons, saving the world one plastic bottle at a time."

Poncho shakes his head. Carter doesn't laugh, either. Joke fail.

"Or re-use. This is 'restore,' to bring back. This is 'redeem,' to fulfill or exchange or gain—the exact translation wasn't clear. And the final, is 'release.'"

I look down at my arm. Yup, chills.

"Release what?" Carter asks. He's in investigation mode, and his forehead has a cute little wrinkle.

Poncho shrugs. "Whatever is needed, I'd wager."

Interesting. Rebirth, recycle, restore, release. That's a lot of really powerful re-words. "So, what do they mean when they are used as one?"

Poncho holds the dagger out to me, and my fingers linger in the air over it before I take it from his hand. "This is the dagger from ancient times used in the Ritual Restitution—" My eyes shoot up at the phrase. "—along with another that is only prophesized about. It does indeed do what you saw it do that to that witch, releases magic, but it also severs a connection, like it did the demon Kriegen. You were right to keep it concealed."

"It's dangerous." *Geesh, Penelope. Way to state the obvious.*

"In the wrong hands, and perhaps even in the right ones."

Carter looks at me, but I'm staring down at the dagger. If Poncho's right, then this can save me. Now more than ever. If it's really the dagger used in the Ritual Restitution, then it's the one I've needed for so long. I've been researching the Restitution for years, the spell that could restore my magic. Not from the void or from Carter or anyone else. I can't believe it. I can do it. All I need is my demon.

"The question remains now, Miss Grey, what will you do with it?"

I feel Poncho's eyes on me before I look up. I feel like there's so much he's not saying.

"And what do you think we should do with it?" Carter asks.

Poncho presses his eyebrows together. "I can't advise you on that. I can only suggest you and Miss Grey keep it safely guarded until the time is right."

"There's going to be a right time?" I raise my eyebrow.

"No," he says, "but there will come a time when you must embrace what is."

"Do you think it could work on demons the same way it worked on the witch in the woods?" I ask.

"Perhaps," he says.

"This severs magic. Maybe we can use the dagger on the Statics?"

"Just go around stabbing Statics?" Carter says, raising an eyebrow.

"Yeah, when you say it that way..." I start. It is a dagger. "Stabby, pointy end that leads to death is probably not a good idea."

The WNN sounds rings out from Carter's phone. I look at mine but I don't have the app on my phone anymore. They took that, too.

Carter clears his throat. "We should go in a minute. I'll be right outside." I nod at Carter and he slips out the door. I trace my fingers over one of the trinkets on Poncho's desk. I'm not really a fan of good-byes or see you laters or whatever this is.

"So, I probably won't be in here anytime soon," I say with a sigh.

"Tired of my company?"

I smile. That's never the reason. For some reason the old guy intrigues, if not entertains, me. "Nah, I'm taking a little forced break from the Enforcers."

Poncho looks closely at the spot where my badges used

to be, and then nods. "Something happened." I don't recount the whole story to him—just mention that they learned my magic isn't quite what they thought. "So, I'm not serving anymore. I'm not even allowed to use the essence, or come on the premises unless summoned or, apparently, even access the WNN." All things witchy are no longer my concern.

With a nod, Poncho grabs my hands and pulls my wrist closely to his eyes. "Ah, you are marked. They must be fearful of what you can do."

"Fearful?" I ask.

Poncho nods. "You are not the first, and you will not be the last."

"They were talking about marking the Statics as well. What does it do exactly? They didn't really explain the mark when they gave it to me."

He doesn't respond, merely looks me. This is a great time for him to lose his limited communication ability. Poncho holds up a finger to me and moves across the room. From his desk, he pulls out a large, round thing. I'm not quite sure what it is.

"For you," he says, holding it out to me. I look down at the weird contraption in my hands. It's gray and plastic, an oval shaped walkie-talkie from those movies in the '90s where they were so big and awkward they could never have been useful.

"What is it?"

"It's a relay. It will allow you to communicate with me, directly. Or whoever has this portion," he says. He holds up a rectangular piece that looks like it should connect to my oval one.

"So, it's a cell phone?"

"It's more than that."

"Like a friendship bracelet," I smile, but Poncho's eye narrow. "Is it timey-wimey?" He gives me a look of confusion at my *Dr. Who* reference. Never mind. "Why are you giving it to me?"

Poncho looks at me closely. His eyes are more human in that moment than I've ever seen them. "It is my destiny."

There's that word again. "Destiny to what?"

"Serve, assist, guide."

"Your destiny is to help me? Why?"

Poncho's eyes link with mine directly, and around the brown, I see some green. Demon green. But it's not menacing—it's soft, like Carter's. "Some destinies are chosen for us. Others we choose. All are left up to us to interpret and develop."

I glance from Poncho to the communicator in my hands. "Which one is yours?"

Poncho smiles. "That's still to be decided."

I shake my head, confused already. Carter opens the office door and pokes his head in. "We need to go, Pen."

"See you later, Poncho." I push the gray round thing into my bag as Carter and I turn away.

"Be wise, Miss Grey," Poncho says.

"I'm always wise," I say, and Poncho laughs. A real laugh. He laughs so loudly that Carter and I both stop and look back at him. I'm almost insulted. I can never make him laugh at my jokes, but when I'm not joking, apparently it's mass hysteria.

• • •

All I have to do is open the door. Open the door, go into the house, tell Gran and Pop that I'm not an Enforcer. Under normal circumstances, Gran would be thrilled. Ever since my mom died, she's never wanted Connie or me to be Enforcers, especially when I didn't have my own magic. She'd probably throw a party, but this—because they saw me use the void—that's not going to be a good reason. She doesn't even know that I *can* use the void.

How am I going to tell her?

"I can go in with you," Carter offers.

I puff out my chest. "I'm fine."

"You sure? You've been holding that door handle for twenty minutes," he says. I look from my hand, still readied to open his car door, and then to his face. He's smiling so big. It's almost enough to make me forget how sucky all this is.

Almost.

"What do I tell them?"

"Don't tell them anything," he says without hesitation.

I scoff. "Right. Don't tell them that I've just exposed everyone in my whole family to the Triad. Because that would have absolutely no repercussions later."

"I'm serious," he says, his eyes steady on mine. "Look, the Triad swore no one will find out. They have no evidence that you've done anything wrong."

"Except that they all saw me use the void."

"But they can't prove anything right now. My dad is going to keep it quiet."

Right. His dad. "How are you so sure of that?"

His jaw stiffens. "I just am. So, until there's a reason to say something, say nothing."

It's not the worst idea ever. If no one is going to find

out, then it at least buys me some time. My family doesn't have to know anything until we stand somewhere solid, and they don't have to worry. "What do I do every day when I'm supposed to be patrolling with you?"

"Anything you want."

Anything I want? That's a foreign concept. I've only ever wanted to be an Enforcer. I practiced, trained, eat, slept, lived, breathed my goal. Now? "What else would I do? Figure out what this marking is…" I can't get into the library anymore.

"I can work on that. Meanwhile, it's summer. Go explore the city, go to museums, do nothing. It's D.C.—there's a ton to do. Tell them when you're ready."

He says it with such certainty that I feel in control of this. I smile. "I like the way you think, Carter Prescott."

"Thank you," he smirks. "Is that all you like?"

"I can think of a few other things." I waggle my eyebrows. "Maybe you can come with me tomorrow? We can go into the city."

Carter's smile drops. "Can't. I told Dad I'd be around. We're supposed to be figuring out a schedule."

"With your dad?"

He tightens his hand around the steering wheel until his knuckles are pale. Then he lets go. "I'm not an Enforcer anymore, either, Pen. He said he couldn't have me wandering around the city without a purpose."

He's not an Enforcer, either. I was so wrapped up my own thing that I didn't even wonder what it meant for him. I take his hand. "Carter, I'm sorry. I didn't even think that you'd lose your standing, too. I should have."

"I don't care."

"Maybe we can talk to them and they can give you a new place to—"

"It's fine, Pen," he says, his voice harsher than before. "I don't even want to do it without you. Dad will find a job for me to do."

He hates all of that. "Is this why your dad agreed?"

He nods and I look away. I've forced Carter to do something he hates, with his dad, who he hates. I'm basically the worst girlfriend ever.

Carter pulls at me until I look at him. His eyes are dancing, his chin overgrown with scruff and a smile on his face. "What?"

His hand falls away from my face, and he kisses me. It's soft until our bodies realize that we're connected, and then mine craves it more. I lean into him across the space of the car. He's right—it doesn't matter. In this moment he's all I know. He's some kind of certainty and it's all I have. My fingers get lost in his shaggy hair, and his light scruff scratches my cheek. His hands are on my cheek and my neck and in my hair. He's the only other person who understands what I'm going through, and I don't want to stop feeling like I'm part of him.

When he pulls away from our kiss, we both gasp for air and he rests his forehead against mine. Between breaths he gently kisses my lips. Once, twice. "You are more than an Enforcer," he says hoarsely.

"You're more than a Prescott," I say. I look at him, and I can't explain how gorgeous he is when his eyes are bright and his lips are swollen and he's out of breath. I did that. Kissing is way better than magic. It will probably always be.

Chapter Sixteen

Carter

I make a pit stop back at the Nucleus House before I go home. Pen's idea to look for information about the mark was a good one. I vaguely remember hearing about it in school, but the ritual being ancient is all I remember.

"Mr. Prescott, I'm surprised to see you here," Poncho says when I come in. Those two cats that are always near him.

"I need to do some research," I say.

Poncho nods. "I already have the materials ready." He points to a table stacked with books. How does he know what I'm looking for? "Miss Grey, correct?" He nods toward the table again.

I toss my backpack on the table and take a seat. There

are twenty books that are already open to pages or have bookmarks stuffed in between them. At least Poncho made it easier for me. The first one I grab is thick and bound with green leather that's cracked and faded in areas. Turning to the page he's marked, I wonder how he knew I'd be here. Pen must have told him what happened to her, but how did he know I'd be back looking for information?

The first documented instance of witch marking took place in 1270 AD when Hiltrude Carlingina secured her daughter's marriage to a duke for the safety of their family following her sister's revelation into witchcraft. The daughter, Theodora the Kind, could not permit her powers to be acknowledged by the Duke of Pomeria. Carlingina marked Theodora the Kind to bind her powers until the birth of an heir, a move that would secure their standing at court and re-establish the family name. After one year of marriage and no heir, the mark began to alter the behavior of Theodora the Kind.

It is documented that she became unbalanced, paranoid, and attempted to take her own life twice in the same fortnight. Carlingina, who was trapped in North Africa during a crusade, was unable to return to her daughter for two years. By the time she returned, Theodora the Kind was deceased.

The next book recaps instances of marking during the Black Death. Apparently, across many of these passages, they all went a little crazy.

Poncho watches me from across the library. His look is familiar, but I can't place it.

February 1692-May 1693 were the dark times of the Salem witch trials in New England. It is said in witch community, that these events in history are "the black mark on witchdom...as many innocents, those we swore to protect, died for our salvation."

Twenty-one were accused of witchcraft and executed. Only two of these victims were actual witches. Seven were found guilty and then pardoned. Nine escaped, while another twenty-five were found not guilty. This only accounts for a portion of the 72 victims involved in the Salem witch trials, and only eleven of which were true witches.

The first two witches to die in the proceedings were Bridget Bishop and Sarah Good. After their death, the survivors fled New England or hid magical abilities. Halfway through the trials, witches began self-marking until they were able to flee. Many witches refused to identify Nons as the real witches or to leave their homes, and many of those died. Approximately thirty-one who were marked died, many say because of the length of time they were constrained by the mark.

Good's daughter, Dorothy (or Dorcas, as it was incidentally misprinted on her warrant) was only four at the time of her accusation. For nine months the child was locked up, and Non historians believe that this caused her descent into insanity. In fact, it was that she was marked.

Her aunt, at the stirrings of the trials, bound the girl's magic to keep her a secret. The longer the mark remained, compared with her age at the time, the more increased the results.

After she was released on bond, the mark was removed and within months she recovered. She was never found guilty.

I take a breath and slam the book closed. The mark caused witches to die, and now they've marked Pen. They want to mark Statics. The Triad must be aware of what the mark did to past witches—they must know the risks. And yet they're willing to take a chance on the girl I love and hundreds of Statics.

Poncho is across the table from me when I look up. "Why would they bind magic?"

With a nod, Poncho stands straighter, fingers gripping the top of the chair. "Sometimes there are fates worse than death."

"Which means what?"

Poncho either ignores the question, or thinks on it. "The Salem Witch Trials were an interesting part of history, don't you think? Those Nons and their crusade against witches. I've always wondered if it wasn't the witchcraft they were afraid of."

"What would it be then?"

His eyes focus into small slits. "What everyone, Non and witch and demon, is afraid of. Especially the more important they are."

There's only one thing my dad is afraid of. One thing that motivates him as well. "The loss of power."

Poncho doesn't respond. "You can leave those there when you are finished."

"I'm done now," I say, moving from the table. My dad has made it clear how far he'd go to keep his position, and to keep our secret. Would he go so far as to risk Penelope? Yes, I think he would if he was afraid that she could knock down his world. Even if it meant killing her.

"Thank you, Poncho."

He waves me off. "I did nothing, Mr. Prescott."

It's obvious to me as I leave that there's a bigger issue going on. Vassago warned me last night, and Poncho just now. I'm going to find out what.

. . .

Dinner is tense. All evening I've been thinking about what I read. The longer Pen is marked, the more dangerous it's going to be for her.

"Tomorrow, we'll need to be at the Nucleus House by eight," Dad says, his fork scratching on his plate. "I have a day packed with meetings and you should attend them," he takes a bite. "I've told the Triad that since you are no longer needed for Enforcer duties, you'll be attending all our sessions. They were pleased that you've finally stepped up."

"You forced my hand," I say, tossing down my fork.

His face is steady and unmoving. "You volunteered it."

"Call it whatever you want. I don't recall you marking Penelope part of the deal."

Dad seems unfazed as he eats. "Yes, well, there are two other leaders who make decisions. It was the only way we could come to a compromise. Sabrina wanted to eliminate her immediately. Neutralizing was the best temporary option."

"And the investigation?"

"Procedural," Dad says, sipping his wine. "The council will find nothing when they complete their search."

"What then? You let her go like nothing happened?"

Dad narrows his eyes on me, chewing his food. "I have the ability to make people stop asking questions. I will spin this best I can when the time is right."

I scoff. "Glad you can use that skill for some good."

Dad puts his fork down. "William, you need to snap out of this. I am not the villain here."

"You sure?"

He shakes his head. "I didn't turn in your girlfriend. In fact, I have been more than helpful in her protection. You were the one who volunteered up your stance against the Triad to save her—I didn't force you into that, either. I've put my neck on the line for that girl, and you treat with me contempt. How long will this vendetta against me last?"

"Well, you lied to me about mom for seventeen years—so maybe in the same amount of time."

He drops his fork. Finally. A human reaction. "She made her decision. It was not us. One day, you'll understand why I told you what I did."

Sometimes I don't know how I'm his son. "I understand it now, Dad. It was about always you."

"Did you not see the way they treated the girl today? How they looked at her? I am protecting you."

He honestly thinks that? My whole life he's only cared about the Prescott name, and about how I carry it on. About where we end up, what they say about us, but it's never been about me.

"You were protecting yourself," I say.

Dad stiffens in his seat. "You knew what your mother was all along. I told you she was dead because she was. That thing was not your mother. It was a demon. And now it's gone forever, which is good for us both. It was no longer the woman I loved, the woman who gave birth to you. It was a betrayer. There is nothing it could have offered you."

"Yet you haven't denied anything she told me down there." He can't try to deny it. My dad used my mom to have me, she said he never really loved her, and then he got rid of her. He's always trying to craft everyone around him. He's right that Kriegen had nothing to offer me—I would've never joined her in the demon world—but at least, with her, I had the choice.

He sighs and his eyes soften. For a second it's almost like he has emotions for someone other than himself. "In fact, I can't. I did do those things to your mother."

"So, here I am then, stuck between a dead demon mother and the father who turned her into that. It's no wonder you can't see real evil and go around marking innocent girls. That mark could hurt or even kill her. And you don't even know what will happen if it's done to the Statics."

I want him to defend himself, or tell me I'm wrong. To be someone other than whom I think he is. He doesn't even blink, only moves to take another bite of his chicken.

"Were you ever NOT a son of a bitch?" I'm over this. I can't sit in this room with him.

"Son," Dad calls when I'm at the door. I freeze but don't give him the satisfaction of looking back. "Tomorrow we leave at seven-thirty. You are to be presentable at my side as a Prescott. As the future leader of the Triad. I expect nothing less."

And now we're back to exactly what I knew all along mattered: image. I look over my shoulder at him. He looks small at the table, alone in the big room. "And tomorrow, Dad, I will be a Prescott. Just like you always taught me."

After I walked out on my dad, I ended up doing the only thing I know, the only thing I have left: finding demons. It usually clears my head, but I can't stop thinking about Kriegen and about what happened to Penelope. About my life.

Protecting Pen means that I've had to give in to every thing my dad's always wanted for me. I hate it.

I've spent my whole life watching how he does everything the Prescott way. Watching him treat other people like dirt. He's never been anything other than what people think he should be, and expecting the same in turn. When I was old enough, I had to become that, too. A Prescott. I jump and people do it. I say a word and they obey it. I throw out my last name and they listen.

I finally found a way out of that the last couple years when I started hunting…and then I met Penelope. She didn't expect me to be anything more than I am. Now I've lost all of that. Now, I'm right next to him, doing exactly what he wants. How long will it be until I become exactly what he is?

What about what I want to be? That should be considered, and it isn't. Not if doesn't fit into the image he's built.

Screw him.

I already hate tomorrow. And the next day. And the one after that.

I won't stand up next to my father, to take his place or to pretend like I support the Triad or the council. Not when they've blacklisted so many people. When they've targeted Penelope. Penelope.

At least I still have her.

The demon tries to get away from me. I'd almost forgotten what I was doing here. I'm back now. I press the knife into its throat. "You can kill all of us that you want but it won't change anything you're feeling."

I turn back to look at its discolored Non body. "You have no clue what I'm feeling."

"Aye, but it doesn't take much to see that you're out to prove yourself. Not with all that hatred. Hatred is powerful, but it can destroy you faster than any demon. This won't make you feel better."

"What is this, therapy? I'm about to kill you."

"Then do it," the demon hisses.

I don't let it speak another word before I stab the knife into its heart and mutter the incantation so it explodes.

The demon was wrong.

That did make me feel better.

Chapter Seventeen

PENELOPE

When I wake up I expect to feel like a piece of me is missing, the way it would feel if I'd lost a limb. I'm not an Enforcer anymore — my magic is bound. I should be sad, or angry, but I don't feel any different. I still feel like me. Me with a supercharge. Even with the magic bound from the marking, the void tickles under my skin like a soft hum in the background. I don't feel powerless. I feel like I could lift a car or bust through a wall.

I run my finger across the gold band on my wrist. If I can feel the magic, then maybe I'm still able to use the void. This is the chance to try. On the other side of the room is a vase of fake, bright, sparkly purple flowers. I'll start out small. Eyes open, I stare at the vase and imagine it blowing up in my head. Cracking down the center along the middle and then splintering off into other sections before it shatters. Once the image is clear, I push it out the same way I always do. The magic responds, building up toward my skin and making it itch, sort of like a sunburn.

But nothing happens.

The mark really does keep all of my magic from working. What's the point of having both kinds if I can't use either one?

The whole family is in the kitchen when I get downstairs. Gran smiles up at me when I come in and points to the muffins, but I make a beeline to the coffee. Priorities.

"Connie, can't you put the phone down while you eat? You won't malfunction without it."

My sister looks up from her cell phone. She's been addicted to some game on there for a week now. "You don't know that, Gran." She smiles when she says it and takes a bite of bacon. "One more level."

Gran rolls her eyes and takes a sip of her coffee. Pop's newspaper ruffles as he huffs. "Penelope, come look at this," he says. I move to look over his shoulder at the paper, but all I'm seeing is a Garfield comic. Pop does not read Garfield, and the WNN doesn't print Garfield.

"What do you think?" he asks, pointing at the panel where Garfield is sleeping.

I think my ban means I can't even read the paper.

My heart races because I can't say that I can't read the paper. If I admit it then they'll ask why, and I'll have to tell them. "I have a little headache."

Pop laughs. "My thoughts exactly."

Wait—that just worked? I take a sip of my coffee but say nothing else. Over the rim of my cup, I watch Gran shake her head and look at me. Like she senses I'm off. How can she know? Then she smiles my direction, and my anxiety falls away slightly. I need to get out of here, before I give myself away.

"Don't you have testing today?" I say to Connie. She nods my way and I can see the nerves on her face.

Everything would've been fine if it had all gone as we'd planned—me and Connie taking the test together, me using her magic, us passing. There'd be no demons after me, no Statics with magic, no me with only the hum of magic I can't access under my skin. The irony of that isn't lost on me.

"Well, good luck," I say to Connie. She doesn't need it. Day one of exams is verbal questions. She can totally ace this part.

Her eyes meet mine across the room and she smiles. "I'm a Grey. I don't need luck."

"You should go—both of you—before you're late," Gran says.

Connie grabs a muffin from the basket in front of her. "Want to ride together?"

Right. We're both going to the Nucleus House—at least we would be if I was still an Enforcer. Everyone stares at me, waiting for an answer. It shouldn't even be a question. In all honesty, I don't think I can get close to the Nucleus House. What if I can't even see it? Crap on a stick.

"I'm not sure how long I'll be there today, or how long you'll be there. Probably better to drive separately," I say. "But we'll hang out after. We can watch a movie."

Gran looks like she's going to protest, but my phone rings. Saved by the freaking bell. "It's Ric. I'll see you all later."

I answer the phone and close the door behind me. It's a pretty day today, not the usual sweltering heat for August, so I'm going to walk to six blocks the metro.

"I miss you already."

"It's only been a day…" But I miss him, too.

"What can I say? It's hot in Texas."

"That's a weird comment," I say.

He pauses. "It—I don't want to be here."

I should've read the subtext. How did I miss that? "But your dad must be glad you're there."

Ric sighs on the line. "Sure, you can say that I guess. Step-diva has been over-attentive. I wish she wouldn't try to so hard."

"Maybe she wants you to like her. That's not too crazy."

"I don't even like myself right now, let alone her."

I'm not sure what to say to that. "I like you," I whisper.

"Too bad you're hundreds of miles way with all the hot guys."

"Find a hot guy. Flirting, relaxing, and resting—that's what this trip is for. Doctor's orders."

He scoffs. "It's babysitting. I'm a burden to everyone now. The last thing I want to do is relax because when I stop I think about Maple, and then I think about how we buried her two days ago and I'm exiled to Texas. And how now that she's gone I have nothing."

"That's not true—"

"It is true," he says, almost shouting. "I've lost my partner. I feel that every single day. The Triad will have to decide if they can re-pair me, and I have to decide if I can handle that."

"Of course you can. You've worked your whole life for this."

"And one week in, my partner dies. What does that say about me?"

My brain scrambles to find the right thing to say, and fails. "It was a freak accident. You didn't do anything."

"Exactly."

I exhale. "Ric."

"Forget it."

"I know you feel lost, but I'm here. You have me."

"And you have Carter." He practically spits his name. He doesn't mean it that way, but it stings all the same. Maybe I am a bad friend. A bad person. A horrible witch.

"I get how it feels to lose someone that important."

"Oh. So, you've lost a partner, someone who you were bonded with magically, and they died and you lost the one thing you've spent your whole life working for and somehow you feel like it's all haunting you? You did all that you didn't tell me?"

"No, but — "

"Then, I promise you don't understand anything that I'm feeling."

There's silence on the line. There's nothing else to say. "I'm trying to be supportive."

"I don't need your support. I need you stop trying to feel this pain and feel your own."

"What's that mean?" I ask, sudden anger flaring up me.

"I played a hand in killing Maple. We all did. You don't feel what I feel. Her death doesn't even affect you. I have to wake up every day knowing she's dead and I'm alive. You don't understand what that's like."

"Ric…"

"I've got to go," he says quickly, and then he hangs up.

I stare at my phone. I understand more of that than he knows.

. . .

I am not fit for museums. My attention span is too short. Maybe if Ric or Connie were with me then we could make it work, flit around and joke at the weird naked-painted people with disproportionate bodies. Alone, though, it doesn't work. After about thirty minutes, I couldn't read little signs or be excited by pictures. I was in and out of the first two museums in an hour. The Air and Space Museum was more fun—at least there I could touch things and listen to Whoopi Goldberg take me on a journey through the stars in the Planetarium. But still.

How do people do this all day? All this walking and looking at stuff that doesn't make any sense unless you read the explanatory signs, but the print is so small and people are pushy and all up in your space with funky breath. And my feet ache. This is definitely not fun.

I need to be useful. I have salt, and while I may be marked, I'm not completely incapable. I've not had magic before and been fine. I can get answers from a demon without magic.

I cross the street and pass the line of people at the District Taco truck. My stomach growls and I wonder how much queso they can pour over my nachos. Pouring it directly into my mouth would be easier, but I'm sure that goes against some sort of sanitary code.

A smell fills my nose—not the carne asado deliciousness,

but sulfur. A demon. Perfect timing, since that's exactly what I wanted.

I glance left, and there's a flash of light. I look over and on the sidewalk is a demon. The mauve one. Again. Lia must be bored, or desperate. She waves at me, and I pull my bag higher on my shoulder and walk toward it. If the mauve demon goes insane, I have salt. I can still use salt—and I can run. Lia could probably catch me, but I'd have a head start. But Lia's insistent about being around me, so she must not have immediate plans to kill me. She's definitely had opportunity. Or maybe I don't scare her. I should work on that.

"Why are you here?"

"To talk," Lia says.

"We've already done that."

She points at my arm. "Still new, yes? Yesterday, from the looks of it."

I raise my eyebrow. "Stalking me?"

Lia smiles, sinking back into the shadow of the building so she's less visible. "No, I have a life. But demons can see the markings when they're fresh. Under three days, still? Any longer and it fades. It's been a long time since I've seen that. What'd you do to make the Triad angry?"

I cross my arms and stuff my marked hand under my armpit. "None of your business."

"I need your assistance, and now you need me even more than before," she nods toward the mark on my wrist.

"I don't have magic—I can't access anything," I hold up my arm as a reminder. "Marked. That's sort of what it does."

"But you can," Lia says. I huff because I have tried. It did nothing. "That only blocks the essence, not the void. And what I want to propose requires only one. I can help you access the void."

A Non walks by me in ripped leather pants and flip-flops and turns her nose up. Great. She's the one wearing leather—in August—and I'm the crazy one.

I look around the mall. A few other people are starting to stare. "We're done with this. I'm not interested, so stop asking me."

"Fine," Lia says, "but you're making the wrong choice. You think you can trust your own kind? You can't. They've marked you, singled you out, practically sent you away. Why? I'm the only one who can help you."

"I don't need you, and I'm not broken," I snap. Lia stares at me. "You can leave now."

And then she flickers away.

My phone beeps with a text from my sister.

Got dismissed in the questioning round of testing. Not going to be an Enforcer. :(

That makes two of us.

• • •

I sit in the grass on the hilltop and look around me. This place is beautiful. The whole city is alive at my feet and the Washington Monument rises above it all like a beacon. It will never stop being an amazing place.

"Hey beautiful, come here often?" Carter says and I turn to see him in the distance of the trees. Under his brown leather jacket is a blue and green plaid shirt. He needs to wear plaid more often. I saw him yesterday, but it feels like longer because so much has happened today.

"Sometimes," I say, playing along. "But you probably haven't noticed me."

Carter stuffs his hands in his pockets and moves toward me with a slight smile. It's like this really sexy glide thing. Do guys have lessons on how to be hot?

"I would've noticed you," he says. Even though he's playing, the words make my stomach feel like I'm floating.

"I'm usually with my boyfriend, and he should be here any moment. You should look out for him."

"Boyfriend? Well, that's a bummer."

"Sure is," I say.

"Tell me, mystery girl, would your boyfriend do this?"

Then he's near where I'm sitting in a second, and my heart is already pounding when he kisses me. This isn't like the one in the alley—not as hungry and desperate and stolen in tension. This kiss is a connection. I feed into it, nipping at his bottom lip as he pulls away with a smile.

"My boyfriend does that all the time," I say breathlessly. I'm not sure if it is the right thing to say, but I can't really think.

"Good. Because you are beautiful and he should. He probably thinks about you all the time."

"I think about him," I say.

Carter smiles and pushes a piece of hair behind my ear. My heart pounding, he leans into me and runs his hand across my cheek until my chin rests between his thumb, which trails lightly over my bottom lip and makes me shiver. Man, he is so hot sometimes. Or all the time. "I love you," he says.

It's not the first time Carter's said he loves me, but each time he says it I get what those books mean. What those movies are portraying. That moment when you have wings and the whole world beneath you is rainbows and unicorns and you're Mary-freaking-Poppins in glittery shoes living on cotton candy clouds. It's kind of a magic that even witches don't have. And when I look into his eyes, I see it there. It's sort of crazy how tangible love is. I never expected that before I had it.

"I love you, too."

The space between us closes. His lips are against mine again, and my tongue slides against his. My fingers roam up his neck, and my body leans into him. This is what I want. Me and Carter. Everything else can work itself out. Our bodies fold together, warmth seeps through the layers of fabric. His hand trails the line of my waist where my shirt rises, and his touch sends chills up my spine. Every part of me responds to his touch, from my head to my stomach to my toes.

When we finally part for air, we're both panting and I rest my head against his shoulder. His fingers lace against mine and we sit. Both of us smiling like idiots. He kisses the top of my head, and this is exactly what I needed. A break away with my boyfriend. The kissing helps.

"How was today?" I ask him. First day on the job with his dad.

"Less than exciting, but I have to be back in an hour for another meeting," he says with a sigh. "I brought dinner." He runs back across the field and returns with a picnic basket.

He opens the basket and starts pulling out food. Some selections from each of my favorites; chips and queso from District Taco, pizza from Lost Dog Café, bacon cheddar scones from Best Buns, and ice cream from Toby's. This is so sweet. I kiss him again.

"Thank you," I say.

"For that, I will do this over and over and over," he says,

pushing a piece of hair behind my ear.

"This is the best date ever, and technically, it's our first."

Carter shakes his head. "That's not possible."

I nod. "We've never actually been on a date—unless you count training sessions, impromptu demon hunting, and nearly dying."

He laughs. "If you don't count that then I definitely need to step it up. Consider me on." He passes me the chips and queso. "What did you do today?"

I bite my lip, everything feels like it shifted with that simple question. "I tried that whole museum thing, but it was a bust. I had some coffee, and it was a day that everyone will be jealous of forever."

But all of the demon's words play in my head. *I'm the only one who can help you.* Help me what? What does she know? Carter says something and then looks at me. I totally missed that. "Huh?"

"I said, you're still going to come with me to the Observance, right? It's the dance of the century, according to every single person I saw today," Carter says.

"I wouldn't miss it. Or you in a tux."

"We need to make sure we have parties all the time."

I shake my head. "I hate dresses."

Carter kisses my temple. "Come in pants or dressed as a monkey if you want. Be my date and dance with me."

"You don't even have to ask."

"You won't change your mind in the next twenty days, will you?"

I smile. "Only if I get a better offer."

He puts a hand over his heart and falls over my legs, fake dying. I revive him with a kiss.

Chapter Eighteen

CARTER

"Let's discuss the Static problem," Dad says. He looks at me from across the room, and I sit up in the chair, pushing last night with Pen to the back of my mind so I can focus. I hate the way they call it "the Static problem." As if it's nothing more than an inconvenience or the flu.

Sacra, one of the ten on the council, stands. "The people are worried," Sacra says. "When will it affect the Statics we are close to, or the ones who are so removed from our society they aren't even aware this is happening?"

And so the argument continues. Here we go again. Three days of discussion and we're still asking the same questions. I don't mind them talking if we're getting somewhere, but it's all circular. The same bullshit, another way, back to the same way, another day.

Kenneth Slade stands next. "And what will we do about it? What's the plan? The Observance is in twenty days. How do you propose to have this settled by then, so the celebrations aren't disrupted?"

"This is why we have proposed the marking as a plan of action," Sabrina says. "It makes the most sense and gives us time to figure out how to undo whatever is happening."

I glare at her. It's not a solution. She keeps pushing it, but two days ago the council wanted other options. Even to them it seemed extreme. Too bad we have none yet.

"Many of us wonder about the image that presents," Buckley James says as he stands.

"Image?" Dad asks.

Buckley squares his shoulders. "If we start marking witches, it makes us appear like we have no other alternative. Dare I say it's a move of fear rather than prevention?"

Ten points to Buckley. The Triad told the council about the marking—but not every piece. At the words 'bound magic,' they dismissed it. Anytime an innate piece of DNA is removed from a witch, negative consequences follow. Based on what was discussed in the meeting two days ago, it was enough to make them all reject the course of action.

I look at Dad, and his jaw is tense. That's how he gets when he doesn't like the ideas being questioned, all coiled up and ready to pounce.

"We need to take action. This is out of control," another voice calls out, while Mrs. Bentham adds from her seat, "What about Containment? We move the Statics, whether they've manifested or not, to a secure location."

"That's a horrible idea," I say without thinking. Every

single person in the room looks at me. Dad is angry, which I can tell from his face, but it's his normal state with me. I throw my hands in the air. "If you'd like to put a bunch of people with uncontrollable magic in a building and lock them up, then be my guest. I have a feeling you won't like that outcome."

"Do you have another suggestion then?" Rafe asks, his eyes locked on mine.

I shift in my seat. I start to say no, but then I see Ellore staring at me from the council seats. She's the one really behind this marking idea, and I hate it. We don't even know what the marks will do. I want to not speak up, to not give in to my father's plan for me, but I hear Pen telling me that I can change how things are.

"Actually, yes," I say. I sit up straight in my chair. "The answer is not to separate the Statics, but to embrace and guide them."

I sound like a hippie, but it's true.

Too bad no one else thinks that. The whole room roars into talking at once. I can't make out what any one person is saying. Some look angry, others excited, and I haven't even finished the idea yet.

"Quiet," Dad yells over the room. They don't stop talking until he stands and bellows the word, magically magnifying his voice. As soon as they stop talking, he looks at me. "Continue."

I stand so I look more commanding. That's what Dad does when he wants to look in control. *Imagine you are the most important voice in the room and you will become that.* "If we teach them how to use the magic they've obtained, then they can be in control of it."

A few people in the council roll their eyes at my sentence. I make mental notes of their names in my head, along with a reminder that closed-minded people are not welcome in the future.

"Statics are exiled as soon as they are eighteen and cut off from everything in our world. They don't have our knowledge or experience, and this is a chance for us to fix that, to give them the training and tools they need. We need to teach them how to use magic." It strikes me that I do believe those words. I didn't even know that I did. Not until I've said them.

Sabrina shakes her head. "You want us to teach the Statics how to use magic?"

I glance at her. "Hold on, wait…Yes, I think that's what I just said."

A few people chuckle, but she glares at me in response. Bethany Targen stands from the council seats and pushes her glasses up higher on her nose. "You expect us all to give up our time to teach the Statics how to use their magic. They aren't supposed to have magic in the first place."

"And yet they do," Rafe says. "Magic is not ours to command, but to borrow and use for good."

"They are out there without training, manifesting at random moments, accidentally killing Nons and Enforcers. Every day they don't feel like they have anywhere safe and accepting to go is another day they remain quiet and risk exposing all witches. I don't see how there's another way," I say. Even I am a little surprised by how much I care about this. I hadn't really thought about it before, but it could work. It has to work. For too long our community has pushed away people who need us. Like Emmaline Spencer, Penelope's great-great-great-whatever-grandma, and my mom, too. They certainly can't be the only ones.

"If we teach them magic, how do we even have any guarantee that this will work?"

"Yeah, what if our efforts are wasted?"

"Or what if it works?" I ask. "You could all be hailed as innovators, fearless, and willing."

Everyone considers that for a moment. *Make them think it's for their benefit and they will always step up. At our core, we are selfish beings. Play on that.* A few of the council members whisper back and forth. It's really working.

"But they're Statics," Nick Vantage says. "They shouldn't even be here anyway."

"And you're an asshole, but we let you stay."

A few people in the council giggle again, and I see a warning look from Dad out of the corner of my eye. I don't give a shit what he thinks. "For centuries we've pushed away Statics. Even without magic, they're still our blood, yet we exile them like they are worse than demons. This is our chance to make up for that—and it benefits us. This will increase our numbers, make us stronger. Think of the amount of Statics we could add to our numbers. Demons won't take us down if we make the Statics our allies."

For the first time, without command, the whole room is quiet, everyone looking at me. Some of them look angry, others relieved, and all of them seem to be assessing what I said. That's huge, considering the audience. I have them right where I want them, and now, Dad's best lesson ever: *Lay out the stakes, make them painful and desperate, and then you always win.*

"The marking is unstable. Containment is not a valid

option. If we don't teach them, then the alternative is exposure. Either they expose us by wandering around with uncontrollable magic, or we expose ourselves because we've tried to contain the uncontrollable and they cause some accident that makes the news in a way that even we can't cover up." When I finish, I lean back and prop my legs up on the table to piss off Dad and Nick Vantage a little more. "I hope you all will make the right decision."

The council members whisper among themselves. The Triad looks back and forth to each other. Dad clears his throat. My stomach twists a little. Is that nerves?

"All in agreement to teach the Statics as a trial phase, please rise."

Rafe stands, followed by my dad, and slowly all of the council stands. I watch them pop up one at a time, and lower my feet to the floor. They're listening to me? To me? Even the asshole? Soon the whole room is standing, even Sabrina, so I jump up, too.

Dad looks at me. "Then, it is decided. We'll start the initiative, and with your guidance, Carter, I think it will be a good one."

Did my dad just call me Carter *and* tell me I had a good idea in the same sentence? The Statics having magic isn't the only thing that's weird around here.

· · ·

During my lunch break, I pull out the demon tracker I made on my phone and search for Vassago. He's in a coffee shop not that far from the Nucleus House. When I get there, his old man form with the dirty beard to his knees and singular striped sock looks out of place. He looks up.

"I was hoping you could help me," I say. Vassago points at a chair across from him and I sit.

"What do you seek?" he asks.

I cross my arms. "Information about the marking."

His eyes widen but then he points at the chair. Vassago doesn't say anything, so I jump right in. "Has a halfling ever received it? I was doing some research, and it seems to have negative effects on witches. Does it do the same to halflings? Is it worse?"

Vassago stares at me momentarily. "When magic wants something, it will get it. Everything belongs in a certain place."

"What does that mean?"

He only nods in response. "Magic is a gift." Then he picks up whatever he's drinking, and looks away from me. I remain there, hoping for tangible clues, but he doesn't speak, and eventually, I leave.

Chapter Nineteen

While I wait for Connie to get home, I stare at the mark on my pinky. The little black dot seems bigger than it was yesterday. What are you, little black dot? I'm still looking at my finger when Connie plops down on the couch next to me and grabs my hand.

"Ouch. Slam it in a car door again?"

I scoff. "That was once and I was twelve." She stares into the distance of the living room, her face heavier.

"Let's watch *Breakfast at Tifftany's* tonight, since we couldn't last night," she says.

I nod, and she moves from the couch, plucking the DVD from the shelf. "Sorry about your Enforcer exams. What happened in there yesterday?"

She sighs and bunches up her shoulders, tossing the movie on the coffee table and sitting on the corner of it. "I thought I'd have it. It was the oral quizzes, but I got flustered. Totally blanked and took too long."

I reach out and take her hand. "I know how much it meant to you." My mind drifts back to our conversation a few days back. *Or how much I thought it meant.*

Connie pulls her hand away. It's not like her to be the non-touchy one. That's usually me. "I thought I'd get farther than day one."

My sister is way too smart to get flustered. It must have been a doozy. "What was the question?"

Connie glances at me and then away, shifting in her chair. I stare at her. Seriously. What's all this suspense about? Her lips open, like she's about to answer, but then she pulls out her phone and raises an eyebrow toward me. I look at the screen, and it looks like she's checking an e-mail.

"Where's your phone? When this thing rings you're on it like white on rice."

Must be the WNN. *Lie, Penelope, quick.*

"Battery's dead," I say, and she tilts her phone my direction. Right. I should be able to see words there. I can't see anything. But if she knows that then I'll have to explain it. Crap.

I start coughing and move from the couch and grab some water. Foolproof plan.

Then Connie gasps. "No freaking way."

"What?"

Her eyes are wide when they land on mine. "Taylor Plum is dead."

Taylor Plum is dead. Wait. What? "What happened?"

She shakes her head. "Read it to me," I say, coughing again for good measure.

"Taylor Plum, Static, 16, and sister of renown Enforcer Shira Plum, was found dead in the bike path on Four Mile Run. Plum was fleeing Enforcers after it was revealed that her magic manifested. Witnesses say it seemed that she was using magic when she glowed with a white light, and then collapsed. Enforcers say she was dead upon their arrival."

Whoa. We saw her five days ago. She had magic then, but she definitely didn't glow. There's only one situation that witches glow, at least in my experience, and that's when the void is involved.

"So, the magic killed her?"

"Maybe," Connie says, scrolling down her phone.

My phone sings out from across the room and Connie glances at me as I move to grab it off the coffee table. "I thought it was dead."

"Guess not," I shrug. "Ric."

"I-can't-believe-Taylor-Plum-is-dead-how-did-this-happen?" Translation: he's freaking out, too.

I shrug even though he can't see me. I'm trying to keep my cool, but my mind is crazed with ideas. Scenarios, reasons, explanations. I'm not sure which of them are right or if I even want any of them to be.

"No idea."

"Do you think it was the magic?" he asks. "I mean, that's the only thing abnormal. What if other Statics start to die?"

Suddenly, I wish it was anything else. A car accident. Being struck by lightening. A demon attack, even. At least all of those things have a better explanation. "It could've been non-magical."

"Like a heart attack," Connie adds.

"Exactly. Like a heart attack," I repeat to Ric.

"She was fifteen—and she ran cross-country."

Panic forms in my chest. If the magic killed her…"It could've been anything. A brain aneurysm, bad sushi, a bee sting," I say.

"A bee sting? Really, Penelope?"

"Maybe she was allergic."

"Or it was the magic."

"It could've been anything." Anything else, besides magic, because if it was the magic and I released the magic, then isn't it my fault she's dead? She's dead and Maple's dead and Ric is gone, and all of that is on me.

"I wish I was there to help out with this. Whatever's going on, it's big. I should be there."

"You're better where you are. Right now you're not an Enforcer, so all of this isn't your concern. Get better and stay safe," I say.

"Safe isn't always ideal," Ric says back.

"But safe is alive, and alive is what's important."

He's quiet on the other end of the line, a deep breath fills my ear as he inhales. "Is it?"

I don't say yes, because I'm not sure anymore.

Chapter Twenty

This is on us.

I stare at Pen's text one more time. Taylor Plum is dead, and Pen feels like we're responsible. I was going to tell her about the mark tonight, but I can't throw this on her right now. If Taylor Plum died using magic, then why? How do we stop it? And can we?

"Carter," Pen says, coming up over the hill. I hug as soon she's near, but she pulls away from my arms too quickly. It makes sense, with everything, but I don't like it. If she's pulling away from me already, then all the other things I have to tell her will not be easy.

Pen shakes her head. "She got magic and she died."

"We'll figure it out."

She shakes her head, and I see the glimmer of tears in her eyes. "Figure it out? You keep saying that but we have no information! We did this, somehow, Carter. We spread that magic from De'Intero. Maybe we should come forward and tell everyone what's happening."

I try to pull her closer again. "We can't do that."

Pen jerks away from me. "Why not? We can save them."

"How? From what? This morning the council wanted us to round up all the Statics and mark them all and—"

Her eyes widen. "That's perfect. Let's do that. We can at least contain the magic that way."

"Pen, no, it's not the solution."

"Why?" she asks.

Now's my chance to tell her what the mark will do to her, what it's done to anyone in history who's had it. "Pen, the marking doesn't—"

"Block the void," a voice calls from the darkness. Pen and I both look around, and the mauve demon steps out of the shadows. "Sorry to interrupt."

That demon. Again.

"What are you doing here?" Pen asks.

"Finishing some business with you from yesterday. And him, I guess," She nods toward me, and looks down at our still entwined hands. "Do you mind? I don't want to disappear."

I smirk. Last time we held hands and felt threatened we made all those demons disappear. I drop Pen's hand, but stand close. The demon walks around us, its eyes out on the horizon. It's still talking to Pen? "It's beautiful up here. Almost like heaven. Or so I would think."

"What's happening?" Pen asks. I hear the anxiety in her voice. For a second, I wonder if she's right about telling everyone. The Triad can clean up our mess—but at what cost? Everything, I tell myself. Sharing the truth with them is going to make everything worse because we'll have to tell them how we know, who we are, what we've done. It's only a last resort.

The mauve demon sighs. "I told you that you could trust me. I'm trying to prove that." It steps toward us and looks at Pen. "This mess with your unfortunate witches is because of the pair of you."

I step forward between Mauve and Pen. I don't like the way the demon looks at her, like she's a piece of meat or a prize. This is wrong. My hand itches. It's hard to be around a demon and not put it out of its misery. "Demons aren't usually so forthcoming with information," I say.

It smirks at me. "I'm not a usual demon. We're after the same goal here."

"Which is?" I ask.

A smile. I really want to slit its throat. "That Static who died today? She's only the beginning. It will change them."

"Change them into what?" Pens ask.

The demon shrugs as if it's bored. "If you take something pure and taint it with something else, how long will it take until it changes? A day, a month, a year?"

Turn them into demons? The Statics will turn? Pen's face darkens. Not good is an understatement. Considering the way she talks about how that magic feels, they'd be crazy, powerful ones. "How do we stop it?" I ask. The demon smiles, puts a hand up in the air to stop us from talking. "I'm not here to answer your questions. I'm here because you owe me and I have a proposition."

Pen takes my hand again, and the mauve demon looks

horrified. It's only a second, but the message is clear.

"I'm not in the business of making deals with demons. So, thanks, but no thanks," Pen says.

"What do you want?" I ask. I don't trust it, but we can at least hear it out. Pen glances at me in disbelief that I'm even indulging the demon. I'm surprised too, if I'm honest. But information is key here. We need to get as many details we can about what's going on.

The mauve demon crosses its arms. "To be restored," it says to me. My eyes widen as it steps toward Pen. "You can do that, Penelope."

She's quiet for a moment. "How?"

"The Restitution."

That spell. The one that is supposed to bring back Pen's magic. She was planning to do that before she met me. "You have the black dagger. You have the spell. Now you only need the demon who did this to me."

Pen shakes her head. "I don't have power for that."

The demon chuckles. I hate demons. "You do. You have access, and all you have to do is let me guide you. I can teach you how to use the void, and you can harness it." The demon grabs her hand. "I want to lead you to what you were meant to be."

Pen jerks her hand away.

"What do you mean? How can the Restitution help you?"

The demon shoots me a look and I cross my arms.

"The Restitution brings back what was before," it adds. "For a demon, it can return them to their previous state. For a witch without magic," it says with a pause long enough to make Pen look. "It can make them whole. There will never be need for the Triad to question you again. You'll be completely one of them. A whole witch."

I glance at Pen, and she's listening now. Fully attentive. Pen being a whole witch is all she's wanted, and somehow I think this demon knows exactly how to spin this. This is its move.

Chapter Twenty-One

I don't know how to handle this.

This is exactly what I've always thought I'd never have. If this is possible, then I can't ignore Lia. If she knows how to do the ritual, where to find my demon, and how to undo all of this, then I need to explore that. I don't want use the void, or to be sought after or dangerous. I wanted to fit in, not to be a freaking target. But I can't do that if my own people won't let me in.

I can't do that with the mark, without magic, on my own.

And I can't do anything if Statics are dying.

But this is a demon. It seems too good to be true, and Gran always says things that seem too good to be true probably are. Lia grabs my hand again, and Carter tenses. I look from her scaly mauve one to my human one.

"I will give you information. I've proven that I'm valuable. I have information you need—like where the demons are and what they search for—but I can't risk my life for nothing. You don't have long to act. Things are just beginning. If you think I suck, then you don't want to meet the big guy."

I scoff, pulling my hand away. "I find it hard to believe that your kind gets even worse than the ones I've met."

Lia crosses her arms, but my heart is pounding. She's offering me a chance. Even if it seems impossible, I've never had a demon on my side before.

"It's only going to get worse before it gets better. You two lovebirds have unleashed one crazy ass can of worms, and the other demons won't give you opportunities to fix it."

"The other demons?" Carter asks, as he clenches his fist.

Lia nods. "The demons are torn. Some of them will come for you, and their plans aren't good ones. Others—a few others—are banding forces to protect you."

This is all too much. Demons aware of who I am, let alone be for me or against me? "Why do they care about me at all?" I ask.

"Some of us feel like you should be protected. What you did in De'Intero? You have major power."

Carter crosses his arms. "And you want to give her more?"

"I want to be free," Lia snaps, her normally blue eyes flashing a bright green. "If a witch getting stronger magic makes that happen, then that's not my problem. It's theirs."

I don't know what to think.

"You just said this was all for yourself. Why should she

trust you?"

Lia steps toward Carter. "I'm not the enemy here. I'm telling you the facts. Some demons are for you, others will destroy you, and I promise the last thing you need is Azsis to come here."

Azsis. My demon. The one who stole my powers, who killed my parents. The demon who destroyed my entire life. I take a deep breath so I can try to process this. This is the first time any demon has said his name openly, that he's still alive. This is the biggest breakthrough in, well, ever. I've spent most of my life looking for him, and she drops his name like that.

Oh, crap. I've been looking so long, I'd almost forgotten to be scared of him. He *killed my parents*. *Stole* my magic. Turned Emmaline Spencer *into a demon*. He's after me, too, now. He could come here and finish the job that he started.

Carter puts a hand on my shoulder.

"You know Azsis?"

The smile on her face is enough to tell me that she knew exactly what to say. "Of him. I told you Kriegen was middle management. Azsis is the prince of hell, right under Lucifer and he's got his own level of hell."

Azsis, my demon, is alive. He's the assistant ruler of hell, and all of this feels so much bigger than I can even understand right now. Lia can find him. She'll help me. All I have to do is restore her humanity, and then my magic — and outsmart an ancient psycho demon in the process while I'm marked and have no magic. Yeah, no big deal.

"If we say no, then you've harmed your own kind by telling us all of this," Carter says.

Lia looks at Carter. She doesn't seem to like him much.

"I'm trying to prove that not all demons are evil. Some of us are innocent. It should be reassuring, as a demon yourself."

I steal a glance at Carter. I don't ever think of him as a demon, or myself, but we both are. It's part of us, halflings, even if we hate it.

"We can find another way. There have to be other demons that have information about what's happening. We can investigate all of this our own way," Carter whispers.

"They won't answer you, Carter Prescott. Not with years of hunting our kind. They won't come near you, and now they're on strict orders from higher up the chain," Lia scoffs and glances between the two of us. "The pair of you surprise me." Then, to Carter, "All I'm doing is giving your girlfriend what she wants. The Restitution. It will restore her magic as well as me to my old form, to my life. And in fixing herself, you can fix this mess the two of you have caused with the Statics."

"How, exactly?" Carter asks.

"The magic that caused it came from her—from the void. If she doesn't have the void anymore, then it stands to reason that the magic produced from her using it would be undone. The Restitution restores everything. It's a reset button."

Carter scoffs. "But at what cost to her?"

"None," she says.

"That's not how magic works. There's a balance," I say. Even with all of this new information, that's a constant.

"There is—the balance is even. A life for a life. Blood for blood. A demon," she points to herself, "for a witch." My heart pounds in my ears. This is insane. It's even more insane because it makes sense. She makes sense.

"You should go," Carter says.

Lia nods. "I'll come back. Think on it." She turns to walk away and the looks back. "And Penelope," she adds, "never say never."

And then she flickers out.

. . .

Carter and I walk through the streets of downtown. We've found two demons, but they told us nothing about the Statics, or about the magic. I feel that Lia is right. None of the demons will tell us anything, while she's already given us more information than we ever knew before.

People will keep dying, and each death is on us. Maybe it's not a bad idea to take the offer.

"Don't agree to anything," Carter says, staring at me as if he's reading my mind.

"I'm not."

Carter sighs. "You act before you think."

I step away from him, allowing space between us.

"And in the meantime, how many Statics will die? The demon had a point."

"Maybe, but why would the demon be so forthcoming unless it wanted more than what it was saying?"

I shrug. "Maybe it has selfishly pure intentions. If it really only longs to be restored, then why should it lie?"

He touches my arm so I freeze, and he closes the space between us. His breathe is close to my face, so close that it sends a shudder through me. I want him to kiss me, right now, even in the midst of our disagreement on this. When I'm with him, the rest of the world can slip away, at least for a moment. He lowers his face toward mine, and as his lips are nearly there, he pulls away slightly.

"It's also weird that that demon knows the one thing you were waiting for. You've been thinking about the Restitution for your whole life. Now it's suddenly the one thing that can save everyone?" I step back from him, moment swiftly ended. "And this demon somehow can randomly find Azsis."

Azsis is out there. He's not a dream, or a ghost, he's a real demon. The fact that Lia can get to him means that I can still fix it. "When you say it that way, it does sound suspicious."

"Of course it does. It is suspicious."

"That doesn't mean it's not real," I snap, crossing my arms.

"It doesn't mean it is real."

"But it could be," I say. "That's enough for me not to dismiss this."

"I'm not saying dismiss it. I'm saying we research and evaluate." Carter rests his hands on my shoulders. "Promise me. No deals with demons unless we are clear that this is the *only* way."

He's right. I shouldn't jump into this blindly. Not until I have proof about what Lia is saying. But it's hard to ignore the fact that Statics could die from this magic. If what Lia says ends up being true, then I don't want to see how many die before we have the proof Carter so desperately needs.

"I promise," I say.

Chapter Twenty-Two

Not sleeping is a constant problem for me. Tonight is no exception, aside from seeing Pen's face when I close my eyes. The way she looked when that demon offered to make her become a whole witch. Even though she promised not to make any deals, I know her—she'll do whatever she thinks is right.

Which is why I have to show her this is wrong.

"Mr. Prescott," Poncho says, his voice heavy, a stocking cap on his head. "It's late."

"Yeah," I shove my hands into my pockets. I'm not sure why I'm here now. I guess answers equate to the library. "I couldn't sleep."

Poncho *hmms*. "I don't sleep much myself. There are things that haunt whether we are asleep or awake."

I'm really too tired to deal with his non-sentences. "Can I do some reading?"

Poncho spreads out his arms, as if welcoming me. "I'm around, if you need anything."

Just some quiet. But I don't say that. I don't respond at all. Poncho turns away from me, and I head toward one of the computers. Where do I start? I pull out the list of words that Vassago used from my pocket.

CHECK. REMAIN. DAGGER. MAUVE.
OBSERVANCE. QUEEN.

Staring at them, I expect them to make sense and form some kind of message. I need to move the king in a check, so if the king is Pen then who is the queen? The color mauve is obviously the demon, and the dagger is connected. The demon mentioned the dagger. "You have the dagger," when it talked about the Restitution. How did it even know we had the dagger?

Is the Restitution really a reset button? If so, then what does it mean for us? If it really can reset everything, then that means it also resets us. She won't need my magic, and that's good for her, but I can't shake the bad feeling. And if Pen doesn't need my magic, how long will she need me?

Always. She loves me. But if she didn't need me would she still love me?

Stop being stupid, Carter.

The demon is trying to get into my head. It's trying to make me doubt, and I won't let it win. Not when it's obviously lying. I stare at the list and replay the conversation with the demon in my head. She said some things that don't make sense.

We made it happen. What we did was release the magic, and that magic went into the Statics. It's killing them. Can tainted magic really change them into demons? Is that the same thing as the Transformation from a witch to a demon?

I'm sure other people have tried this, but I open the search on the computer.

SEARCH___

HOW DOES MAGIC WORK?

A few hits pop up about the power witches possess. We learn that magic is eteneral during our Special Topics classes, the lessons weaved into our time at school. When a witch dies, the essence doesn't die. It's replenished to the elements where it awaits a new life in an empty host with the ability to contain the magic. Magic is reused, a continuous unending cycle. That's basically all the article says. A few more say the same, but with different words.

Magic is basically reincarnated from witch to witch. And maybe that means demon to demon.

If the magic left the demons, it went somewhere else.

SEARCH___

WITCHES INTO DEMONS

It's a long-shot but we're due for a miracle. I rub my eyes as the computer pulls up results. They are only articles about witches that went to the other side. Names, dates, details. Not what I'm looking for.

I glance back at Vassago's list and look at my search bar.

SEARCH___

OBSERVANCE KING QUEEN

There are no coincidences. There's no way everything happening now, with the Observance coming up, is random chance. If Vassago's message has a meaning, maybe this will tell me what. The search only loads ten results, but that's more than nothing. I click on the first.

The Observance dates back to the creation of witches, when we had the first encounter with the demon king, Lucifer. The fallen and his followers were adamant to stop witches, to take control of the Nons, and to reign. It was on this day the witches first discovered the use of salt as a demonic tool.

And now we celebrate that date every hundred years. Useless.

I scroll through the hits and the first four are more history I've already learned about.

The fifth one, though, it's actually new information. I sit up in my chair.

With Lucifer, fell Taliel, an angel more enamored with the betrayer than God. Lucifer and Taliel built an empire, changed their names to demon, and Lucifer ruled as king of demons. Taliel served his king in all manners, but as Lucifer declared his need for a queen, for one powerful enough to rule beside him, Taliel became jealous. He alone deserved the attentions of the King.

The demon sought to claim a witch, and it was during this time the first witch killed a demon using salt, and their celebration of the Observance was birthed. This new form of murder was a surprise to the demons. As the search for a queen intensified, so too did their death rate at the hands of witches.

As Lucifer spread his search across the masses, Taliel grew tired of the king's search. He grew impatient, tired of being pushed aside, and he longed for his old life. Taliel attempted to re-enter heaven. Lucifer, however, discovered this betrayal. As he was about to be ended, Taliel made a promise to Lucifer: Taliel had prepared a gift. The gift was given to Lucifer in bargain for Taliel's life, but it would take centuries to be revealed. It was the only way Taliel could guarantee his survival, but eventually, Lucifer tired of waiting and killed him anyway. The gift has still not been received, nor is its origin known.

That's weird. I run a hand through my hair. If Vassago gave me that message about the void and the gift. His other clue was the Observance. If this article is right, then all these pieces are connected. The Observance and the gift could go together. Maybe this gift will come during the Observance? That's less than a month from now. My head hurts.

Poncho clears his throat behind me and I jump in the chair. I forgot he was here.

"I'll be retiring for the evening," he says.

"I should go home, too."

I click on the button and hide my search results. But even when they're gone from the screen they're in my head.

"You found what you were looking for?" Poncho asks.

With a sigh I say, "I have no idea."

Chapter Twenty-Three

"Earth to Penelope," Connie stares at me over her ice cream the next day. Her eyes are wide, like she's seen a ghost.

"What?"

"You going to eat that?" she points at my ice cream.

I sigh. "I ordered it, didn't I?

"You've barely touched it. That's a rare thing," she says.

She knows me too well. "I'm letting it melt," I say, trying to cover. If she doesn't buy it, she doesn't question me.

Connie shifts in her chair as her phone rings out a high-low-high sound. I don't have to be able to see the messages of more Statics dying or manifesting. That's all it is now. I'm really glad that I can't see the names. It's already too much to carry around knowing the fact that I could change this. I rub my wrist. This stupid mark makes everything worse. If I had magic I could do…something.

"I found the best dress for the Observance. It's blue. Do you have one?" she asks.

I shrug. The Observance seems far away and there are so many things happening that it's hard to be excited. "I'm not worried about it yet."

"You'll get to go with Carter at least. Built-in dance partner. We can go shopping for one if you want." Connie pauses and sighs. "What happened today? You seem more distracted than usual."

"Nothing." Everything.

Her nose crinkles up. "You sure? Because you can tell me." I don't answer. I don't want her involved in any of this. Not more than she already is.

"And moody," she says. "I've never seen my sister not eat ice cream. You're not on your period so that doesn't explain the mood swings."

I remain silent as she raises an eyebrow at me. "Are you and Carter fighting? Did you guys break up?"

"No. Just this once can you stop?" I snap.

She holds her hands up in defense and 'rawrs' at me. I hate being rawr'd at. I twist the spoon around in the ice cream. It's already changed consistencies, almost a milkshake now, but I can't eat it. My stomach is in lumps and the thought of eating this makes me want to vomit. Sadly, I admit ice cream doesn't solve everything.

"I can make all this better," Connie smiles, "with laser tag."

"I'm not interested."

"Come on, Penelope. This is supposed to be my day

because I failed my test. We didn't watch the movie because of everything with Taylor. You said whatever I wanted, and I want a break."

Connie is leaning halfway across the table, trying to coax me. "Come on. Let's do *something* besides sit here and mope. Laser tag or pedicures or a movie. We still have to pick up the pizza for Gran."

"Fine." I give in and throw away my ice cream. It's a sad day when a girl can't eat her ice cream.

I follow Connie out the door. Lucky us, pizza and ice cream and laser tag all on the same block. She's practically skipping, she's so happy. Laser tag has never made her this happy. I doubt it would cheer her up after she failed her exams—yet there she is smiling. Almost free.

I freeze. "You did it on purpose."

"What?"

"You blew the test. Why would you do that?"

Connie crosses her arms slowly. "You won't get it."

I lean into her, and pull her around the corner. "Try me."

Connie stares at me, eyes wide like they usually are when she's nervous. "Being an Enforcer was your dream, Penelope, not mine."

Our conversation about what I'd do without being an Enforcer repeats in my head. I should've seen it then. I knew then that she was having doubts, but I never asked her. I should've followed up. "What happened?"

She huffs. "You never asked me what my dream was. No one has. We're the Grey girls. Obviously we'd be Enforcers like our parents," she pauses. "I knew you needed me to be one, so I went along with it. I thought I did want it. But then you got Carter and you didn't need me," she says, the words rushing out like she'd been holding them in all this time, about to burst. "I was waiting for the exams to come, and I realized that it wasn't what I wanted to do. I don't have to be an Enforcer. I'm happy being a regular witch."

We walk down the back street toward the laser tag and those words sit on my chest. Something else I can never be. Not an Enforcer and not a regular witch. Silence fills the space between. I sort of admire Connie for what she did. I could never walk away like that and go find an entirely new plan.

"What would you like, then?"

She laughs. "No idea! I'm not even seventeen yet, Penelope. You're older than me. Can you say being an Enforcer is what you want to do forever? Risk your life for other people who will never know that you're doing it, even if you die for them?"

I can't say that because it's not my life anymore. Can I even say I felt that way before? My goal was to get my magic back, and that was it. Did I ever really want to do the job, or just to feel like I had a purpose? Those are different things, aren't they?

"I don't know," I respond. Connie looks surprised by the answer, and there's so much more she'd be surprised about. "I'm sorry. I didn't realize that I was pushing what I wanted on you."

Connie smiles, her hair bouncing as she hugs me. "I didn't, either. When I did, I decided I would fail. Then I'd be able to get where I wanted to go. Wherever that is."

She's more understanding than I am. My sister is so much smarter than me.

"I do get it," I say. Connie looks surprised. "I mean, I've

always tried to be more than I was."

"You were pretty fantastic before too, you know," she says to me.

"You too, little sis. You get it from me." I wrap one arm around her elbow and shove my other hand in her face like a microphone. "You won the superbowl, what will you do next?"

She laughs as we walk. "Go to Disneyworld. Or maybe I'll go crazy and do college with Nons. That could be an adventure."

"It's definitely an adventure," I say. In that moment, I feel like I should tell her everything. That I'm as lost as she is, and why I've been so moody. "Connie, something happened."

The high-low-high notes ring from her phone. Immediately, Connie's is already in her hand, and I huff. "Oh my gosh," Connie says.

"What?" I ask. I reach for my phone from my pocket out of habit, but Connie grabs my arm. "Smell that?"

I freeze. A demon is nearby. For a second I wonder if it's Lia, but I don't think she's so desperate that she'd make two appearances in such a short time span. Connie squeezes my arm, and then a demon appears in front us, bright red and teeth bared. Definitely not the mauve demon. Or friendly.

Before either of us can move, it runs toward us faster than I've seen a demon move. It's almost a blur. I call on the magic, and I almost feel it all moving inside me, building up. When I try to release it nothing happens. The mark keeps it from coming. Stupid.

Connie's face grows fierce and then she zaps magic toward the demon. It growls at her and I jump out of the way. Connie calls on the wind to push it away from us — and I can't do anything. Great. What the hell am I supposed to do now? I scan the area for an object to use against it, but I don't see any iron. It's worthless to try, but maybe if I keep trying to use the magic then it will work.

My sister screams as the demon tosses her down the street and she slides across the cement.

Screw this. You do not mess with my sister.

I hurl myself at the demon, and kick it in the head. It stumbles backward. Even if I don't have magic at all, I still have my ninja moves. My fist flies into the demon's stomach, and it doubles over. I kick it again, bringing it to its knees, and then run toward Connie, who's getting up from the ground. I don't make it far before the demon draws me toward it. My whole body feels like it's on a string, and I try not to move, but the demon magic is stronger. How the heck is it doing this? It jerks its hand, and I land hard at its feet.

The demon bends over me, drool falling onto my face, which is less than appealing. When it's close enough, I kick up my legs and wrap them around its neck, dropping it to the ground. I punch toward it, but the demon grabs my leg and hurls me down. I toss whatever salt I can pull from my necklace toward the demon's face. It howls and covers its ears, backing away slowly. It recovers quickly, thanks to my pitiful amount of salt, and its eyes narrow at me in anger. It takes a step forward and then stops, immobilized, and looks up at the sky, arms stretching back away from its body.

I look up and Connie's hand is out in the air. I don't know what magic she's doing, but the demon hates it. I move as quickly as I can to stand by my sister.

Connie drops her hand and the demon stumbles forward.

"Let's kill this thing," she says. It growls at us and Connie takes my hand before I can protest. I start to pull my hand away but it the stupid mark will stop it. I can go along with it and she'll expel the demon all on her own.

My sister takes charge of the whole situation and I stand there watching. In a normal situation, I'd feel her magic stirring mine. I don't feel anything. It's the first time that the marking feels real, even though I haven't had magic for days. I don't have anything, not even the little stir from Connie. The Triad has taken away the only piece of myself that made me a witch. Without magic, what am I?

"Virtute angeli ad infernum unde venistis," Connie yells into the air, her hands pointed toward the cowering demon.

As soon as the words are said, I feel magic. My skin is on fire, insanely hot. I feel the burning under my skin, the same way it felt when I was in the testing, and a small cry escapes my mouth.

A bright light fills the small space and the demon howls, the worst sound I've ever heard. Nails on a chalkboard mixed with white noise mixed with that note the fat lady sings in all those operas. Connie drops my hand and covers her ears, but I can't move. My whole body is on fire, exuding a bright white light and I have no idea how to stop it. The void is pouring from me—and I can't contain it. It's a tsunami escaping through a keyhole. It hurts, but it feels good at the same time. Release. Like pent-up energy and emotion finally expressed.

Connie yells my name, and I look at her, but it's hard to see her in the brightness of the light. What the hell is happening? She moves closer toward me and I open my mouth to yell no. As soon as I do, her body is tossed across the parking lot—by me—and into the brick side of the building.

"Connie," I yell, but the white light doesn't stop. I can't make it stop. My sister isn't moving. Why isn't she moving?

The world starts spinning, and I feel like I'm floating. I see my sister on the ground.

The slight blue of the sky beyond the rooftops.

Demon guts covering the sides of everything. When did it die?

Gray concrete.

And then I see nothing.

Chapter Twenty-Four

The heart monitor is a constant steady beeping. That sound has become this soothing noise. As long as it's beeping then she's breathing. Breathing means alive. Alive means I stay right here. I run my hand over Pen's hair. I expect her to wake up and demand a cookie. Whatever happened to her, I just want her to wake up. It's been thirty-six hours since those Nons found her and Connie behind the pizza place, and I want her to wake up.

I glance up and Dad's face appears in the window on the door again. He stares in, and I stare out. I haven't talked to him much since Pen got put in the hospital, but the last we spoke he'd asked if there was something he should know about her. I said no. I had him agree the Triad wouldn't tell

Pen's grandparents that she had been marked. And then he said, "That girl is trouble." As much as I'd wanted to, I refrained from flipping him off.

After a few seconds, he walks away from the window. The Triad has been here since yesterday. They don't know what happened out there, either, or why. Was it a demon? Was it Connie?

Or was it something else?

Given all that I know about the mark, she shouldn't have magic. But the demon had said the void would still be working with the mark. If Pen does have magic, even though she's completely separated from the essence, then she's using the void. I can't use the void that way. I can't even access it, but Pen can. If Pen was involved in what happened out there, if she used the void to do all this, then it's a game-changer. Not that I'm even sure what game we're playing anymore.

The door opens and Frank comes in. "Any change?" I ask about Connie.

"Connie is stable, finally," he says. He looks down at Penelope and I see the exhaustion in his eyes. I can't imagine what it's like for him to have both of his granddaughters in the hospital without explanation. "This is really hard on Deb," he says. He's not looking at me. He's probably talking to himself, but I listen anyway. "She's in there with Connie now. You watch your kids go after these impossible things, and you worry about what could happen to them, but then it happens. When it was Genevieve, we didn't even have this moment of wondering. She was just gone. I don't know what's worse…"

"Pen and Connie aren't going to die," I say, still holding

Pen's hand. She won't die. Neither of them will. They can't. Frank looks at me. "They won't. They're strong girls, and Penelope's too stubborn."

Frank cracks a smile and rests his hand on my shoulder. "You're a good boy, Carter. I'm glad she has you."

"I couldn't imagine not having her."

"Penelope's always been guarded, but not with you. Ever since you came around, she's been more open. Less afraid. Almost as if she feels safe."

I don't know what to say to that so I don't say anything.

"Can you tell me one thing?"

"What's that?"

Frank nods toward the door. "Why is the Triad parading outside in the hallway?"

His eyes are dark, narrowed in on me. He's suspicious because this isn't typical of them. I look from him and out the tiny window. Sabrina's face is there for a moment. Even from the other side of the door I can sense her attitude problem. I look back toward Frank.

"Maybe they're worried."

He puts his shoulders back. "About my granddaughters when there are Statics dying?"

I don't move my gaze away from his. We both know it's more than what I'm saying.

There's a pressure in my hand. The monitor beeps next to me and Frank and I both look down. Pen's eyes are wide open.

"Penelope," Frank says, laughter seeping through his smile. He kisses Pen's forehead softly. For a moment, I feel like I'm intruding, but then she looks at me, too. That's all I need to break into a smile. She's awake. I don't know what would've happened if I'd lost her, and now I'll never have to.

"What happened?" she asks in a whisper, looking between her grandpa and me.

"Let's get the doctors first," Frank says. He kisses her cheek and bounces out the room. One less thing to worry about for him.

Pen looks at me, waiting for me to tell her. She tries to sit up in the bed, but barely moves an inch. "Some Nons found you and Connie behind the pizza place two days ago."

"Two days?"

I nod, forcing down the feeling in my throat. "There were demon remains on the scene. You and Connie were both unconscious. You don't remember it?"

She scrunches up her nose. "Not really. Connie—where is she?"

"In a room next door. She hasn't woken up yet," I say. Pen nods her head slowly. "I thought you...we were all worried."

She squeezes my hand. "I'm too stubborn to leave yet."

"That's what I said," I say with a smile.

"I need to be here to make your life interesting."

"A little less interesting wouldn't be a bad thing," I say. I run my hand over her cheek. She's so beautiful, and she's right here. "Whatever happened, whatever happens, I love you."

"Why are you talking like I'm in trouble?"

"Because we have some questions," Rafe Ezrati says. He stands in the doorway of Penelope's doorway with Sabina and my dad. Pen's eyes widen.

I cross my arms but don't move from her bed. "Right now? She just woke up."

"We'll only be a moment," Sabrina says.

I shake my head, about to protest. How can they come in here right now? She's been awake four seconds. Pen puts her hand over mine and holds her head up high.

"What's your question?"

"Do you remember what happened out there?" Rafe asks.

I study Pen's face as she thinks, nose scrunched up, eyes wide and then a sigh. "I remember a demon. Connie and I were going to play laser tag and get pizza and it came out of nowhere. I fought it. She used magic on it. Then, I was waking up here."

Sabrina crosses her arms, and exchanges a look with my dad and Rafe. "That's all you remember?"

She nods. "That's all."

"You didn't try to do magic?" Dad asks. He doesn't even look at me. His gaze is totally focused on Penelope.

"I don't have magic, remember? You marked me. It's probably the reason my sister and I are in hospital beds right now. It's like you're against me when I did nothing wrong."

Rafe shakes his head. "Miss Grey, we are not against you."

"Then give me my magic back."

I look between Penelope and the Triad. If they are trying to get her on their side, they're doing a shitty job of it.

"We can't do that yet, Miss Grey. Not until our investigation is concluded."

Pen looks away from them as Frank comes back in with the doctor. He looks at the Triad and then at Pen. That look is in his eyes again. The one from earlier, where he seems to know more is happening. "Can you give my granddaughter a moment before you berate her?"

"We are finished here," Sabrina says.

A noise from across the hall fills the awkward silence. It's Deborah yelling for a doctor. Pen's doctor leaves the room, followed by her grandpa and Pen squeezes my hand. "What's happening over there?"

"She'll be fine," I say.

Pen shakes her head, tears in her eyes. "Are you sure?"

No, but I don't tell her that. Connie was stabilized before Pen woke up. The last two days have been this constant back and forth for her.

The tears slide down on her red face, this new determination there with the worry, and in all the time I've known her, I've never seen her that angry. She looks at the Triad. "You took my magic. You made it so I couldn't help my sister when that demon came, and if she dies, I will never forgive you. I will make sure that her death haunts the three of you forever."

"Remember your place, Miss Grey," Dad says.

"Oh, I have not forgotten," she says, and shakes her head. "You can get out now."

Before he leaves, Dad tosses me a look. The Triad's not even close to finished with this. Whatever they are looking for, whatever the reason for being here, they'll be back.

. . .

"I want to see Connie," she says. Pen's been awake and Connie's been stable for the last ten hours. Deborah and I sit on each side of Penelope's bed. Her color is back.

"You're not strong enough to be up," Deborah says.

"Please," her voice cracks. "Just a minute. I need to see her."

"I'll have to check with your doctor," Deborah says.

Penelope nods and Deborah kisses her cheek before leaving.

"I have a question," I say, looking down at Pen's hand. She *hmms*. I hold up her hand. "What's this spot?" Her eyes widen as she looks at her fingernail. Her whole pinky fingernail is covered in black. "I'm pretty sure that's new."

"Maybe I stubbed my finger?" she whispers. I run a finger over the spot but it doesn't seem swollen. A bruise would at least be sensitive.

"You feel okay?"

"I feel fine," she says. "Stop worrying about me."

I shrug. "That's hard to do."

"When's the last time you went home?"

"I don't want to go home." My dad is there, and she's here. It's hands down no contest for where I want to be.

"You should shower, sleep. Everyone looks so tired."

I shake my head. "I don't want to leave."

Pen touches my cheek, a soft smile on her lips. "It's only a few hours. I promise you can come back in the morning."

"Penelope."

"William," she says back. I hate when she plays that card.

I sigh. "I don't want to leave you."

"I'll be fine. Gran and Pop are here. You go get some rest. I already have to worry about them, so please don't make me worry about you," she says.

I look at her, and she's not going to change her mind. Honestly, I could use a shower. And food that's not from a vending machine. She's safe with her grandparents here. The

Triad's gone, and whatever questions I need to answer can wait another few hours.

"I'll be back first thing."

"Great."

"And you'll call me if you need anything?"

"Yes."

I press a kiss to her forehead. "I don't want to leave."

"I love you, too," she says.

I lean in and kiss her. I can't help it. Not knowing if she was going to live, waiting for her to wake up, to tell me those words again, to see her smile, it was all almost gone. Her hand moves up around my neck and she pulls herself up into my kiss. What started as a simple way to be closer to her sends my whole body on alert. Her fingers twist in the back of my hair, and I kiss her deeper. I want to be closer to her. To never let her go. I want her to tell me to stay, even though she won't.

"Ahem," Deborah clears her throat from the door. I pull away from Pen, but I don't look away from her. I'm not ready. Her hand rests on my arm and I don't know how I was anything before her.

"They said you could see Connie."

Penelope nods and I kiss again her softly. Once is never enough. "I'll see you in the morning."

Chapter Twenty-Five

Connie is connected to tubes and wires and machines. Tears fill up my eyes as soon as Gran wheels me into her room. I did this to her with the void. I didn't even know I had the power. It hadn't worked since I was marked. If I had… accident or not, it was me. She's here because of me. I was supposed to protect her.

"Just a few minutes, Penelope."

I nod softly and Gran leaves me next to Connie's bed. I take her hand, and it's drier than usual. Connie would never let her skin get so dry. I'll have to make sure Gran puts some lotion on them.

Steady beeps fill the room and I watch the dots move. It should be an encouragement, but it's not. "I'm so sorry,

Con," I whisper.

I told Carter and the Triad and everyone else that I didn't remember what happened. I was lying. I remember everything. That demon attacked us, and when Connie touched me, all the magic I'd been trying to call on came out. I can still see the way she looked at me when the magic started pouring out. Like I was a monster, dangerous. She was afraid of me. I could hear it in her voice as she pleaded with me to stop. I couldn't stop. I couldn't stop and now Connie's injured. The void did this, and it came from me. I almost killed my sister.

I hold back a sob and squeeze Connie's hand. Hers in mind reminds me of being a kid.

When Mom was alive, there was a day where she was going to take us to the park. I was five and Connie was four and we insisted that we had to walk there without her holding our hands. "Behind us," I'd insisted, and Mom didn't fight me. Instead, she tied Connie's hand to mine and looked at me. I can still her face, soft and round and peachy, when she said, "You're holding her hand now. Protect your sister. Don't let her wander off."

We walked the two blocks to the park, hands tied together. Mom was behind us the whole way, but I felt invincible, strong, and I was ready to keep Connie safe. I was in such a hurry to get there that Connie couldn't keep up and she fell, scratched her leg on the sidewalk. She cried, and I helped her up. I promised that we'd make it to the swings and then it would be all better. She believed me.

"Believe me now, Con," I say to her.

I'm going to make this all better, too. I stroke her hair. Connie would not be happy about looking like she does right now. Dark circles under her eyes, hair all over the place and an unflattering hospital gown. I should braid it, pigtails, like when we were younger. She never needed it because her hair has always had this curl, but mine did. She wanted to be like me.

"What are you doing?" Gran asks.

I pull one side of Connie's hair through my fingers. "Connie wouldn't like this. I'm braiding her hair. We need a little concealer under her eyes, some lip gloss."

"There's no point right now in— "

"Gran. Don't. She would want to look better." I don't mean to say it harshly, but I'm almost yelling. My sister is in a hospital bed because of me and I can't help it. I'm supposed to protect her, and instead, I did this to her.

"I bet there's some in her purse," Gran says. She's back a moment later and hands me some concealer. I apply to it Connie's face, but Gran surprises me by braiding the other side of Connie's hair. "You're right. She wouldn't want to look unkempt."

I pull my gaze away from Gran's tired face. No one should have to deal with this.

For a second, I think about telling Gran what happened. That I'm marked. That I did this, but then I stare at her and see the worry she carries. I can't add that to her plate. Not right now.

Her cell phone rings and she makes a little annoyed sound when she checks it. She passes it to me, still ringing. "Ric," she says. "He's called every few hours."

Hand shaking, I take the phone and answer.

"Thank God," he breaths into the receiver. I can hear the relief in his voice. "It's you. You're awake."

"It's me," I whisper, squeezing the phone tighter in my grasp.

He sighs on the line. "I thought I lost you. I couldn't do that again. I couldn't."

"I'm alive, and I'm right here," I say. He thinks I'm talking to him, but I'm really reminding myself.

• • •

Hospitals are creepy at night. Even though I've been moved from ICU, it's unsettling that people are dying around me. That, plus the fact that every time I close my eyes, someone else is in my room, checking my vitals, checking my blood pressure, checking my IV, poking at me to make sure I'm still alive. Spoiler: I am.

Even when there's no one in my room, I hear them. Walking outside, and the beeping. Sounds of people crying out in their sleep, or awake and in pain. They echo through the long hallways and I'm supposed to be able to sleep. Right.

It doesn't help that every time I try to sleep, I dream that I'm back in the street, tossing my sister into a wall with my magic. Only in my dream I'm more destructive. I'm light and power that ripples across everything, turning over cars, knocking out Nons, destroying the witches who try to stop me. I don't want to dream about that.

I pretend I'm somewhere else. Cuddled into Carter's arms or eating burritos with Ric or shopping with my sister. Anywhere else that's not a hospital.

"Penelope," a voice says. It's one I recognize, even though I shouldn't, and my eyes bolt open. Lia stands at the end of my bed. "Sorry to interrupt your beauty sleep, but you're a popular girl. It's hard to get in."

"Then leave." I don't want her here.

There's a silent pause in the room and then, "How's your sister?"

The sound of my heartbeat fills my ears. "You know about that?"

"Everyone does. You used the void, a lot of it."

I shake my head. "Can you fix her?"

Lia walks around my bed to the left side of me so she's closer. "You have to use the void to undo magic done by the void."

"Then you can heal her."

She shakes her head. "You're the one who wielded the magic. You call the magic back to yourself and undo it."

This is so frustrating. "But I don't know what I did. I didn't even mean to do it."

"I told you that you needed me."

I scoff. "You knew this would happen?"

"No," she says. "But I told you that you still had the void. You can't deny this part of yourself. In fact, you have to embrace it and fully become one with the void."

"Meaning…?"

The demon leans into me. "You have to become a demon by being connected fully and only to the void. Temporarily, at least." I stare at Lia. That's not what I want to hear.

"I'm not going to do that. No way," I say. This is crazy talk. Become a demon? No.

"This is for your sister, and for the Statics. You want to save them? This is the way."

I close my eyes. Lia told me the same thing before. I

didn't have a chance to figure out what any of it meant since our last talk on the hill. How many Statics have manifested or died in the time I've been asleep?

"How did they even get the power from me?" I ask.

"You passed it to them, at least that's what I can gather. That power from the demons that disappeared had to go somewhere—and you were the nearest doorway for the magic to get out. Maybe you came into contact with one or two Statics, empty vessels built for magic they don't have."

Taylor Plum. She was always so friendly, and she hugged me in the Nucleus House. She hugged me, got power, and died. She was going to a Static meeting so she could've passed it on to them—I really did give her magic. I killed her. And she killed Maple, and Ric is gone and my sister is dying next door. My own stubbornness, my determination to have magic, to be an Enforcer, to find Azsis—all of this is because of me.

Despair crushes my chest, and I breathe in as much as air as I can. It's not enough.

"You're saying I can undo all of the things that have happened. How? The dead can't come back to life."

Lia shakes her head. "No, you can't bring back the dead—but more can be prevented. You need to perform the Restitution and undo it all, reset everything that was before. To do that, you need to use the void."

"Why do you want to be human so badly?" All the guilt, all the sadness, I really think that being a demon would mean none of that.

She runs a finger along the edge of the hospital bed and circles around me, lost in thought. Was what her life like that Lia wants to return so badly? "We all make mistakes. We all wish we could undo whatever it was we did, Non, witch, and demon alike. I had a life. A good life, and I can have it again. You can have the power you've always wanted. You can save your sister, and all the Statics."

I swallow back all of my fears, and the uncertainty about how crazy this sounds. It is crazy.

"How does this work? You said I had to become a demon?" I ask. I need to make sure I fully understand what I'm doing here. Why is it worth me risking all that I am, even for my sister?

"The Restitution will remove the void from me, making me human. That magic has to go somewhere, so we'll make it go into you. You'll have complete control over the void."

"I'll be a full demon."

"You'll be a new demon, essentially. It will strip away whatever remains of your essence, whatever connections you had before. You'll reset everything that was before. Then, you'll have the void and the power to undo it."

"And I'll be a demon."

"Temporarily," she says. "Until you capture Azsis and do the whole thing again to restore your full essence. It's a cycle, a balance."

I'll become a demon. A full T-total demon. "You're sure that's how it works? That it will reset everything with my sister and all the Statics?"

"Yes," she says. "The magic you put out there belongs to you. If you have enough power, you can call it all back. The more control you have, the more powerful you'll be. Right now, it controls you."

"This is too much," I say. I feel like I'm losing my mind. I shouldn't agree to this, to becoming a demon—even for an hour—but what are my other options? A scaly hand appears on my forearm and I never imagined being consoled by a demon. She pulls her hand away quickly, only to grab my own hand instead.

Lia holds my hand in the air between us. My pinky fingernail is completely black now, and from it, a couple small lines that trail down to my top knuckle. It's gotten worse.

"What is that?" I ask.

"The void," she says.

I run my finger down the black marks on my skin. In my skin, rather. "Is it turning my blood black?"

Lia nods. "It's a powerful magic. Until you learn to command it, to manipulate it, and accept it, it will consume you."

I can't believe I'm even considering this. I jerk my hand away from the demon's. "I don't want this."

"I respect your decision. Be prepared then for what's to come." The demon turns to walk away. *Good, leave. I don't need you.* But it's a lie.

"What's to come?" I ask.

Mauve turns around to me. "Your sister and those Statics that are dying? That's the beginning. How many people you will have destroyed by your magic before you accept that you are more? That you have demon blood and demon magic? You can't ignore it—the void won't let you."

"If I do this," I say, "how long until we can fix Connie?"

"She has a timeline," Lia stares at me before continuing. "Thirty days, or less, before it kills her. She can't sustain the void. We should do it on the Observance, that would give us plenty of time, and it's a powerful night for magic."

I inhale and close my eyes. Thirty days or less until my sister dies. We've already wasted almost three being asleep. "Even though she's technically a halfling, too?"

"You and she aren't the same. She has an essence—you do not. Halflings have two magics fighting inside them—Carter has that, too—and the essence will always win that fight. But when more void is added, as it was with Connie, it becomes stronger. The essence will fight that. It will fight for her. It's the fighting that kills her."

"But not me, since I don't have an essence. It's free reign for the void."

Lia nods. "Exactly. If a full-blooded witch had been hit with the same power that Connie was, he or she would already be dead. The demon part of your sister is saving her life, temporarily."

In the silence, the clock on the wall is practically taunting me. Tick tock. My sister is on a timeline. Tick tock. I have to save her. Time is running out. I'm in a race here to become one with the void. To become a temporary demon, or let them all be destroyed.

I can't live with that for the rest of my life. I can't live knowing I did nothing to save them all, and I could've.

"Okay," I say. "I'll do it."

Lia smiles and moves toward me. "There's a way we make deals with demons," she says.

"I'm not kissing you," I snap.

"No kissing required unless you're a Non," she says. One of Lia's claws appears and she sticks herself with it. Blood drips from the tip of her finger.

"A blood oath."

"Unbreakable," she says. "I, Lia, will teach you, Penelope,

how to harness the void and save your sister, then you will help me with my task." She pushes the point of her finger toward me and I gulp. This is a big deal. No going back on a blood oath. What would Carter say if he found out what I was doing? What would anyone say? They'd definitely not approve.

But it's the only way for them and for me.

I press the tip of the Lia's claw into my finger until my own blood comes out.

"I swear on my blood," she says.

"I swear on my blood," I repeat, and then our fingers meet so the blood intermingles. As soon as it touches, there's a shock and a spark of light between us. I'm now sealed into a promise with a demon.

"You can call me when you're out of here," the demon says.

You can call me stupid.

Chapter Twenty-Six

Carter

Penelope seems off. For the last six days, ever since she got out of the hospital, she's been somewhere else even when she's sitting next to me. She's been snappy and giving short one-word answers. She's worried, but I want her to talk to me. She used to tell me things, now it's like I'm a stranger.

She sits across from me, staring off into nothing. I stretch my hand across the table to grab hers. She pulls away from me.

It's been like that, too.

"Hey," I say, pulling at her sleeve until she looks at me. That's another thing. She's been wearing long sleeves for a week. It's August. I'm trying not to be invasive, but with Connie, the Statics, and Pen being marked, there's a lot going on. But there's this look in her eyes. A little broken, but desperate and determined. It's a look that reminds me of my dad, of what happens when who he really is seeps out behind the mask of arrogance. Those moments, rare as they are, are the hardest to process.

I tap my fingers on the side of my coffee cup. "Where's your head?"

"I'm fine. It's been a long week. I feel like I should be doing something."

"You've only been out of the hospital six days, Pen. Take care of yourself first."

She flashes a weak, and fake, smile. That's become the norm for her, but I see through it the same way she can see through mine. "You're right, but it's hard."

Pen rubs her wrist where the mark is. I can't see the gold anymore, but I know it's still there. Maybe that's the problem. The mark. I think back on the articles I read. The effects happened over time. I should tell her. I've been trying to tell her for days.

"Can you turn that thing off?" Pen snaps, pointing at my phone. It's vibrating again. The WNN is in full swing with Statics. I snatch up my phone from the table and look at the time.

"I need to go, anyway," I say. "Static class today," I say, kissing her cheek gently.

She nods and picks up her coffee cup. "I should check in with Gran and Pop, go see Connie."

Now's not the time to tell her. Besides, what if it's not the mark? It could be the stress of everything. If I tell her then I'll be making it worse, especially when it turns out to be nothing. "I'll see you later."

As I get in my car, I have the realization that this is one more thing I have in common with my dad. We'll both keep the truth a secret if it means saving someone we love.

• • •

Classes for the Statics started three days ago. Today's the first day we've had double digit attendance: Twelve. It doesn't seem like many in the scheme of things, but it is. At least they're coming.

"Let's start with the control formulas," I say. If they can't control their magic, then they can't do anything.

The class jumps into action, spreading out across the training room. Four newbies partner up with some of the Statics from the first classes. The first day is the hardest. The void, even when it's tainted like this is, doesn't work like the essence. Somehow this magic is in between. The essence creates by pulling from the elements, and the void from nothing. This is more essence, but also tainted by thoughts. It would all be so much easier if Pen could be here.

I watch as one kid in the class, Ash, starts a simulation demon attack with a newbie. She moves quicker than most Enforcers I've seen. Her magic is strong, and she's learned control quickly. The whole simulation is over in less than a minute, and the newbies' eyes are huge.

"Good job, Ash," I yell out. She gives me a thumbs up.

Around the room, this is the standard. Simulations and training, using techniques to move items and learn basic control. I stop in the back corner and watch a boy named JC. He's young, maybe thirteen, and the only one in his family that hasn't had magic. Until now. He's been here every day.

JC turns on the simulation and dives around a demon, under another's legs and is on his feet in seconds. He slides across the floor, grabbing a salt gun from the rack on the wall. The two demons lunge toward him, but he calls out a spell and sends one into the wall. The other uses magic on him and knocks the gun from his hand. The demon snarls, and moves across the room in a second. JC is ready, and uses magic to hang him from the ceiling. In a swift movement, he tosses salt and yells the incantation, and simulation demon explodes. Demon two sneaks around the back of the room behind his back, but JC calls up the gun with the magic and pulls the trigger as soon as it hits his palm. No more demons.

Everyone cheers as he finishes and he stands there with a big smile. The others slap him on the back and then go back to their other places. As I turn away, I notice the look on his face change and it makes me pause. He stumbles forward.

"JC?"

He looks over at me, eyes wide and face pale. Shit. "JC!"

Wordlessly, he caves to his knees and falls over. I race over to him, but he's already sprawled out on the ground. I know before I touch him that he's already dead.

• • •

My dad's quiet. I sit across from him in his office, but neither of us speak. It's a rare thing to see him worried. I can't say that I've seen it much before in my life. He buries his head in his hands, not making a noise, and I sit there, staring, not sure what to say. While I'm still processing his reaction, he pops his head up, clears his throat, straightens out his jacket, and looks at me. Moment's over, I guess.

There's a knock on the door before Sabrina and Rafe come in without waiting for a response.

"JC's parents have taken him home. They are such faithful servants, it's a shame this happened," Rafe says.

Sabrina looks at him. "Perhaps we were wrong to encourage the use of magic in this way."

"It's not wrong. They're learning. It's been three days." I say. I can't believe her sometimes.

She puts her hands on her hips. "Three days and how many have come? This isn't solving the problem."

I stand and the chair scratches the floor. "You haven't even given it a chance."

"How many have died during your 'chance'?" Sabrina says cooly, even though she's only inches from my face. It's been three days. They can't expect it to work out overnight.

"Sixty," Dad says, and all three of us look at him. "Sixty Statics have died in five days."

"And how many more must die before we take action?" Sabrina asks, turning away from me to my dad. This is bullshit. He can't be listening to this. Dad's eyes look between us before he stands.

"What action would you like to take?"

"What?" I shout. This is wrong.

Rafe holds out his hands in front of him. "Whatever the cause, it's obvious that the magic is behind it. It's the magic we must control."

"The solution is to get rid of the magic," Sabrina says. She means the mark, even if she doesn't say it, back to the original plan. "It will prevent any further deaths and any further disruptions."

Rafe, Sabrina, and Dad all share a glance. Dad sighs,

his whole body moving, and strokes a hand over his bushy beard. He can't be considering this.

"I've researched the mark. It made all the witches who had it crazy. You're asking for trouble if you pass it around to everyone. You have no idea what the response will be. This isn't normal magic, you've said it yourself," I say.

"You researched it?" Dad asks.

"You gave it to Penelope," as if that's all the explanation he needs. That's not the point of this conversation at all. "Besides, you'll never have enough time or magic to mark all the Statics."

Sabrina crosses her arms. "I've already trained the reserves. I did it in case your plan failed, which it has. Victor, I know he's your son, but think about the good of everyone. Our world is in danger."

I shoot her a glance. She's trained them on giving the mark? Dad looks as surprised as I am. She can't go behind his back like that, can she?

"How many are trained?" he asks.

"Father."

"Forty Enforcers," Sabrina says, barely containing her smile.

I lean into my dad, hands pressed on the desk. "Don't do this. It could kill them," I say.

"They'll die anyway," Sabrina says.

The room is quiet. Rafe doesn't say anything. Dad rests two fingers on his temple, thinking. What's there to think about? This is dangerous.

Dad straightens his posture. "Gather them, and split the city up into sections. We'll start tonight."

I can't believe him. All of them. I leave the room and let the door slam behind me.

Chapter Twenty-Seven

PENELOPE

I'm in my car when a buzzing sound goes off. But it's not my phone. I tinker around until I find the large, round, gray communicator—relay—buzzing under the passenger seat. I'd forgotten about that thing. I stare it at it, at the small red blinking button. Did it blink before? I press my finger against the red button, and then the car spins. Literally spins. Or maybe I'm spinning. Then I'm not in the car—I'm on the library floor.

Whoa.

Seak rubs his face against my arm. I'm in the library. How am I in the library?

"What the heck was that?" I ask.

"Relay," Poncho says. I look up from the floor toward

his rounded face. He holds a hand out. "Hello, Miss Grey."

I take his hand and he guides me up. "You didn't tell me it did that."

"Didn't I?" he says, and then he shrugs. "It does a multitude of things."

I stare at the plastic thing and then slide it into my pocket. Half of it sticks it out.

"I've been calling you all morning," Poncho says. I follow him through the library back to the information desk.

"What's so important?"

He stops and turns to face me. "I have found the cause of your sister's condition."

I swallow the lump in my throat. "You have? Who asked you to look?"

"Mr. Prescott," he says.

A sinking feeling falls into the pit of my stomach. If he's looking into what happened to Connie, how long will it be until he discovers I'm what happened? And if he learns that, then what if he learns that I took the deal with Lia? The nervousness sets my magic on alert, like an arrow taut on a bowstring. "What did you find?"

Poncho leans into me. "Traces of the void." He pauses. "The void is a powerful magic, much different than the essence. It exists without rather than within. A pure magic that can kill."

"Kill?"

He nods. "Witches can't handle such pure magic. The void is a seeping poison to the heart. The contact slowly shuts down the body over days. Most victims don't survive long."

Don't survive… "How long?"

"The longest case was twenty days, but that witch was a halfling. Halflings are still susceptible to the magic. The void and the essence will always battle, since only one can have control. The battle between the two magics is what kills someone."

This is pretty much what Lia told me. Connie's been in a coma for eight days. I freeze, eyes on Poncho. I've never told him directly what I am, but I always assumed he knew. I can't tell from his face whether he's testing me.

"Why are you telling me all this?" I cross my arms, hoping it shows more of whatever point I'm trying to make. I'm not even sure right now. The void stirs within me.

His eyes are on me, and I feel like he's looking through me. "Perhaps it is a demon seeking to finish what Kriegen started."

Kriegen. She wanted to convert me and Carter. "Kriegen's dead."

"Indeed," he says, voice very still. "I will continue to look into it, per Mr. Prescott's request. I do suggest that you keep that dagger hidden. If a demon is after you and your sister, it could be for that, since it too links back to Kriegen."

He's not completely wrong. Lia needs the dagger, but she needs me, too. "I will," I say. My eyes drift to the clock. I'm late for Lia. Poncho stares at me. "Anything else?"

"You should continue with your day. You don't want to be late for your plans." I freeze. How does he know I have plans? I start to question him, but he holds up a hand. "You looked at the clock, Miss Grey."

Right. I glance at it again, directly above his head. He never misses anything. "See you later."

"I am here should you need me as you are aware that I

am here to guide you."

"Your destiny," I say. "I almost forgot."

"Yes, and yours. For it is underway."

I swallow, nervous and on edge suddenly.

Poncho only smiles. "Have a good day, Miss Grey."

· · ·

Lia is waiting in the woods off the trails in the same place where I first saw Kriegen use the dagger. It's a good location, secluded, with open space and not many eyes. At first, I could still see the red-headed witch that died and the dagger releasing her essence into the atmosphere. Now, after four days of meeting with Lia, it seems like a distant memory. It's not lost on me that this is where everything changed, and now, it's where I'm changing.

"You're late," Lia says. Her voice comes from above me and when I find her, she's sitting up in a tree. I think about giving her a reason, but I don't think she needs one. She's not my keeper. Lia jumps down from the tree and lands on her feet.

"Let's not waste time talking," she says. We walk to the center of the open space and she faces me. "Start where we left off yesterday. Remember what you did?"

I nod and exhale.

We started out with small things. I demonstrated how I'd been using the void by calling up images in my head and then projecting them out. She told me that was incomplete and weak. I'd always thought the void created from nothing, and it is, but it creates from what I visualize—from conception, to use, to ending. Apparently, there's a way to use the void without thinking, to have it become part of me and respond. When that happens it—and I—can do way more damage.

Lia said the reason my using the void backfired on Connie was because I didn't have a clear image of how to stop what happening, and I didn't have control of my emotions. When I'm too emotional, the void doesn't know how to respond so it either doesn't, or it goes too crazy to control. She says it's better to feel nothing. With Connie, I was scared, and fear is the most powerful of all emotions. The result of that fear is lying in a coma in a hospital bed.

Lia walks around me in a circle. "I want you to call on the void again, and then close it off immediately. Emotions are a liability, but being able to control them makes you powerful. Our goal here is to make the void be completely connected to you."

Apparently, phenomenal cosmic power requires you to not feel anything. That completely goes against how we're taught to use the essence. The essence is heightened by emotion, the void hindered by it.

"Feel the strongest emotions," she says. Fear, anger, worry, the emotions that command decisions. "Then cut it off, let the void take over."

I nod and focus on the empty space around me. I see an image of a tree falling down, what I want to happen immediately, but no. Not allowed. No images.

Fear. I have a lot of options, and they all flood through me. I need to pick one moment, so I focus in on when I was a child. Each time I go there, though, back to that moment, I feel myself crack open. Yet I keep going back. For the last four days, I keep going back.

Mommy is singing to me and daddy busts in, and lunges

*at us. Mommy throws me under the bed and starts fighting
him. I'm so scared. I can't see anything, but I can hear it all. I
can hear her. What is daddy doing? Why is he being mean? I
don't want to hear so I cover my ears and mommy screams.
A demon grabs at my feet, pulls me from my spot under the
bed. I'm crying, screaming for mommy, for daddy, but the
demon holds me down. I can't get away. I can't get away.
Mommy whispers magic words, says my name, says please
to the demon. But the demon with the orange eyes laughs
at me. "Watch this," he says to me while his friend tears into
mommy's throat.*

I feel the magic building up, that familiar bursting
sensation right before it flows from my pores. It wants to
come out, but I'm still in my house, still a kid, still afraid.

"Now close off your emotions. Don't feel anything,
Penelope. Let go."

That's easier said than done.

Don't feel anything.

*Be a wall. Be a statue. Be solid and unmoving. Close the
door. Love no one. Fear nothing. Be nothing.*

I force the images of the demons and mom and me away
from my head. I try not to see the blood. I tell child-memory
me to take a breath, to forget, to release it. I push all of those
emotions back down into the box I've built in my head. I
push and push and try to not feel. To not care.

I won't care. I don't. Nothing can harm me.

Then the magic pours out of me in the form of light
and wind. Not with the usual force that it carries, but more
obedient. I try not to enjoy it. But when I see Lia smile, I
break my concentration and the magic stops.

"Good job," Lia says. "But you need to be faster at

gaining control of the emotions and turning them off. When you do that, you'll be unstoppable. Again."

That's what we do over and over. She makes me feel a strong emotion, then makes me close it off. For hours we do this, and when she's satisfied, she allows me to stop.

"Better, but it still takes you too long."

"Sorry, I'm not a robot." It's hard to shut off that pain. To not feel it. She's asking me to harness it into the magic, and that's not done overnight. Not when I've had so much of it.

Lia shakes her head "It's not about being a robot, it's about not having connections. Your emotions are still attached to these people. Demons don't develop feelings. It's the human emotions that make you weaker."

"Demons have no feelings?"

"None," she says. "We have to kill to survive, to continue our population. If we had feelings, then we couldn't do that. The conscience is a tool of destruction. When a demon is made, the old life is gone—for a Non or a witch. The ties that bind them to this world are removed."

"Then why do you want to be a human again?"

"Because I remember what it was like," she says. "The sun on your skin, a first kiss, the way food tastes. I always try to keep it close, and other demons don't. Remembering makes it hard to be powerful. I don't remember my life, particularly, but I can almost remember how it was to be alive. I hang out at this bar called O'Malley's sometimes because being around the living is as close as any of us demons can come to being alive."

"You're alive now."

"Am I?"

I stare at Lia. Her appearance will never allow her to be human again, to live the life she once did. I stand and dust off my pants. That's when I notice the blackness has spread up my hand and over my wrist.

"It's spreading," I say. She takes my hand and examines it.

"You need to master the magic. You have to accept it."

"I'm trying."

"You need to be faster. Three hours a day isn't enough."

I look at the blackness spreading up my hands. "Everyone is going to see this."

Lia takes my hand and runs a finger over the vein. "We can glamour it. We'll have to do it every day, and more frequently as it expands. I'll show you," she says.

She calls on the void and I feel it embrace the space around me. She doesn't say anything, and it's only a second, and then my marks are not visible. Not even to me.

"How do you do that?"

"The same way you will. Devotion to practice," she says, crisply pronouncing every syllable.

I sigh. "Then let's do it again."

• • •

It's nearly three a.m. when I sneak into the house. The stairs creak as I walk up them, and I try to be quiet. My hands are shaky from doing magic all day, and the last thing I need is Gran on my case asking questions about where I was all night. I doubt she'd like my answer of hanging out with a new demon friend who's teaching me how to use demon magic.

"I'm glad you made it home," Pop's voice says. I look up and he's standing at the top of the steps, staring at me. So much for being quiet. "Deborah went to sleep only an hour ago, so you can expect to speak to her when you wake up."

Great. "Sorry, Pop."

He holds up a hand. "Are you hurt?"

"No," I say.

The relief fills his face. I realize that I should be upset that I worried him, but I'm not. "Where were you?" he asked.

I stare at him. He won't like the answer, either, so I lie. "With Carter. Sorry, we fell asleep at his house after I went to the hospital."

Pop's face snaps up to look at me. "You weren't at the hospital, Penelope. But it was your day to check in on her."

I forgot about that. I was supposed to go there, but then Poncho called me in. Normally, I'd be panicky, worried that Pop is upset, but again, I wasn't. "Pop, I can explain."

He shakes his head. "Save it for your grandmother." He rests his hand on my shoulder, and the magic billows near his touch. I step back from his contact, and his eyes seem heavy. "If you're in trouble, Penelope, you can tell us anything."

"There's nothing to tell," I snap quickly.

Pop raises an eyebrow at the sudden outburst. I never talk to him that way. "I was at Carter's, and that's all. I didn't go see Connie because I couldn't handle it. It was a hard day, Pop."

My skin still crawls even when his face softens, and he pats my back. "Get some sleep." And then he goes back into his room, leaving me feeling surprisingly okay with the lie.

Chapter Twenty-Eight

I had to go out with the Enforcers for the first markings. This whole idea is ridiculous, but I had to be there. I need to be able to tell my dad he's wrong. I can't do that unless I see it happening. So, I join Jordan Stark and Annah Jelowski today.

Jordan slaps me on the back when he sees me. The guy is as big as a linebacker and Annah is this girl about half his size, short and stalky. It makes no sense for Council to appoint this to two brand new Enforcers—they were in my training class—but they did.

"This is the first one," Annah says. She rings the doorbell, and Jordan smiles at her. She smiles back. I feel like I'm imposing.

With a shuffle, there's a face in the window and then the door unlocks and a woman appears. "Mr. Prescott, what a nice surprise."

"Mrs. Arthur," I say. The nice old woman from the hospital. Jordan and Annah look pleased that she knows me because this will make it easier for them. Harder for me. "Sorry to intrude."

She *tsks* and opens her door wider. "You and your friends, come on in. I'll make some tea."

"We actually don't have—"

Jordan pushes past me. "Tea sounds great, ma'am." He gives me a dirty look before he goes into her house. We have to mark this old woman. Last time I saw her she didn't even have power, but I told her the Triad cared about her. They don't. I lied. My dad has made me into a liar.

Lindley Arthur's house is full of books. Annah takes a few minutes to look at them all. There are books on shelves built into the walls around the house, on the floor, on the steps. Anywhere and everywhere. I pick up one that's a compilation of three of her novels.

Mrs. Arthur comes back and notices me looking. "I hate that cover," she says. "A pirate series without pirates on the cover. Dreadful. You can take it, dear."

"You have a lot of books," Jordan says.

She snorts. "My to-be-read pile seems to constantly be multiplying."

Jordan smiles, and we all sit, crammed next to each other on her floral couch while she keeps talking about books. Annah nods along, adding a comment. Finally, Mrs. Arthur looks at me. "Why are you here? Is this about the Observance? I have my parts in the Static play all memorized."

"It's not about that," Annah says.

Jordan sits straighter in his spot. I stare at the wall. "Mrs. Arthur, we're here on official business. Reports have indicated that you have manifested with this new magic."

Mrs. Arthur looks at me. "I didn't ask for it, it just happened two days ago, I woke up and there it was. Clear destroyed my whole bedroom wall."

"Yes," Annah says. "We're aware. The Triad has sent us to here to remedy the problem."

Mrs. Arthur jumps up, knocking her little coffee table out of place. "Remedy? Nothing's wrong with me. You go. The lot of you."

She moves across the room, eyes wide and on alert. Jordan takes a step toward her, but I hold him back. Last time I saw a spooked Static, it was Taylor Plum—right before she killed Maple. "Mrs. Arthur," I start. "We're not here to hurt you."

Her head shakes so fast that her hair falls out of its bun. She backs into one of the stacks of books and they fall to the floor. "Leave."

"If you sit down then this will be less painful," Jordan says.

That's the wrong thing to say. Her eyes give her away first, abnormally large and bright, then Mrs. Arthur goes ballistic on the room. The magic shoots from her fingers, knocking a chandelier from the ceiling and Annah has to jump to avoid getting hit. I move toward Mrs. Arthur, but she shoots more magic at me.

"I trusted you."

The words sting, because yes, she did. And I trusted the

Triad to do the right thing for once. We were both wrong.

"I'm sorry," I say.

Before I can act, Jordan zaps her with magic and holds her in place. He and Annah start chanting the same words and the whole time Mrs. Arthur fights against their hold. Around us, the whistle of the tea kettle starts in a low tone. The lights flicker between bright and dim, and her magic shoots out from her hands, bouncing off anything, hitting anything. It's chaos.

"Don't do this to me," she yells, and then the words drift off into screaming. Then her body starts to convulse against the bookshelves.

That's not right. "Let her go," I yell to Jordan over the high pitched, impatient whistle of the tea kettle.

He and Annah stop chanting, and Mrs. Arthur falls to the ground. Her body still moves on the ground and I rush over to her. Her face is stiff, eyes bolting back and forth, but she's unresponsive to me when I say her name or touch her.

"What's wrong with her?" Annah asks, her voice frantic.

"Call someone," I yell.

But when her body stops moving, her face is white, and she's ice cold.

Lindley Arthur is dead.

Chapter Twenty-Nine

On Monday, Lindley Arthur's funeral is packed with witches, Nons, fans, and media coverage. I'd never met the woman before the hospital a few weeks ago, but her books are treasured by the world. I even read one or two of the ones about the little rabbit that wanted to be a duck. But apparently Gran knew her. So, she and Pop and I are packed in a pew along with what feels like every other witch in the tri-state area. There's a tension in the air because the room is aware she died three days ago when some Enforcers marked her.

My tension comes completely from being here with all these witches. The void has been bending more to my desires, but it's still unpredictable. If I lost control in in here…

Out of habit now I rub my fingers around my wrist. The guilt washes through me. I survived and she didn't. More won't. They wouldn't even need to be marked if not for me.

"Take off that ridiculous sweater," Gran says to me, tugging at my black cardigan.

Panic starts to bubble in my stomach, because even though the blackness is glamoured, it could disappear at any moment. I haven't seen Lia today. With the way I've been using the void, the colors have spread. The possibility that someone could see if wears off is too much. *No. No strong emotions. Turn them off. Don't feel anything.*

"Gran, stop it," I say. I try to twist in the seat to show her how impossible it would be to move my arms.

"You've got to be burning up."

She's still fiddling with my sweater. Pulling at the sleeve and the center where it buttons, trying to maneuver it off. I force down the magic or the fear or whatever it is that comes creeping up.

"Gran, let go of me." But she doesn't. With her pulling at my sweater, the people crowded in around me, and the anxiety and magic inside me, I'm going to lose it. "God, just stop it already." I hiss through my teeth and jerk away from her.

Gran's face shifts into a look of surprise, and she drops her hand from me immediately. "What's wrong with you?"

I groan in response, pulling my finally freed sweater closer to myself and shifting away from her. My hands are in my lap, fingernails pressing into my palm against the magic building. I can't lose control in this room. I take long breaths until the rush of my magic feels normal again.

"I don't understand why she's wearing that thing in

August." Gran whispers back to Pop after a beat. And by whisper I mean says it loud enough that I can hear.

"Leave her alone," Pop says.

"I'm cold," I say, fingers still pressed in my fist.

"She's cold, Deb. Let her be," Pop says in that completely pleasant yet completely forceful way. Gran crosses her arms as Pop rests a hand on her knee. He whispers in her ear and it makes her smile and pat his hand.

A feeling settles in my stomach again. Uncertainty. Doubt. Anxiety. This is the right thing to fix the mess I've made, but it's going to cost me my family. Everyone I am trying to protect will turn their back on me. When all of this happens, when I become a demon, they'll never understand it. Maybe Gran will think it's because of the secret with Emmaline Spencer. The one Gran kept the truth about our demonic heritage. I've given them no clues, left them no reasons. I look sidelong at Gran. This will kill her, thinking that she failed me somehow by letting this happen. But Connie will be alive, so maybe that will be enough, and when I'm done, I'll come back to them. Then I can explain it all and ask for their forgiveness. Maybe they'll love me enough to give it to me.

I look up feeling someone stare at me. It's Carter from the front of the room, next to his dad, and he smiles back in my direction. I force my best smile out, and even from across the room I can tell that he doesn't buy it as real.

I'm also going to lose him. He'll never understand, never forgive me. The smart thing to do is to end it now, but I can't do that. I need him. He's the only thing that makes me still feel like myself.

The priest stands in front of the crowd, and I watch the

back of Victor's shoulders for any extra tension. This funeral is for Lindley Arthur, a famed author, and not the funeral of a Static. Victor Prescott's probably glad of it. This way no one can speak out against the Triad in a public way. No one would dare, not with the media. It would expose us.

"It is with a heavy heart we all gather to say good-bye to a woman who changed the face of children's literature. But beyond that, a woman who loved fiercely and died too early."

Because of me, I think.

• • •

I see Carter again afterward in the reception hall, standing next to his father. Even though it's a funeral, they both seem to be "on" today. Aside from the dark circles under Victor's eyes, you wouldn't be able to tell that anything else was happening. Carter waves at me when some bald guy walks away. I take a step toward them but when Victor sees me, he pulls Carter in the opposite direction. Oo-kay then.

I should go after them to show him that I don't go away that easy.

Three steps toward where they stand, and Pop grabs my arm. "We have to go," he whispers.

"Already?" I ask.

His blue eyes are trimmed in red. I can't tell if it's from crying or from trying not to. "It's your sister."

That's all I need to hear. We maneuver through the others and Gran's already at the door waiting for us. We're in the car about to back out when Carter appears at my window. Pop rolls it down for him, and Carter stares among the three of us.

"What's wrong?

I stare at him, trying to speak, but I don't have an answer yet. None of them want to come out of my mouth.

Luckily I don't have to say anything. Pop does.

"It's Connie. We have to go."

I try to keep my emotions down. I can't lose control of the magic.

"You want me to come with you?" He's asking me this, but I can't...*I don't know.* And then the magic I'm forcing down mingles with my own fear about my sister. I look at Carter again, waiting for an answer, and I'm annoyed at him for delaying us. For trying to make me choose between him and her. Whether it's the magic or really me, I feel a sudden surge of anger toward him. The magic wants me to release it, to allow it seek vengeance for whatever I'm feeling. Part of me knows all of this doesn't make sense, but the other part, the part the magic connects with, doesn't care one iota.

"We have to go," I shout.

Pop must take that a sign because he backs the rest of the way out of the spot. Carter watches after us and gets his keys from his pocket, because I see him through the back window of the car. He's going to come.

As he disappears, so does my anger. The magic lulls itself back into that place where it hides until it's trying to destroy my life.

I really could use him with me in case she's...*Oh God I can't even think that. Don't think that.*

But when I glance back out, Victor is standing next to him. They look like they're fighting, but then I'm too far gone to see anything else.

• • •

The doctor is waiting for us in Connie's room when we get there. The beeping is the first thing I notice. It's always first. If it's beeping then she's breathing, then her heart is working and she's alive. I exhale a little when I hear that annoyingly beautiful sound. Then I realize that she's really pale today and there's a new tube running down her throat.

"What's happening?" Pop asks.

"Mr. and Mrs. Warren, it's good you're here. Constance had a seizure today. We were able to stabilize her, but once we did her lung collapsed. That new tube is assisting her in breathing until we're able to fix her lung."

"So, fix it."

"We can't until we're sure she's able to maintain stability."

"She was doing better," Gran says. "You said she was doing better."

"She had been, but now she's rejecting the previous treatment. Honestly, if she keeps progressing at this rate there won't be much more we can do aside from make her comfortable."

"Make her comfortable?" Pop repeats.

"You mean give up on her," I snap. They're suggesting we let her go. The doctor looks away from me, and toward my grandparents.

"Based on the information Penelope gave us before, we believe demon's magic did this. A demon's magic, when used in this direct way, is poisonous to a witch. Pure void is too strong for our hearts. If this is what happened, then it's a miracle she's even survived this long. We're really doing all we can."

"Do more," Gran says. "Whatever it takes. Do whatever it takes."

"There are limits to both magic and medicine, Mrs. Warren."

"She's our granddaughter, so with all due respect, screw the limits. She's sixteen years old. Figure it out," Gran says.

The room is quiet for a good minute before the doctor excuses himself. I stare at my sister. She can't die. I'm doing all of this for her. I'll practice more. I'll talk to Lia and we'll move the timeline up. I will save her. I have to. It's on me.

Wordlessly, I turn to leave. I'm going to find Lia and make it known that I am tired of waiting. We can do the ritual early. Surely, the extra power of the Observance isn't so much that—

"Where are you going?" Gran asks.

I turn around at the door. "I just—I need to think."

Gran doesn't like that answer. She strides toward me in large steps until we're maybe a foot apart. The magic is already on the defensive, waking up again. "Think? Your sister is dying and you need to think?"

Pop reaches out for her. "Deborah, hold it now."

"No, you hold on. Both of you. She's never around anymore. The least you can do is be here, right now. My family has been tormented by demons my whole life. My daughter died from a demon attack. You were nearly killed by one, and now Connie here is fighting for life. I understand more than anyone in this room, and you can't leave right now to *think*."

I want to touch her, but I don't trust the void. "She's going to be fine, Gran."

Gran huffs, neck turning red like it does when she's really angry. "Like you are? I'm glad you're alive — Lord knows my heart couldn't handle both of you still being in these beds."

Gran reaches out for me, and I take a step back. She doesn't pause when I do. The pain is there anyway. "You're the only other person who was there with her. If you suspect something else that you're not saying, if something happened, then tell us now."

I do because I did it. However, I can't say that. If I tell her what's going on, what I'm going to become, she'll lose it. "I don't," I say instead and feel all my old guilt and my new lies with an insane amount of pressure on my heart.

Gran tosses her hands up. "Who are you these days? Sneaking around, out all hours of the day and night. We know you're not an Enforcer, Penelope."

My heart races and the magic stirs. My mind is trying to catch up. I was careful. Someone betrayed me. "What?" I shout.

"Where are you going?" Gran practically spits the words at me.

Anger fights toward the surface like an oasis in the desert. Brief, unexpected, quenching. "How do you know that?"

Gran points toward Pop. "Frank found out last week. What's happening and why would you even try to keep this from us?

I want to cry. I want to scream. I want to strangle someone. It's a barbell pressed down on my chest, a drumming in my head, a nagging at my fingers to let go, a crack of light in a dark room. I want to let the anger out so it can consume them. "Gran you don't understand."

She moves toward me again, and I step away. Feeling like I could explode. "What don't I understand?"

I shake my head. I can't say anything to her about this. I can't tell her. "There's more going on than that. Trust me."

"That's hard to do, considering."

Pop moves closer to Gran, resting a hand on her shoulder. The two of them are near to me, eyes narrowed in like lasers. My sister's machines pulse and beep around me, filling the tiny room with unnatural sounds. Everything feels constricted. I feel too big for this space and too lost in it at the same time.

"I have to go," I say.

"Your sister needs you. She's always been there for you when you needed her. Whatever you have going on can wait," Pop says.

It's the first time he's spoken in a few minutes, and he does that thing with his voice. He knows how to get me. But when I look back at him and I see her in that bed, he's right. Connie would do anything for me, and I'd do anything for her. And that's why I leave.

• • •

I find Lia in a bar she mentioned before with some other demons. They snarl when I approach, but she holds up a hand and they back off.

"This is ballsy—especially for you." She almost looks impressed.

Demons are staring at me, but I ignore all of them. "My sister is getting worse."

She looks at my covered arms and pulls up my long

sleeves. The blackness trails up my arm. "It's spread."

She can't see beyond that, but it goes all the way to my neck and down my waist straight to my knees. "Yes, but it's not happening fast enough. The Observance is in five days, Lia. Five days."

Lia pauses and masks the blackness with her magic. When she opens her eyes, she says, "You better work extra hard then, Penelope. Look, I've told you what you have to do."

"I can't flip off my emotions. I'm not you," I snap.

"Not yet," she says. "But soon. We can't do the ritual until the Observance anyway, so you have five days."

Five days. That's so not what I want to hear.

Lia puts her hand on my shoulder. "Keep working at it. Keep using the magic. I promise you'll be able to save her."

I turn around and leave.

I'm so sick of promises.

Chapter Thirty

CARTER

I park my car outside of the address sent to my phone. I must be crazy for coming here. I don't know who sent the message, but with so much going on, I couldn't overlook it. I open the door and tighten my jacket around my neck against the bitter D.C. wind.

It's 65F outside on a Tuesday, and it leaves a bad taste in my mouth. A change has come like Vassago said it would. I doubt the weather was all that Vassago was referencing, but it could be some kind of omen. It's never this cool in August.

Outside the abandoned building in the middle of H Street, a door's propped open with a rock. I inch my way into the space. Light streams in through the broken windows, and a noise like the clinking of chains fills my ears. Muffled voices echo through the hallway. I grip a knife in my belt, ready for whatever could jump out at me. Demon, Static, or Non, I'm not taking any chances.

I follow the hallway around a left turn, and then a beam of bright white light fills the darkness and blinds me. I cover my eyes, and lean against the wall. The light is hot as it touches my skin, almost burning into me like the sun. I can't place what this is, and as the spot against my coat starts to get uncomfortable, all the heat sensations disappear.

That was not normal.

I pull the knife into my hand, and turn the corner. There's another clinking, louder this time, and a voice yells, "You can do better." And then I creep into the room. I see blond hair across the room next to pink skin. I've got to be imagining this.

"Penelope?" My mind is racing, because standing there next to a chain fence is my girlfriend. My eyes dart around the room and settle on the mauve demon. *Mauve.* Vassago's been warning me about her since day one. "What are you doing here?"

The mauve demon looks from me to Pen, and speaks under its breath what sounds like "awkward." Yeah. Why is Pen here with that demon? What are they doing? What was that light? I start to slide the knife back into my belt, but change my mind. I may need it. I step toward the demon, knife ready. Considering everything, seeing Penelope here is not what I need right now. I told her not to make deals.

"Someone better tell me what's happening right now."

No one speaks at first, and then I move toward it. I have no problem ending this creature here and now. Even if it's supposedly on our side. The demon puts its hands up. "Geesh.

You are impatient. Point that knife somewhere else."

I lower the knife half an inch to show I'm amiable. Really I could slide this in the demon's throat and feel no remorse at all.

"I asked her to come," Pen says. I look over the demon's shoulder at her.

I glance at Pen and try to read her face. She seems nervous. I swear if she went behind my back on that deal…

"You asked her to come? And do what?"

Each second she doesn't answer is a blunt punch to the gut. There's more going on here. I can feel it.

Pen moves toward me. "We were talking, that's all. I wanted to see if she had an update about the Statics that were dying, and if it relates to my sister."

I slide the knife back into my belt. Not because I trust the demon, but because Pen's near me. And I feel irrational. Like I could smash in its smug face. "You think it's connected?"

Pen shrugs. "I think it's worth looking into."

I look toward the demon, who nods. "So, is it related?"

The mauve demon answers. "Unclear, which is what I told her. I'm going to look into it."

"So, basically you're no help at all," I snap.

The mauve demon crosses its arms. "You're spunky. I see why you like him. You can both annoy the world together."

I smirk. "That's a compliment."

"Don't fight with her," Pen says. Her voice is nearly pleading. Since when does she care if I fight with a demon? It's what I do with demons. I pull my gaze toward Pen, and I can't quite pinpoint what's off. Ever since she was marked she's been changing. Becoming more like a stranger. "Why are you calling her here? She's already proven that she doesn't know as much as she thinks."

The mauve demon growls. "That's harsh. I've given you more information than your Triad has."

I ignore the comment and don't look away from Pen. "What was that light?"

"What light?"

Pen's face is blank when she says that, but there's no way she didn't see it. I look from her to the demon again. "That bright light. What was it?"

The demon smiles. "That was the void."

"The void?" I glance at Penelope. If she showed this demon that she can access the void, then we're in more trouble than secret meetings. She can't give a demon that information. I lower my voice. "Did you…?"

Pen shakes her head and I exhale. At least that's one thing I can cross off the list. "She was showing off with her magic. That's all. She's leaving now." Pen glares at the demon.

With a nod, Mauve says, "Until next time, lovebirds," and then she flickers out.

She's barely gone when I say, "I don't like that demon."

I look at Pen, and she takes my hand in hers and pulls me toward the door. "Have you eaten? I could eat."

I stop walking. She's deflecting. I'm a Prescott and we do that better than anyone. "Don't," I say. "What are you doing right now? Here? With that?"

"I told you. I had questions and she's good at getting the answers. How did you even get here?"

I shake my head. "Someone texted me an address."

"Weird," is all she says.

She doesn't make eye contact with me for three seconds. She's hiding a secret, a big one, but what is it? I want her to tell me so I can be here for her. Whatever it is. I'll understand. "Demons don't have the answers to this, Pen."

"Or maybe they do and they aren't sharing," she says.

I shake my head. I can't stand this. She opens her mouth to speak, and then closes it. I stare at Pen, hoping, praying that whatever she's dealing with she'll tell me.

"I'm glad you showed up, though. I missed you. I haven't had time with you since before Lindley's funeral."

So much for that. She's changing the subject on purpose. "It's been crazy with the Observance in five days, and Dad has kept me busy," I say.

"I have you now," she steps toward me. Pen wraps her hands around my neck, fingers trailing at the ends of my hair. I start to ask her what else is happening, but then she presses her lips against mine, and my brain is all Penelope. Her skin under my fingers, her lips pressed against mine. Even with everything else going on, Pen is right here. Still solid. She's what I'm fighting for.

· · ·

An hour later, we're sitting at Guapo's. Pen stares at me across the table, looking bored and angry at the same time. "They're still insistent on the marking? It's obviously causing more harm."

"Unless we figure out another alternative." The thought of it makes me sick. The Statics didn't ask for this magic, they didn't seek it out, and yet they're dying because of it. Because of me and Pen.

Pen taps her finger on the table. There's a small mark I notice, a black one, and I reach out for her hand. She moves it quickly under the table. What was that?

"We can do the Restitution."

I shake my head. "No."

"Lia says I can do it. She thinks that because of my status I can access the void."

"Lia?"

Her eyes focus on mine, sharp and all business. "The mauve demon."

I scoff. "You're on a first name basis with it?"

"Her," Pen says sharply. "And yes. I couldn't keep calling her 'demon.' It's insulting."

I shake my head, still stuck on the fact that Pen calls the demon by its name. "That's what it is: a demon. We don't owe it anything."

She scoffs at me. "She's proven herself truthful over and over again." Her voice is almost sarcastic.

I lean in toward Pen. "That's what makes me nervous."

"I trust her, Carter."

What is Penelope even looking for? None of this makes sense. "That's great, but your trust in her doesn't give me any ideas how to save the Statics."

She crosses her arms. "I've given you an idea, but you don't want to hear it."

"You're right;. I don't." I don't even want to have this conversation. All of this is ludicrous and she would see that if she was thinking straight.

Penelope leans in. "Your dad would be for it. This could solve his problems, even if it cost me."

"I'm not my dad," I snap, and I hate the comparison. Anything he would do, would think is a good idea, isn't something I want to support. Especially at the cost of her.

She knows that.

The food comes and she picks up her fork. I see her fingers again, and realize she didn't answer my question. This time, though, there's nothing really to see. It's only her hand. No blackness.

. . .

"I'm sorry we fought," Pen says outside her house. "I don't want to fight."

"Me, either," I say. I should kiss her. I want to kiss her. I always want to kiss. Hell, even mad I want to take her and kiss her until I forget, but it feels off. I'm not forgetting any of this. I'm going to file it away and figure it out.

Instead I kiss the side of her mouth, where her smile forms. "Together," I say.

She smiles back and wraps her arm around my neck. "You and me."

We do kiss, but it's a slow kiss. A familiar one to remind each other that we're still here. It's a good kiss, don't get me wrong, it's always good. This one though, this one feels fractured. Like we're both doing it because we feel like we need to.

"Tomorrow?" she asks.

I nod as she goes inside. Before the door closes, I realize that I never want to kiss Penelope like that again. Like it's something I need to do as solidarity. I want to kiss her because I can't *not* kiss her.

. . .

After I take Penelope home, I go to see Poncho at the library and tell him all the things I've seen. The way Penelope was hanging out with a demon, the light of the void, the blackness that wasn't really there. He shrugs, not able to offer any assistance. I pull out the list of words from Vassago.

CHECK. REMAIN. DAGGER. MAUVE.
OBSERVANCE. QUEEN.

"These are a warning. I got it the night before Penelope was marked. That mauve demon has been around ever since then. It can't be a coincidence."

Poncho's eyes narrowed in on the page. "You've searched for their connections?"

I nod. "I found an article about a gift, Taliel, and Lucifer, but I think it was one of those mythological beliefs, a story, not real."

"Aren't all things in mythology based on reality?"

"So, it's real? This gift?" Seak jumps on the desk and knocks over some pencils. Poncho bends down to pick them up, muttering at the cat. I wait, impatience building until he's done and standing back up. "Poncho, is it real?"

"Some have faith in it, but it has not come yet."

I take a breath. "Can you show me everything you have in the library on it?"

Poncho's eyes light up and he nods. "You can't possibly read it all in one night."

"Good thing I still have a few days before the Observance" I say.

"Indeed," he says with approval.

Chapter Thirty-One

PENELOPE

I can't feel my toes anymore in my running shoes.

The temperature dropped overnight, and it hasn't gone up. I should stop running, but if I stop then I realize that I have three days. It doesn't feel like enough time to finish connecting to the void, or fix any of the mess I've made. It's all I've been doing since Maple died, trying to clean up messes, but I'm only making them worse. So, running it is.

I spent the entire day yesterday, until Carter interrupted, with Lia. And when he took me home, I went back out with her. Only my face and feet remain unchanged by the void. The glamour I make for the blackness isn't as strong as Lia's yet, so I still need her to do it.

I feel lonely. Everyone is preoccupied with the

Observance. I'm not home when Pop and Gran are there, and since Gran and I aren't really speaking now it's probably for the best. They're always with Connie. I want to go see her, to be with her, but if I'm with her then I'm not practicing, and I'm emotional, which won't save her. I haven't talked to Carter since he dropped me off yesterday, not even a text.

On instinct or auto-pilot, I end up at the Nucleus House. I can't see anything beyond what the Nons see, the Capital of the United States. A white building with gold top. There's no alternate entrance, no magic hiding beneath the surface. At least not for me. Even the Static door, which is usually ten spaces to the left of the main entrance, is a wall. Being marked sucks.

Lia appears beside me. "I hate being this close to so many witches."

She can see them and I can't. I wonder what they're doing. Knowing Mrs. Bentham, I'm sure the whole party will be extraordinary. Even if it's inappropriate to celebrate when so many people are dying.

"Then leave." I'm not really in the mood.

"Someone woke up on the wrong side of the bed," she says back.

I roll my eyes. "Why are you here right now?"

"There's a snag in our procedure," she says. "I can't get one of the herbs—the Dragooni. Apparently, it's out of stock."

"Did you go to Target? They have everything."

I'm still not looking her. My eyes are out there, where I know the witches are. "You need to get us some for the Restitution."

I look toward Lia. Of course she does. I do everything.

"Where do I get it? You're the demon."

A smile creeps up on Lia's face, and I was not trying to be amusing. The fact that she thinks I am annoys me even more. I turn away from her, but she walks alongside me.

"I can't 'get it' like buying a dress, and you can't, either—but you know someone who knows someone who can."

"Who?"

. . .

I release the button on the relay and balance my footing. The lights are off in the library, which is creepy and weird, since the lights have never been off while I'm here. I press my hand against the wall and use it as a guide to Poncho's office. The door is closed, but light shines through the crack of it. He's in there. I knock three times before the door opens.

"Miss Grey, back again," he says, barely looking up from his desk.

"I missed your charm," I say, moving into his office.

"I'm certain."

I stop a few feet from his desk, petting the cats' heads. I shouldn't be surprised that Lia sent me to Poncho.

"You seem to be in thought."

"Yeah, it's been a weird couple of days." To say the least. When I look up, Poncho is watching me, eyebrows taut with concern. I think that's what it is, anyway. It's not entirely easy to tell what someone is thinking by their eyebrows. "What?"

"You are stressed."

"A little busy," I say.

"Secrets have a way of eating at us," he says. Poncho's eyes grow wide, examine me, and then soften. "Why are you here today?"

"I have a question." He waves me on to ask, his attention fully focused on me, and I sit in a large chair. "I'm looking for an herb called Dragooni. Do you know where I can find that?"

He *hmms* and rubs his hands. "Dragooni is forbidden in the witch community. A rare herb with tremendous use, it's only found in the distant mountains of the Himalayans, and can only be plucked from its home by the power of one who serves selflessly."

Perfect. Let me go find a good fairy with selfless morals. "So, that's a no?"

"It is not a no."

I smile. "So, it's a yes?"

"You asked where you could find it. I've answered that," Poncho says, looking back at his desk.

Right. "Can you get some for me?"

Poncho raises his eyebrow. "What is your use for Dragooni?"

I debate lying to him, but then I realize that he's staring at the blackness on my hands—or where it is under the glamour—so he probably already has that answer, too. "I'm getting my magic back."

"That is used in the Restitution," he says.

"That's the last piece I need so I can do it."

He stares at my hand. There's nothing. "This is the path you choose?"

I shuffle my feet and lean against the desk. "Yes," I say.

Poncho seems like he wants to object, but he doesn't. "I can assist you. It will take a couple of days."

"Thank you, Poncho." A couple of days. That will be

right in time for the Observance.

"May I give you some advice?"

"You will anyway," I say.

"Only if you want it."

"Sure, then. What's your advice?"

"You alone can undo what has been caused," he says.

I stare at him. "What does that mean?"

"You sought an answer, and you have found it. It is not in hiding. You alone can undo what is."

"I hate your riddles."

He shrugs. "This is not a riddle."

It is, but okay.

I turn to leave, but pause. "Can you answer one more thing?"

Poncho lowers a pen and nods in my direction. One of the cats rubs up next to his hand and he pets it. "If it is possible."

"You said guiding me was your destiny. Why?"

Seak the cat jumps off the desk toward me, but then stalks off into the stacks. Poncho moves away from the reference desk and sits in a chair closer to where I'm standing. "Our paths intersected long ago, before I knew your parents."

My parents. I push down the pain that bubbles up. What would they think of me now? Not that they could change any of this or make it better. The void is already part of me. I'm part of the void. More demon than witch. I have been for years, and maybe I would've been even without Azsis taking my essence.

I sit next to Poncho. "You've never told me what they were to you."

Poncho rests his hands on the top of the table. "I go back

a long time with your family. I have existed for centuries alongside them, back to Beatrice and Clara." Emmaline Spencer's daughters. My great-great-great-great-great-grandma. That's a long time of being alive, of existing.

"Are you a vampire?" I raise an eyebrow.

"Those are fictional," he says. I start to say I'm joking, but he keeps talking. "Demons do not always age the same as humans."

Demon. He's never admitted that out loud to me.

"What are days for us could be years for you. I was not, back then, connected to this witch world. I was but a boy when they were living, and barely a man when your grandmother was a child."

He knew child-Gran? What was that like? I bet she was pretty terrifying even then.

"For centuries I served all as a sage—I was sought after by demon and witch and human alike. Sages were highly respected then, honored even, and sages served all, not one. Later, I had to become two in order to serve both sides."

"That's why you became Vassago. Do you have a split personality like some Jekyll and Hyde freakozoid?" He shoots me dagger eyes, and I put up a hand in defense. "What happened that made you become two people?"

Poncho's eyes get that far-off look in them. Not like a prophecy, but like a memory. "I am not two, I am one. I am myself, the one before you, but times changed. The belief in the power of a sage for Nons decreased, witches avoided all things demonic, and only with the demons I found a welcoming home," he says. "Then, sixty years ago I saw a vision. Witches killing other witches and turning demonic. In my vision, it was chaos, and I, being a servant of all, knew

I should come forward—but if I spoke up, then I risked my life. So, I said nothing, did nothing. Until it happened."

He means when the family name went bad because of Emmaline Spencer's choices. Gran was a child when it all started. A bunch of witches woke up and claimed they were demonic. They killed other witches, and the Enforcers went on a hunt for halflings. The Triad wiped it out of history as much as they could, like they still wipe out halflings when they find them.

Poncho knew that was going to happen.

"I came to the Triad and offered my assistance. We prevented deaths, and I traded them for a favor to be paid later, and went home." He pauses and moves from the table. I watch as he walks around the room, seemingly nervous. "But home was not the same. I was no longer welcome there. One demon in particular, with a fascination for souvenirs from his victims, wished for my exile. He saw me as a betrayer, and refused to let me into the inner circles of our life. We battled, as demons do, and he won. He was much stronger than me, for I was not a fighter but a guide. I was banished and then given refuge here, in exchange for what I'd done."

He gestures around the library, arms out, when he finishes.

"Is he gone now, this demon? Is that why you can go outside?"

Poncho's eyes focus on mine. "He's not gone. Not yet. Poncho Alistair is only safe here."

"So, Vassago is how you go outside. And all those files in the computer about Vassago?"

Poncho disappears into the stacks for a moment and returns with Hyde. He walks back toward the table, but doesn't sit. "They were intentionally placed there once I was sent here. Sages have a purpose, and even though I am locked away here, I must serve. Vassago is how I fulfill that role, a service to all. I knew a time was coming when I would be needed again. I developed a new image so I could fill the role needed for any who sought guidance."

"So, which one is the real you—Vassago or Poncho?"

"Both are me. I am both. We can be each other, yet neither."

I roll my eyes. "That makes no sense."

"Not all things make sense in this world," he says.

I tap my fingers along the tabletop. He didn't tell me anything about my parents, but him being a sage makes everything clearer. It's the reason he talks in riddles—the reason he can only answer certain questions. Sages have a purpose.

"I first met your parents when they were in training, and there was special quality about them both," he says. My ears seem to perk up and I sit up straighter in the chair. I can almost see them in here, how they looked back then, talking with Poncho like I am now. "It was only a short period after they were Paired before they got married. We didn't really speak much until around that time. They would come in to research cases, and I provided them with sources, as I do with everyone who seeks my help. Your parents came to me once they discovered they were pregnant with you."

"With me?"

He nods. "I remember the day. They came in looking for information. Genevieve was highly distraught, Owen demanding. He was usually the quiet one. We worked on that one until after you were born. I held you once."

"Sweet," I say with a smile.

"You spit up on me."

Or not. Should I apologize for that or would it be weird?

"Why were they upset?" About me, is what I leave out. I don't know anything about that. Did they want me? Were the ready? Was I a burden more than a joy? My parents were amazing, so the thought of that makes me a little sick.

"I can't remember." Wait…that's not cool. "I should get that," he says.

"Get what—" And then the phone rings. Sneaky.

Emmaline Spencer had a secret. Her daughters had secrets. Gran had a secret. My parents had a secret. I have secrets. Maybe all the Warren women are woven and bonded with secrets.

When he hangs up I whisper, "Was it the demon bloodline thing?" He blinks. "The reason my parents were upset. Because I already know about that so…"

He considers this for a moment and then says, "I'm certain it must have been. I will inform you when the Dragooni arrives."

And that is when I know it wasn't.

Back outside, I call Ric. I haven't talked to him for a week now since he's been in Texas with the injury, and with this new information about my parents I need him to reassure me. He answers on the third ring.

"I miss you," I say.

"Come visit," he says. "I'm finally up and moving. We can have a dance party."

That sounds remarkable. "I can't leave right now. It's not a good time."

"I wish I could be there with you right now." I wish that too, but I don't say it. I don't say anything, for a long second, because my mind is racing. If he was here or I was there, maybe none of this would be happening. "Connie's going to pull through this, Penelope."

Connie. I wasn't even thinking about her for once and now I am. The way she used to follow us around when we were kids, and Ric was my only other friend so I'd get mad at her for wanting to be around him. Really, she wanted to be around me. "You can't be certain of that."

"You're right, I can't."

Silence fills the line. That's not what I want him to say. I want him to say she's going to be perfect. That all of this will be over soon or I'll wake up to find it's all been some horrible nightmare. A fake one instead of a real one.

"Ric, I think I did something stupid."

He's quiet and for a second I wonder if he heard me. My heart is racing with the possibility of him knowing, of telling someone. "What? I'm the king of stupid."

"I can't tell you."

"Okay…"

"I mean, I can't. But I want to."

"What is it?"

Silence again. He's waiting on the line and I'm not even sure what I'm going to say or where to start. The beginning, I guess.

"There's this demon." And as soon as I say it I regret it. I can't see his face, but I can imagine it. Twisted and hard. Just like Carter's. Like mine used to be.

"That mauve one?"

I open my mouth then pause. I've never mentioned any of this before. "You know about that?"

"Carter may have mentioned it."

Carter…wait. "You talk to Carter?"

"Only once. He called me yesterday and asked me if you'd mentioned anyone named Lia. That's the mauve demon's name, right?"

I can't believe Carter's been talking to Ric about me. About me. And trying to find out information about the demon. Nerves liquefy to red hot anger. That's not his place to talk to my best friend for information. Ric doesn't have information, but that's not the point. Carter doesn't trust me.

In my silence, Ric says, "Are you hanging out with a demon? What's going on there?"

"Nothing," I snap. I can't believe I almost told him about this. I won't now that I know he could turn around and tell Carter.

"Penelope, you can tell me if you're in trouble."

"I already said I couldn't," I yell into the phone.

Ric's voice gets higher, more frantic. "So, you are in trouble?"

"No," I snap. "God. Just forget it."

He cusses at me and that pisses me off even more. "What's going on? Carter and I love you. Your Gran said that you—"

"You've been talking to Gran too?"

He must hear the annoyance in my voice because his tone softens. "A couple times. We're all worried about you."

Everyone has been talking about me to each other behind my back. They're all plotting against me. "Don't be.

I'm fine. You know what? I'm amazing."

"You don't sound fine or amazing."

I hit him where I know it will cause the most pain. I want him to feel how I do right now. "You aren't even here, Ric. You don't know anything about me."

His words rush out on the line. "You're right. I'm sorry that I was injured on your patrol, and my partner died and I had to leave against my will. How selfish of me, Penelope. You've been my best friend forever, so sue me for being worried. At least you have people who worry about you. Where have you been the last month? You haven't called to ask how I'm doing, how I'm coping. You've been playing with demons."

"Screw you. You know nothing."

"Tell me."

"I shouldn't have called."

And then I hang up.

I don't need him. I don't need anyone checking up on me. I'll do what I planned to do and save my sister and then the Statics. I don't need anyone to tell me it's right or wrong. I have to undo this, or no one else will.

Chapter Thirty-Two

Two days until the Observance. Beyond my duties with my father, I've spent all my time reading books. My eyes are heavy as I turn the page.

A sage foretold of Taliel's chosen. It is said that the gift will be given during the Observance between midnight and dawn. During this time, a singular witch will be born. This sole witch will have enough power to eliminate the void or the essence forever. The control of this witch, the side to which the being pledges loyalty, will receive the prize, for the other side will cease to be. The eternal struggle between good and evil would be no more. This witch alone will be able to choose which side, good or evil, essence or void, will remain. The other will be destroyed.

Shit.

I straighten up in my chair. This is the jackpot. I've read pieces of pieces, but nothing like this.

This sole witch will not yet be made by the eighteenth year, and will be able to access both sides of the magic. This witch shall be willing and have used both sides of the magics before. When chosen, the witch will be at the center source for either side, void or essence, and from there use the opposite magic and ritual to destroy the other side, as only one can exist at a time within a source without complication.

I look up and Poncho is standing across from me, eyes on me. "If this is true, then it happens in two days." Penelope. She's this. She can use both sides. She has before, anyway, all she'd have to do is choose.

How has the Triad kept this a secret? "I've never heard about any of this before."

Because the Triad, since our creation, only tells half-truths and keeps things buried. They cover up situations, lie instead of fix them. I'm the perfect example.

My mind flashes through all the warnings that my dad ever gave me about halflings. *Dangerous. Deadly. Abominations. Feared.* The way there'd be a kid in my classes who was there one day and gone the next. When I was younger, Dad would tell me they moved. After I learned what I was, he told me that they were killed. All those halflings. That they were a threat, and he never told me why. I never asked, either. I couldn't.

"This is why they get rid of halflings, isn't it?" I ask.

Poncho nods. "Every Triad, past and present, has been aware of this legend. Current leaders may not remember the full story, but it's why Enforcer testing is mandatory. The reason it was created to begin with."

"They were looking for the most powerful witch," I say.

It makes sense now. They've been adamant for decades about everyone being tested for the role of Enforcer. It's the perfect way to discover halflings. They're controlled by the fear of this sole witch. If someone existed with that much power, then it could destroy the whole world we've built. The Triad looks for halflings, gets rid of them so they can't threaten life, and continues to exist. Fear keeps us all alive, and it keeps the Triad blind in their prejudice.

Poncho nods. "The leaders of the past were adamant about responding to this threat, and they pulled out the strongest witches as Enforcers, a way to search for warning signs that one may be more than a normal witch."

I cross my arms. "Surely the current Triad is aware of this threat, too."

Poncho crinkles his eyes and his brow furrows. "When you wait centuries for a thing that never happens, it often gets forgotten. If such a witch were to exist, the power would shift. A choice for demons or for witches that would rid the threat of the other forever. There would no longer be a war."

And this is why they're acting weird. They don't want to react poorly to the Statics, because what if one of them ends up being this gift? So, they mark them, keep them from becoming powerful. And Penelope—it's the same thing. If she can't access the void, then she can't be the threat to end the witches.

"It's Penelope," I say. I look at Poncho. All the warnings from Vassago make sense now.

CHECK. REMAIN. DAGGER. MAUVE.
OBSERVANCE. QUEEN.

The mauve demon is using her. She's the gift, the queen Lucifer was looking for—she's the sole witch who can destroy the other side.

Magic is a balance.

If the void is destroyed and there are no demons, there'd be no need for witches. We were only created because of the demons. But they were here first. If we didn't have magic, if they succeed in destroying the essence, then they'd be the most powerful beings again. The earth would be their playground. That can't happen.

This is why I'm in a checkmate: I have to save her or lose her.

I grab my bag. I have to go find Penelope. I have to tell her. I pause and look at Poncho. "This choice will destroy all witches if she chooses the void?" Poncho nods. "And all demons, if she goes the other way?"

Poncho nods. "Anyone with a connection to the void."

The void…"Even halflings?"

"Even so." He says.

That includes Pen. And me.

• • •

Pen is using the void, and she's changing because of it. Even though her essence is bound by the mark, the void isn't affected. The demon said as much. If Pen really is the one who should be able to access both sides, the gift from Taliel to Lucifer, then I need to figure out how to stop her and the threat she poses to witches and demons everywhere. She can't know she's a threat to everything, can she? Would Pen still do this if she knew it would wipe out a whole race? She wouldn't. I have to believe she wouldn't.

I walk past some tourists pointing at the Washington Monument. I can't find Pen. She'd never be here, but she's not anywhere else, either. Not at St. Elmo's. Or home. Her car isn't parked at any of the trails, so she's not on a run. She's not at the mall. She's not getting ice cream or pizza, and she's not on the hill. She wouldn't be here, either, but demons are sometimes. If she's not answering any of my calls then my only hope is to find the mauve demon.

The light on my demon tracker blinks a steady blue pulse. Vassago is nearby. He's not the one I thought I'd find, but maybe that's better.

There are people everywhere. Tourists and locals who came to spend the summer in the city. A mist of rain starts to fall, but no one seems deterred by it. The weather has been unpredictable all month. I weave through the crowds at the Washington Monument toward the Smithsonian, but the blinking stops. Wrong way.

I follow the tracker in the other direction, past the monuments, until I'm standing near a perfect rectangle of water. The Reflecting Pool. At one end is the Washington Monument and the Lincoln Memorial is at the other end. I stuff the tracker in my pocket and walk toward the steps of the Memorial.

Why is Vassago hanging out here?

The steps of the Memorial are full of people taking pictures. It's always busy over here, everyone wanting to see this place. I came here a lot as a kid with my dad. It was before I knew I was supposed to hate him, before he took me sailing when I was ten and told me I was a halfling, and that it was a secret I had to protect for always.

I push past the people and in toward the statue of Lincoln. The room is always quieter than I imagine it will be, everyone taking in what this spot represents. I glance around them all and seek out Vassago. I don't see him, so like everyone else, I read the words carved into the wall of the Gettysburg Address.

There's a shuffle behind me and I look over my shoulder. I recognize his long, dirty beard first, and then he nods toward the exit. I follow him out and around the side of the Memorial to see a large plaid blanket and a Scrabble.

"You've got to be kidding me," I mutter. I'm sick of this. For weeks it feels like everything in my life is a puzzle.

Vassago points to the blanket and then sits down on one side. "I thought it would keep us warmer," he says, patting the blanket.

"You said a storm was coming," I say. "What's going on?"

He looks pointedly at me. "Sit."

I'm obviously not getting answers any other way, so I take a seat on the blanket. Vassago starts unpacking the board and grabs the little bag of letters.

"You knew Penelope would be involved in whatever is happening, didn't you?"

He shakes his head. "I did."

I blink. He really answered my question. "You answered. You never do that directly."

"You never ask questions I can answer properly."

"I ask you questions all the time."

Vassago smirks. "I am only to give guidance when the proper questions are asked. To get the answer, you must ask the right questions."

"Why? What makes that the rule?"

"It is what I am. A servant of all, an unbiased party who knows what others do not until they seek the answer."

"You're a sage."

Sages were popular centuries ago. Witches often sought them out to find direction for the future or get information. Even in history, they could only answer directly if the right question was asked. They aren't allowed to freely share knowledge. The sphinx was their creation, the riddler of Greek mythology. Now it all makes sense. I clear my throat. "The mauve demon is involved with her," I frown, poking at the memory. "She's changing. Angrier, distrusting, desperate, and it's not because she was marked, but because of the void."

Vassago simply looks at me. "You go first," he says, passing the bag of letters.

I shake my head. "You this time."

With a nod, Vassago draws some of the letters. He stares at the board for a moment and then places the words down. INDEED.

I stare at the word. That was convenient.

"One hundred and four points," Vassago says.

The void is changing Penelope. The magic is making her someone so unlike herself. Why? And even more importantly, how do I stop it? I look at my letters and play VOID off his D. "How do I stop this?"

Vassago pulls some new letters out of the bag. I don't

take my eyes off him. "I've always enjoyed the Observance. It's an important time for witches and demons and Nons."

UNABLE, he plays off the E in his first word.

"I can't stop it," I say. I thought I'd at least get a clue about how to prevent all of this. "The demons want Pen to destroy witches. And I could somehow convince her to destroy the void, then demons die, but witches can't exist without demons. Magic is a balance. What do I do?"

"The answer is already one you have been given."

I close my eyes and exhale. I can't do this. I can't sit here and try to figure out his answers to riddles to solve a puzzle. I thought I liked puzzles, but I don't.

"Your turn, Mr. Prescott." I open my eyes and stare at him. That voice was Poncho's, not Vassago's. I shake my head. There's no way that's possible. My mind is playing tricks on me.

"Poncho?" I whisper, even though this is crazy.

"Vassago at the moment," he says.

What the hell? "You're both people?" Whoever-this-is gives me a quick nod. I tighten one of my hands into a fist. "How?"

"Your turn."

"You have to tell me something."

But he doesn't say anything. He doesn't blink. I'm supposed to accept that Poncho and Vassago are the same person?

"There is not an explanation for every mystery in the universe. Sometimes there is, but having it will prevent you from believing on your own."

"That's all you're going to say?" Again, nothing. It's like staring at a wall. This is frustrating. I throw the word

DEMON on the board off the N.

"When she does the Restitution, what will happen to her?"

Vassago puts the word BALANCE on the board. "A balance of magic. Magic is a scale. If she is going to harness the void, then she must give up good. To give is to take, and to take is to give. A life for a life, or a magic for a magic."

"The mauve demon is involved," I say. I put DEAL on the board. Poncho nods. Penelope made a deal. She made a deal with a demon. "If I can't stop it, then how do I save Penelope?"

Vassago considers this for a moment. "I told you that answer last time."

BALLOON

The story from my childhood. Red balloon, blue balloon. I changed the color, but he said I couldn't change this, couldn't stop it. That doesn't make sense. I put FATE on the board.

"Why is this happening to Penelope? Of all the halflings in the world, why her?"

MARK

"Because she's marked?"

"There is more than one way to have a mark. Some are literal, some visual, while others exist internally. Others are fated."

I play YAMS because I have nothing else. Only his words matter anyway.

"What marked her? What made them want her?"

Vassago cracks his neck. "There are forces at play that are larger than you and Miss Grey. It all goes back to the beginning, to Taliel and Lucifer's desire to have more."

PROPHECY

I play TURN. But I let his words sink in. The desire for more. The gift and the sole witch. "She's only doing to this for her sister and the Statics. Is there another way to save them?"

RESET

I can reset it. "What do I need to do it?"

"Only two more days until the Observance. What is your favorite part? I enjoy the feast and the festival of lights."

I play THREE.

"What do I need to reset everything?"

"It's a momentous day for witches and demons."

He plays DAGGER. Again. His words matter, and this one has been used in both of our games. The dagger is the ultimate weapon against both sides. I need to get it.

"Where is Penelope right now?" I ask.

Vassago is staring again, unable or unwilling to answer. "For the win," he says.

I draw out the remaining letters and lay out THANKS on the board, then stand to leave as Vassago gives me a nod. I have to find Pen and get the dagger if I have any chance of saving her from all of this.

Chapter Thirty-Three

PENELOPE

It's right after sunrise when the relay disk buzzes again. My heart leaps because this means that Poncho got the herb, in time, too, since the Observance is tomorrow. I push the button and land on solid ground in the library, Poncho is only a few feet away from me, but it feels less like home than it used to.

"Miss Grey, you made it," he says.

I nod. I don't have time or energy for pleasantries. "Did you get the Dragooni?"

Poncho bows his head and holds out the plant to me. It's long and flowing, like a willow branch, but covered in bright tangerine flowers. As I take it from his hand, he pauses. "Are you certain this is your path?"

"My sister is dying. Statics are dying."

"Answer one thing, Miss Grey. Is this really for them, or is it for yourself? The void is not your magic. It is not what you have been told. Once you do this, there is no going back."

Part of me thinks he's right. The other part, the part with a sister on the line and the void magic that's already flowing through me, that part hates him. "There's already no going back."

He shakes his head. "It is only too late to turn around if you are lost."

"I'm sure," I say. Sage or not, that doesn't mean anything to me. Seak, the cat who never liked me, rubs against my leg. Finally, some attention.

"I see," he says, staring at the cat. Then Poncho turns around and leaves me.

. . .

When I connect with the void this time, it feels like my skin, bones, and muscle all separate from one another. It's becoming so easy to let go, to not feel anything except the magic. There's nothing to tie me together or hold me down and I'm weightless. But I'm whole. Like that part of me that I've been missing has finally appeared and woven the pieces of myself. I'm empty and I'm completely full.

"Great job, Penelope," Lia says as the void fades away from me, leaving me feeling normal again. She moves toward me across the open space of the woods, her eyes wide.

Letting go of the void is a painful withdrawal. Or what withdrawal seems like it could be. My skin crawls, burns and longs for more of it. There's this loss that's immediate when I'm done using it, and the more I'm able to connect with it the more intense it gets. My whole body burns with the power, especially along my veins where the blackness flows. It's nearly spread to all of me now — almost there.

A source with this much power will definitely save my sister. This is right, even though others will think it's wrong.

"When I first heard the rumors about you being able to directly access the source, I didn't think it was true. No demon has been able to do that," Lia says. Her eyes pierce into mine for a moment.

"So you've said before," I say.

"You really are remarkable."

"I hear that a lot," I say. She shakes her head, but she had to have thought it was a little funny. Carter would've thought it was funny.

"If only you could block out everything else, you'd be unstoppable."

I don't remark on that because my thoughts haven't changed. One more day. One more.

"That's enough Dragooni, right?" I ask, pointing to the little stack of yellow flowers.

She nods. "It's perfect. I knew you could do it."

"Glad I didn't disappoint," I say, chugging some water. The void may be amazing, but it's also exhausting. "I'll work some more tonight. I'll be ready by tomorrow," I say. Only my face is unmarked, but as soon as I master the void it will all clear up. When that happens, I'll be ready, and it has to happen tomorrow.

"Before you go to the Observance, come find me. I have a present for you."

"I love presents. What is it?"

"A surprise."

I frown. "Surprises aren't so much my thing."

"This one will be worth it," Lia says. "See you tomorrow."

. . .

My nerves are shot already. I was so excited earlier. This is what I've been waiting for. This is what I've known was the best way to accomplish it. Maybe it was seeing Poncho, or my fight with Ric. I can't pinpoint it, but now I feel sick. Not magic sick. Like I'm making a bad decision sick. I'm voluntarily becoming a demon, and no sane person would do that. What am I thinking? What Poncho said about turning around, I can still stop this.

But if I stop this then my sister dies.

That's not an option.

I order a double scoop of coconut chocolate chip and scan the small ice cream parlor while I wait to pay. I freeze when I see some other Enforcers from my testing period in the far corner. I recognize James McEllory immediately with his bright red hair, and his partner, Jenna Lakes. Annah Jelowski whispers to the table, and then Jordan Stark waves at me, and points to an empty chair near them. I can't sit there. I have to get out of here.

Annah rushes over to me as I pay. "Penelope. Long time no see. How's your sister?"

I gulp back my fear. *No emotions*. "She's hanging in there."

She touches my arm softly, and then leads me toward her table. So much for not coming over. "We miss you and Carter at meetings. When the council told us what happened, we were all pretty shocked. It was nice of them to let you take some time off. After everything," Anna says. Nice, sure.

That's how they're spinning it.

"Very *nice*," I spit. I hope they feel the venom of it.

"Ready for the Observance tomorrow?" Jordan asks.

"I have the best dress," Jenna adds.

I judge her with my eyes. I hope she feels the judgment. A dress is the one thing that doesn't matter right now. "Oh yeah. I enjoy celebrating while everyone around me dies."

They all look at me like I'm insane for saying the unspeakable—that people are dying. It's not like it's a lie. Then all of their phones go off. They all look at once so I know it's the WNN. I debate pulling out my phone and playing along, but there's no point. They know I'm away, so maybe that's a good enough reason not to look.

But then Jenna's face goes white, and James looks up at me in his usual accusatory way. Anna whispers, "no way" under her breath—but not well if I can hear her. It's Jordan Stark's expression that gets me, though. The complete and utter disgust. I've seen that look before.

My phone vibrates in my pocket. I ignore it, even though there's a chill through my body that they know. *They know*. Then Jenna asks, "Is this true?"

"What is it?" I ask. My heart is racing, but I try to push down the anxiety. I can't feel it. I don't want to feel it. My phone vibrates again so I pull it out of my pocket, all of their eyes on me. I can't see the WNN, obviously, but I have a text from Pop and from Ric saying the same thing. But it's the third one, the one that comes in from Carter while I'm holding my phone that resonates the most.

Someone told the WNN you're a halfling.

I look up from my phone toward the four people sitting across from me. Jordan's face is mimicked on everyone's. The revulsion.

"I have to go," I say.

I drop my ice cream on the table before I run, and I don't look back.

Chapter Thirty-Four

CARTER

Pen texts me back a few minutes later, asking me to meet her in our spot. I leave the library without even saying good-bye to Poncho. He'll understand. The elevator takes forever, so I push the button again and again to make sure it's on the way.

How did this happen?

That update is burnt into my eyes.

PENELOPE GREY IS A HALFLING.

Who would tell the WNN? And why?

This stupid elevator is taking forever.

She can't handle this right now. Whatever's going on with her, this is going to make it worse.

I stare at the numbers. Three more floors. It jerks to a stop, and starts going back up. Wait, what? I push the buttons, but they don't change. I need to get out of here.

The doors ding open and my father is standing on the other side. Shit.

"My office. Now."

His lips are in a tight line, and his shoulders back. He means business right now, and I'm positive it has to do with Penelope.

Dad slams the office door behind him, and before I even sit down he's already talking. "Who submitted that information to the WNN?"

I cross my arms. "You?"

My dad shakes his head. "I wouldn't do that."

I scoff. "I didn't do it."

"And Miss Grey?"

Is he really asking me this? "Did she out herself? No. She's not stupid, Dad." Why am I even still here? I need to go to her, so I move toward the door.

"Someone sent that. A day before the Observance and now this mess to clean up."

I turn around to him. He always makes it about him. "Undo the rumor. Send out a retraction to fix this." He has the power, so he might as well use it for good.

Dad's eyes narrow in on me. "You aren't to see her anymore."

"What? No way."

Dad shakes his head, stepping toward me in the small space of his office. "You have to end it with that girl. It's the only way to keep your secret."

"No," I say. Not even an option.

"You are my priority."

That's always his excuse. This isn't about him or me. Penelope needs me. Now more than ever. I'm the only one who knows what's really going on with the demons. He can't keep her from me when I can help her out of this mess.

"My relationship with Penelope isn't your business." I turn the doorknob.

Dad slams his fist on his desk, and it makes me turn around. He doesn't lose it very often. "It is when you share a secret. If people start to question her then how long until they question you? Everyone close to the girl is guilty by association. I can't protect you, Carter, not if you're with her. You want to lose all you've been building here?"

"You mean all the ideas I've had and you've barely let me try? Yeah, what a loss."

"We'll need you, son, to lead the Statics after the Observance."

I can't believe this. Only he'd stoop this low. "So, you're bribing me. She isn't a toy that you can threaten to take away."

"She is exactly that," Dad yells, his eyes wide. This makes his thoughts about her and me very clear. He doesn't think I'm serious about her, about not following his path. "I don't have to threaten it—I make the laws. One word from me and she's gone anyway. Don't risk yourself or this family."

Why can't he understand this? "I can't do that. She needs me."

Dad stands and puts his hand on my shoulder. "I've done a lot of fighting for you. To keep you safe and with me. Will you sacrifice that for a girl?"

"Yes," I say without hesitation.

Dad sighs, lowering his hand. "Please don't be with her publicly until this settles. I will find out who revealed this information. This is for your own good. It's only until after the Observance, only one day. We need to make it through this event unscathed. This is an important sign of hope that our kind needs right now."

I can tell he means it, even if I don't want him to be sincere. "If I say no?"

"You can't say no. It's this or she's gone completely."

I step back from him. "Then I don't have a choice, do I, other than to bow to the great Triad leader?" Then I bow, purposefully. I want him to know that I hate this decision as much him. He's wasting my time when Penelope needs me. I'll do whatever it takes to get out of this room.

Dad lowers his voice. "Don't forget your place."

I stand up and shoot him a look of disdain. "It's hard to forget it when I haven't even found it yet."

"I can tell you where it isn't—with Penelope Grey."

"Got it," I say, pushing past him to open the door.

Dad moves out of the way and straightens his blazer. "Be sure that it sinks in."

"Consider it ingrained." I say as I close the door.

Chapter Thirty-Five

Standing on the hilltop isn't peaceful. It's chaos. Everything below seems to want to swallow me whole. Every witch knows I'm a halfling. I wring my hands. What am I going to do?

"Pen," Carter says.

Then, I'm in his arms. He holds me close, and I miss his familiar scent of nutmeg. He's been busy, mostly protecting me, and I've done nothing to deserve it.

"Everyone knows," I whisper in his ear. It's ironic, because I'm not even sure who I am anymore. I'm so confused by all of this. The magic plunges around in my stomach, and the motion is enough to make me sick.

"I know," is all he says.

"How long until they learn what I did? They'll all really hate me then."

"They won't find out, and they won't hate you. It's all going to be okay."

I pull away from him. "How can you say that? Stop saying that."

There really is no worse expression. It's not going to work out. It's not.

"Penelope," he whispers.

"Nothing is 'okay.' Nothing will work out. This is a mess. A mess. I've pulled you into all this," I say.

Into the fire with me. Into the demons. Into the lies, the void, the Statics, my betrayal. Everything. The void feels like it's crawling under my skin, and I pull my arms toward myself to stop the sensation.

"I don't see how this can get any worse now," I say, mostly to myself. Except, even as I say that, I don't accept it as true. Poncho could get in trouble for communicating with me. Carter could be discovered. Connie could die. My family could be destroyed. Everything, really, can only get worse from here.

Then he exhales, and my eyes meet his. "I left my dad from here," he starts. He scrubs a hand down his neck, and my stomach is a pit. "Because of all this, my dad has decided that I can't be with you—in public."

"What?"

"He says it's too dangerous for me, for him."

I pull away. I can't hear this. No. He's all I have right now. He can't do this to me. He can't leave me.

I knew he would leave me. I knew it.

Carter grabs my hand. "I told him I wouldn't, and he

threatened you. It's until the Observance is over. One day. Dad's desperate to keep his secret about my mom, and I'm going to do whatever it takes to keep you safe. It was the only way, Pen."

"For you to not date me?" I scream it at him. All the words in my head are jumbled together with the magic brewing and the anger.

"To pretend," he looks at me. "I wouldn't give you up."

But you just did. "Then why are you even here right now? If Daddy forbade you." Everything comes out louder than I mean it to.

Carter squeezes my hand and locks eyes with me. "Believe me when I say I'd do anything for you." I shake my head and he rests each of his hands on my cheeks. "Say the word and I'll walk you into the Observance myself. Screw him."

Don't feel. Calm down, Penelope.

"It's fine."

"It's not fine," he says, dropping his hands. "It sucks. He sucks. All of this."

I close my eyes. Push down my emotions. I won't feel anything. I won't feel anything. I won't feel anything.

If I say it enough then maybe it will be true.

"You said there was more."

Carter sighs. I hate that sigh. I hate everything.

"There are some things I've learned, and I've been trying to tell you for weeks."

His phone beeps and I roll my eyes. "Answer it."

"No," he says.

"It could be your dad," I say. My chest feels like it is caving in. Carter reaches for me, this look of pity on his face.

I shake my head. I don't want his pity. That's worse than anything else. I want him to leave me alone. "You said you can't be with me. Answer it."

He does and turns his back. I look over the city, and my eyes fill with tears. Wrong move. Answering it means Carter's giving me up. Just like that. I don't want him to leave me.

I hear him yell into the phone. The way he talks to me, looks at me, understands what I'm feeling without me saying it. No one else can do that. And I'm lying to him about everything. If I tell him that I really do know what's going on with Connie, what's really going on, then maybe he'll be able to let me go. It'll be easier now, then when I'm a demon. Maybe it will make it easier for both of us. He's risking everything for me, and I'm about to be gone.

He hangs up the phone and I look toward him. This is my chance to finally set him free.

"Carter, I need to tell you now," I say as he steps closer toward me. "I'm doing the Restitution."

He steps away from me. "What?"

I might as well get out with it. "I'm almost ready. That's what I've been planning and working on all this time with Lia."

"You can't," he says. The strain in his forehead, the strain in his jaw, the blaze in his eyes all say more than his words. His whole body screams at me. I hate it, but now I've come too far. "You can't do that. Not right now."

My stomach is bouncing, swaying. I need him to understand this. "It's the only way."

"The only way to what?"

I stare at him. How is he not getting this? "To save my sister, and the Statics."

"How is that exactly?"

I look away, so I don't have to see his face. Seeing his reaction is worse than hearing it. "I'll restore Lia, and then take her place long enough to get to Azsis. And when I do, everything will be back to normal. Undone."

He's staring at me when I look back. He thinks I'm crazy. Maybe this is crazy.

"You can't do this," he finally says. When he does, I notice the look in his eye is the same as the one Jordan Stark wore. Disgust. "I *am* a demon. So are you. This is for Connie, and everyone else."

"This isn't the way," he says, shaking his head. "Not like this."

I choose not to look at his eyes anymore. Not even to look at him. I don't need his approval for this, or his support. I knew he wouldn't understand what I'm doing. That's why I didn't tell him. He doesn't have a sister to worry about. He's never had anyone like that. I keep my gaze focused on everything else in front of me. On the city. On the cars. On the trees in the breeze. "It's the only way to have everything fixed."

He scoffs beside me, but I still don't look. "I know what this is really about—the magic."

I can't believe he's even suggesting that. Yes, I like the magic—but it's my sister. "No, it's about Connie. I'd do this even if I couldn't get my magic back." He tries to grab me but I sidestep from him. If I can barely look at him, then I definitely can't touch him. "I thought you'd understand. Out of everyone, I thought you would get why I need to do this."

"I don't," he says.

It's proof that I was wrong before. I'm too much of a girl,

controlled by desire and emotions. He doesn't understand me, because if he did then he'd get how much I need this. For Connie, for the Statics, and yes, even for myself. I can't live with all the things I've done when I have a chance to fix them.

"This won't undo anything," he practically whispers but it echoes through the darkness. "You don't have all the details," I say, finally looking back at him. Bad decision. Our eyes meeting makes it easy to want to be a simple girl. It makes me remember the cute, annoying boy who pursued me and kept my secret and loved me. The one I had before when I was the old me.

Carter sighs, but his eyes are still blazing with energy and emotion. With a nod, he reaches out for my hand. "Listen, tell me what's happening. I need to understand. How can you do it?"

"I've been working with the Lia to learn the void."

Carter squeezes my hand, and his eyes widen. "You can't trust her."

"Then who can I trust?" I shout. It echoes through the trees and disappears somewhere over the hill.

"Me," he whispers.

I laugh, and it's totally in a funny-ironic-hateful way. From the brokenness and anger on his face, he picks up on it. "You gave me up for your dad, Carter, so no. I can't."

"Penelope, don't walk away. Don't do this."

Chapter Thirty-Six

CARTER

Penelope looks at me, and I don't know who she is anymore. She's angry, and it practically comes off her in waves. This isn't her. Not this girl right here in front of me. This girl saying she's giving up her life for a demon.

That's it. They're trying to get her to come to their side. She's the sole witch, and if she chooses to work for the demons, then they'll destroy the witches. I've been trying to tell her for weeks now about the pieces of information that I put together, and I didn't fully understand, but now I do. This was the plan all along—to get her to their side.

"What you're doing with the Restitution and the demons, it's not what you think it is."

Her face gets red, and I swear for a moment her eyes

flash a shade of green. I have to be imagining that. "You're desperate to keep me from my magic. You'd risk my sister for that?"

"That is so not what this about. The demons are using you to get to the dagger. That's all they want."

Then, she's in my face, inches from it. Her skin is red, her eyes large and hot. She's not being rational. "Listen to yourself. I can't, Carter. This is over. I'm done."

I freeze when she walks away. As if she punched me in the gut. "What are you talking about?" She's not thinking. "No. No way. I'm not walking away from you right now."

"You don't have to," she says with a pause. "I'm walking away from you."

This isn't her talking. It's not her. "Penelope."

"I don't want to pretend—and you aren't supposed to be around me anyway. I'm doing you a favor."

I grab her hand. She tries to pull it away from me, but she can't. I'm holding too tightly. I need her to listen. "This isn't you. You aren't thinking straight. It's the void and the demons want the dagger and—"

"Stop it."

But I won't stop. Not now that I've finally got her listening. "They've had their eyes on you for months. It's all been for this. The Restitution isn't going to undo any of this. It's going to hurt people."

She shakes her head and tries to pull away from me. Her arm twists my hand around, but I don't let go. That's when I see it. Her pinky nail is completely black, and this dark trail travels up her hand. I slide up her sleeve. It's over her wrist, up her arm...

"What's this?"

She tries to pull her hand away, but I hold on to it and draw her closer. I run my fingers over the black in her veins. I did see something before. This is not good. Whatever it is. "What is this?"

"Let me go," she hisses through clenched teeth. But I don't.

"Penelope, what—what is this?" She bites her lip, and doesn't answer me. That first mark on her nail appeared after our test, when she used the void. "This is the magic, isn't it? The void."

She tries to get loose from me again. I refuse to let go.

"Tell me," I say.

"I said let go," she shouts, and when she does, a bright light shoots out of her. It knocks me to the ground and knocks the wind out of me. Holy shit. That was her, that light in the warehouse. She really can control it. I start to stand, slowly, but my mind is racing.

"Did I hurt you, too?" she says, her voice full of panic.

Suddenly, I realize she's what happened to Connie. The way she's looking at me, on the verge of tears and her face red. A wild, uncontrollable fear dances in her eyes. It's the same wide-eyed readiness that Lindley Arthur had. It's the same look Taylor Plum had that day.

I hold out my hands so she doesn't think I'm trying to harm her, and so she can see me. "I'm fine," I say, trying my best to sound assuring. Even from a few feet away I can tell she's shaking. She looks like Taylor when she killed Maple, nervous and terrified. "I'm fine, Pen."

She nods, wrapping her hands around her stomach. I move toward her slowly. "We can fix this. I can protect you."

Like a switch, those words change her. She jerks her

head up and pushes me away. "I don't need you to protect me. It's too late. This is done."

I shake my head. Her face is so steady, so emotionless, so unlike her. "I told you once I'd fight for you, and I meant it. Even now."

I take another step forward, watching the tears streaming down her cheek.

"Don't. Don't come near me. Don't follow me."

"Pen—"

Then she runs.

Chapter Thirty-Seven

PENELOPE

Black veins creep over my chin and up my cheek. That last jolt with Carter has nearly put me over the edge. I pull a hood over my head and try to blend in as I walk through Clarendon, people moving in and out of shops around me. The void is ready. I feel it as if it's crawling under my skin, waiting. I make a fist with my hands.

The void guides me, burning and itching and waiting for release. With each step I take, each inch I move, it gets hungrier. The blackness seems to be tingling, like a beacon leading me forward, or calling the other demons to me. I'm a trail of breadcrumbs. A rainbow leading to a pot of gold.

I pass a man on the street that I recognize from Enforcer meetings. The void stirs in my stomach. Even though I don't want to, I stop in the middle of the street and watch as he approaches. He notices me staring and his gaze rest on me while he walks. Does he recognize me? I walk faster, the void burning in my fingers, my arm, all down the trail that it's created through my body. It wants out. It wants to fight that Enforcer.

I won't do that. I squeeze my hand tighter until the fingernails stab into my palm.

"Is everything all right, miss?"

I nod, not sure I can manage to talk. *Please walk past me.*

Instinct says to run, but if I run then he'll chase me. So, I nod with a smile, and then I stay frozen in the spot on the sidewalk until the Enforcer passes. I stay frozen there until the magic settles down enough that I don't feel like puking on my own shoes. Until I can't feel my fingers from squeezing them so hard. When I'm able, I walk toward Lia where should be. This is almost over, only a few more hours. But now Carter knows the plan. Is what he said true? That she's using me? He wouldn't lie to me. *But he doesn't understand.* I push the thought away. I need to get to Lia, to ask her, to get answers.

The whole time I head in the direction of her favorite hangout, I can't shake the feeling he's more right than Lia is. The void scares me a little. It's not even fully part of me yet, and I have to fight it so hard. That should make me stop, but Connie is still on my mind. It's not about me or what I have to go through. This is about my sister, about the Statics.

The wind is harsh and bitter as I get off the metro, almost cold. So far from the norm for August. The usual steam of the summer sun is gone, and I miss it. I miss a lot of things.

The magic tingles at my skin, making me feel more on

edge than usual. The magic seems to be trying to rip its way out of me, and every inch of blackness burns through me. I am water on a cloth, soaking through.

I scratch at my arm. It's almost like the void is alive and flowing through me. It's never felt like this before, this uncontrollable. Walking doesn't lead me anywhere I recognize from the other night, and I turn down one of the V-split streets. The smell hits my nostrils immediately, the scent of sulfur so strong it feels like I'm standing in it. The bar must be closed now for it to be that strong.

I pay closer attention to the buildings as I walk, trying to find things that look familiar, but I don't get very far. A demon jumps out from the shadows in the small space between buildings. Its nails carve into the skin on my shoulder before it slams me against the brick wall of the building. The void bubbles and fills me, on the brink of running over, like my stomach is a pot of boiling water.

"You sm—"

"Smell good, I've heard," I say.

The demon smiles, sniffing my neck. "I've heard about you."

"Let me go," I say. Being near this demon makes my insides go crazier. It moves closer and I knee it in the stomach. It lurches away from me, but then, out of nowhere, three more appear. I stand straight up as one of the demons races toward me. The magic billows like a storm. If the void wants out, then I'll let it out.

I don't even have to aim. I stop fighting it, stop feeling any sort of emotions, let go of Carter and Ric and Gran, and my dreams, and all the people and things that have failed me. I don't need them, or want them. A second later the magic is flowing out of my fingers, bright and beautiful and seductive. This time, it's not too bright for me to see. Not like with Connie. This time it's clear, and I'm present. All three of the demons go flying across the alley. I feel invincible as I move toward one of the demons. I'm going to end him. To end all of the demons and the problems they caused me. End all of this.

I don't need salt.

I just need the void.

The magic moves out of me toward the demon. Its eyes are wide, scared—of me. The light from the void flows out of my fingers and wraps around the demon's neck. He starts to move, but I move my hand, and his neck breaks.

The other two demons are scattered on the ground, one trying to move, and the magic finds him. I don't have to figure out what I want it to do. The void already seems to have a plan that I'm not aware of. The void lifts them until they're both hanging from their feet. Fine by me. One is lifted into the sky, yards above, and dropped down. Hanged upside down by the void. His feet twitch in the air long after he's dead.

The last demon squirms. "Please," it says.

I look at it, but I don't see it. I don't care. I'm over caring. I want it to suffer, this one demon that has probably made hundreds of thousands of others suffer. I want to know what it's done, and the demon screams as the light of the void floods into its brain through ears and nose and eyes. It screams as the images flash in my head of the lives it's ended. Witches that it has tortured and drained. Nons that it's toyed with, ruined, killed. It's been alive for centuries, killing and surviving. And it's never felt any sort of sorrow.

Even when the victims said the same word, begged to be spared over and over again, it killed anyway.

Now it will experience that feeling. Vengeance and karma and justice.

"Beg me," I say. The voice doesn't feel like mine. It feels deeper, darker, like it's coming from the void and not from me.

The demon's eyes widen. "Please don't kill me. Please. I'll do anything." It begs. I listen, probably for minutes, as the demon repents and pleads and tries to convince me. It does convince me.

I want it dead.

The void wants it dead, too.

With a snap of my fingers, the demon bleeds out. Its heart falls to the ground, separate from its body.

For the first time I really feel like the void and I are one.

I stand there amongst the dead, and my stomach calms. The void is patient again, content with waiting. I am calm. In fact, I am pleased with myself. With the damage. Then, there's a sudden jolt that leaves me breathless, and I stumble backward toward the wall. The familiar burn of the void grows up my chest and my heart beats triple time. I fall to my knees, screaming. My pores are on fire. My ribs contract, tears flow from my eyes and I can't stop them. I'm not sure how much more it lasts, the burning, the pain. Seconds or minutes, maybe. It stops suddenly, and I let out a sob. Then there's a jolt again, and I lean over, gasping for air. The pain disappears.

"Well, well, well," a voice calls. I look over my shoulder and see Lia and another demon, looking from the mess to me. Lia moves toward me and her friend moves around the demons. "Look at this lot. I say, that must have been entertaining."

I don't respond as I look around the alley. Three demons are dead, blood and guts and a once-beating heart on the ground. I did that, the void did that. I glance at Lia, who's only inches from my face. "You good, girl?"

I nod. I guess I am. I should feel sick, feel bad about what I've done, but I don't. They all deserved it. Lia blinks, and then grabs my hand. "Look," she says.

My hands are a normal color. The blackness is gone from my veins. Only a small dot remains on my pinky.

"Why is it gone?" I ask.

"It's done," she says, examining my arms. She says it with awe and pride. Like she was uncertain it would actually work. "You and the void are connected now. You can control it."

"Perfect timing too," the other demon says. I look across the alley toward it. It's clad in the skin of a middle-aged woman, but beyond the skin of the woman, I see demon underneath. The Non is completely gone.

"Who's that?"

"I'm Bemnel," it says. Even though it's in the body of a woman, the voice is obviously male, deep and scratchy. And Irish, apparently. "Mighty good job. She said it was so, and here you is."

Lia looks me over. "How'd you end up here?"

I stand and dust myself off. I don't feel any different, yet I feel completely new. It's a strange feeling, almost like this is who I was supposed to be all along. Conduit of the void, a demon. "I was looking for you. Carter said you were using me, and lying about my sister."

Bemnel snorts across the alley.

"We had a blood oath, didn't we?" Lia says. An oath. She was very specific to include my sister. I shake my head. How could I let Carter get to me like that? I haven't come this far to doubt Lia now.

"Sorry, I—"

"I'm guessing loverboy and you are on the outs," she says.

"He doesn't get it."

Lia moves closer and strokes my hair the way my mom used to. It's strange that she would know that. "About Carter," she says. "He's demon enemy number one. Blacklisted. He's probably jealous that we actually like you."

"That doesn't sound like Carter."

She shrugs. "Maybe you don't know him the way you think you do." I exhale at that comment. "He's trying to make you doubt me because he probably wants something you have."

My mind races. What do I have that he doesn't? "There's nothing that…" Wait. Wait. I look at Lia. "The dagger. He mentioned the dagger."

She takes my wrist. "Let's go," she says, and Bemnel waves as we flicker out.

Lia flickers me right into my room, and when we get there, Carter's on the floor with the box I keep under my bed out in the open. The research on Azsis and the Restitution spread out around him.

"Carter," I say. He whips around to see me. This can't be

happening. "What are you doing in here?"

"It's it obvious?" Lia says. "He doesn't trust you."

I don't know this boy anymore. Not this one who would sneak into my house and steal from me. His eyes widen. "That's not what this is."

"What were you looking for?"

"The dagger," he says quickly. I turn toward Lia, who nods. She was right. He wants that dagger. What was all that this morning? Did he report me to the WNN?

"You were taking it? I need it for the Restitution tomorrow," I jerk the box out of his hand.

"I'm sorry, Penelope," Lia says in my ear.

"I'm sorry, too." I say.

Carter shakes his head and takes a step toward me. Part of me wants him to hold me, and the other part, the part that listens to the void, hates him. "Stop this. Don't listen to her. You can't believe anything she says to you."

"No, I can't trust you," I yell. It could be my imagination, but the whole house seems to shake like it used to with Connie when she got angry.

"It's a lie, Penelope. She wants to use it to destroy all of us," he says.

Lia leans into my ear. "Cut off your emotions. Feel nothing for him."

I look at him, at his face and his green eyes, and the lips I used to kiss. The ones that have betrayed me. I don't want to feel that. He's nothing to me now. Nothing but a boy in my room, trying to steal from me. A liar.

And then all the feelings are gone.

"Get out," I yell. He steps toward me, but the void sends him backward with a powerful gust of wind. "GET OUT."

And like that, Carter's out of my house. I hope the landing was painful.

Lia rests a hand on my shoulder. "I'm sure that was difficult."

"It wasn't difficult. It wasn't anything."

She smiles a half-smile. "Good. I'll see you in the morning. You have the address?"

"Morning?"

"For the present," she says, and I nod.

After she's gone, I keep telling myself it was nothing. I repeat it until I can say it with a straight face. Until it starts to feel like nothing.

Chapter Thirty-Eight

CARTER

My father and I stand in the zoo. I look up at him, so happy to be with him, ready to see the lions. "Buy a balloon?" a vendor asks.

Dad gives him a dollar and he hands me a red balloon. I hate red.

"I want blue," I say and the man says he's all out. Dad thanks him, and I want blue. I'm upset that dad won't get me blue. We walk on, and I stare at the balloon, wishing it was blue. A blue balloon. That's what I want. Blue like the sky. Blue like cotton candy. Blue.

And then the balloon changes colors.

Dad doesn't notice at first, not until we're almost at the lions and then he pauses. "I thought that was red," he says.

"I made it blue." I smile. It's exactly what I wanted.

"You made it blue?"

"I wanted blue, and now it's blue."

Dad's face isn't happy. It's upset. I made him mad. Why did I make him mad? He pulls me toward a bench and we sit down. He pulls the string until the balloon is in front of him. "This is not how we use magic," he says to me. "It's not proper, William."

Then he pops it. My balloon.

I cry. "This is not how Prescott men act. Stop crying."

I sit up in bed. I've had that dream every time I sleep, ever since I saw Vassago the other night. The dream is a memory. I was only four, and it'd be years before I understood why that moment was bad. The use of magic in public, and the first time my dad suspected I used the void, even though I had no idea what I was doing. His fear has always been that strong.

It's three a.m. when I toss the covers off and groan as I move. My body hurts from Pen throwing me out of her house. Literally. I laid on the pavement for minutes before I could stand. That magic she used isn't normal. The demons have her now, completely on their side.

I needed that dagger. It was the only way I could stop any of this, since she won't even let me talk to her. If I have the dagger, then the demons don't, and they can't go through with this plan. I have to reach her. I have to make her understand. I'll see her tonight, at the Observance, and I'll tell her then. It's the only place the demon won't be around. Every time I try to talk to her, Lia changes her mind. If she's not around, then Pen will listen to me.

Hopefully. I guess she could retaliate against me again,

but she loves me. She's scared about this other stuff. I can play on that. Use her love and her fear to make a strong move, to get ahead of the demons. Maybe even stop them. If I can't, then there's no hope. There will be no one who can make her listen. Not with Connie in a coma and Ric out of town.

Or maybe there is.

I pull out my cell phone and scroll until I find Frank's number. Her grandpa. She loves him, and underneath, that girl is still there. If all this is for Connie, then maybe he can reason with her. Between him and me, we can do this. There's still time.

I sigh before pushing the call button. Even though it's the middle of the night, Frank answers. *Now or never, Carter.*

"Mr. Warren, it's Carter Prescott."

"Carter, it's late." Frank's voice is heavy on the other line.

"We need to talk about Penelope," I say with a pause. "She's in trouble."

Chapter Thirty-Nine

PENELOPE

The Observance dance starts at eight, in an hour, and the Restitution will start right after midnight, at the witching hour. Midnight to dawn, six hours to do all this. The six hours where the magic is at its height. Then this is all over and Connie is safe.

It's dark in the house except for what comes in from the sky. Even that is in minimum because the sky is overcast. I don't mind the darkness, but Gran and Pop never have liked it. It's quiet, too quiet. Gran and Pop must be at the hospital still. Or again. Time is merely a tool to measure how much longer I have to wait. To count down my sister's life.

I grab my green raincoat, since it's pouring outside, and head for the hallway. I have to go meet Lia for the present.

"Penelope," Gran says, walking into the living room. I roll my eyes and then turn on the bottom step toward her. When did they get back? She and Pop stand there, staring at me like I'm an injured puppy.

"We're so worried about you." She takes a step toward me and I take a step backward. I don't want her to touch me. As I think, that the void starts to stir. Now she definitely can't touch me. *Feel nothing,* I tell myself. *Nothing.*

Pop moves toward me. "We want to talk with you, Penelope. Go sit in the living room."

Gran and Pop stare me down. I don't want a fight, so I go and sit. They follow behind me and sit across from me.

"What is it?" I ask. "I've got to go."

Pop shakes his head, and even though I try not to, I do feel. Pop's always been there. *Feel nothing.* "We ran into Sabrina Stone in the hospital and she asked how you were. She informed us that you were marked. Why wouldn't you tell us?"

"You've been marked for weeks," Gran says, the lines on her face harsher. "Since your sister's accident. You losing your Enforcer badge was one thing, and we'd figured you'd come to us about that when you were ready—but how could you keep that from us?"

There was a reason, but it's hard to grasp and cling to now. I don't need to respond at all. I move toward the door, but Gran still talks at me.

"We're worried, Penelope We've been overlooking some of your actions. We wanted to let you deal with things about your sister and the loss of your dream in your own way, but this isn't dealing with anything," she says.

Now I feel anger. How can she pretend to care about my job, about me being an Enforcer, now that I'm not one anymore? "You didn't want that future for me, anyway. I did you a favor."

"I want you to *have* a future," Gran pleads. "Everyone saw that message that you were a halfling. The phone rang all morning, Penelope. We can't protect you from that. Even if the Triad sent out a retraction, the suspicion will not die that easily. Not for any of us. Things have changed forever."

I force the void to stay down. *Feel nothing. Don't let this control you. You don't owe them.*

"Penelope," Pop says, "stay with us so we can keep you from harm."

I stare between them, and those words are supposed to mean a lot, but they don't. They're scared. Scared of things they don't understand and it's not my job to make them understand. "I don't need any help. I have my own magic now."

I stand to move from them, but Gran grabs my arm. Her face is harsh, older than she usually seems. "Stop lying. We are still your grandparents. What are you doing?"

"The one thing you never wanted," I snap.

Gran takes a step back, like I've hit her. "Which is?"

"What I have to do. I'm embracing who I am."

I see the realization dawn on her face. She stares back at me in horror, and I expect her to comment more on it, but it's Pop, not her, who speaks.

"What have you done?"

He touches my shoulders, one hand on each, and I look at him. I have to. But I don't even want to answer him. I want to go. The void lingers at my fingertips, waiting for me to let it out. My hands start to shake, and I have to leave right now.

"I have to go," I say. I lurch away from him, snatch my

bag from the couch, and move toward the door. The void wants to release, and I force it back with all I can. It's very hot inside, and I feel my shirt sticking to me under my coat. I have to get out of this room and away from them. The magic keeps growing, wanting out, and I can't not feel anything for them. Not for him.

Magic zaps me in the back, and when I look, Pop is standing with his hand out in the air. "Do not leave. We are not finished."

It's only a second of emotion from me, but that's all it takes. The void wins the war with my body, lights up the dark room, and shoots out of me. I let out a gasp, but I can't stop the magic. Pop falls to the ground, stiff as a board. Gran rushes to him, calling his name, and I stand there. I should go to him, but I don't. I can't. If he's not okay, then I don't want to see it. My whole body is convulsing, and I don't trust the magic. Or myself.

Instead, I open the door to leave.

I force my hands to steady before I move. My entire body has a moment of stillness, an anchor. I shut off the movements, the pain, the emotions. It's the only way to control it.

"Penelope, please." Gran says. "Don't leave us."

Leaving is the only thing I can do to spare them. I'm too dangerous now.

As the door closes behind me, I decide they are strangers. I feel nothing for strangers.

• • •

I meet Lia in some condemned old house near Great Falls Park. The outside is covered in wood that's blackened with rot, bowing and splintering from damage. "This is cozy," I say.

"I don't like to be at the same place more than once. Not now that your people are all suspicious. The last thing we need is an interference."

"Agreed," I say. "Is this the big surprise?"

She shakes her head, and Bemnel steps into the room from the outside.

"An ambush?

"You're on edge today," he says.

"A lot on my mind," I say.

I watch as three more demons step into the run-down once–upon-a-time house. One is gray, one is blue, and one is wearing the skin of a middle aged overweight, balding man. Lia points to me. "This is Penelope Grey."

"Nice to meet you," the gray one says. "I'm Asag." It points to the blue demon. "That's Sharir."

"I can introduce myself, Asag," the blue one says. "I'm Sharir."

"Charmed," I say. Bemnal crosses his arms, watching in amusement.

"Jerry," the one in a man suit says.

"Jerry?" I repeat.

He nods. Whatever, then. No one moves or speaks for another minute, but they all stare at me. Waiting. "Why am I here?"

Bemnel answers instead of Lia. "Because we're a right fun bunch of buggers. You need people on your side, and we're the best lot around."

"The best?"

"Aye, or the most entertaining," he winks.

"Oh, so you do tricks? Show me one."

Sharir leans toward Asag. "I like this one."

Lia puts up her hand. "Enough. Penelope, dear, there's one problem we've been working on for you. The present I mentioned."

"Which is?"

"You are snappy," she says. She takes my wrists and holds them forward. "We're going to remove the mark so Cinderella can go to the ball."

My jaw drops. "You can do that?"

Lia moves her hands in the air like a teetering scale. "We've never done it. I had to gather the right demons, ones who could harness the most magic, but we're resourceful."

"And if you fail?"

She shrugs. "Without it you won't even be able to enter the hall, so it's worth a try."

"But our plan to use the relay was—"

"I was stalling," she says. "Come on. Let us give it a go." I nod, because what else can I do, and Lia smiles. She readjusts the way I'm standing and makes me pose so my wrists are pointed out toward the group of demons. They all gather around me, touch my wrist, and start chanting.

They chant. It feels like hours. Nothing happens.

And then it does. The pain is like knives in my wrists, tightening and pulling my muscles apart. Then it's stiff and tingly. Then it feels like my bones are being broken before mending. It's all happening at once, and I scream against the pain. I'm pretty sure the void comes shooting out of me, but it's all fuzzy until it's all black.

When I wake up, I'm still on the floor, all the demons looking down at me. "Did it work, lass?" Bemnel asks.

I look at my wrists. There's nothing there. It's my wrist without a band.

"I think so," I say.

He smiles. Lia holds out a hand for me. "Let's get ready for the ball."

Chapter Forty

The dance is already in full swing when I show up. The whole area of the Nucleus House is packed with people. Despite the chilly weather, people are still outside in the overflow. Even the impending doom of Static magic can't stop a celebration.

I squeeze through some Enforcers. A few of them look at me, eyebrows raised or face twisted in disgust. I recognize the suspicious looks. They don't know what to believe anymore, about Penelope's halfling status, given and then revoked. Or what that means for me.

Someone says my name as I pass, but I don't stop to pay attention to who it is. I need to find Penelope. She has to be here. She said she would do the Restitution tonight, and if she is the gift prophesized, the sole witch, then I have to stop her. If I can just talk to her one more time, I can try to convince her to listen to me, or I have to stop her. If I can't do it, then there's Plan B: tell my dad. It's the only other option, but I can't think about what they'll do her to stop her.

Some of the other Enforcers slap me on the back as I walk through them. I flash my Prescott smile, and make small talk through the crowds. They all know who I am. Everyone. Someone mentions Penelope's name, but I turn away, heart pounding. The music drowns out most of what they say and carries the words away into the night. I can't start talking about her. I need to stay on task. They can be suspicious if they want, but it won't change anything. I can't focus on that right now.

Waiters in bowties walk around the whole yard outside and through the interior doors with silver trays of food. There are witches and Statics everywhere. When we're all meshed into a room, it's impossible to tell who is who. I like it that way. If this day had gone the way it was supposed to, Pen would be here on my arm and we'd be enjoying this together. This brief moment of unification, where there are no titles, just people.

I glance around the room as Jordan Stark waves me over, then steps away from his group toward me. "Prescott, we were just talking about you."

"Yeah? All good things about how you can't compare to me?" I ask with a smile. They all laugh. I don't know anymore if it's because of my charm or because of my name. I guess it doesn't matter.

"That program with the Statics, they said in the meeting

today it was coming back. I want to help out. We all do."

It's coming back? I missed that meeting today, but I stare at Jordan, waiting for a joke. He's serious. "Why?"

Jordan looks toward the ground. "I knew Taylor Plum. Shira's pretty torn up about it, and I want to be there to support them after Mrs. Arthur. Besides, with Maple and Ric and all the others, well, I see where you're coming from."

"Yeah, definitely. Let's talk about it later."

Jordan smiles. "Cool." He takes a step closer. "And that stuff with your girlfriend..." I don't respond, just stare at him. "Did you know she was a halfling?"

I glance away from him and my eyes scan the room, and I'm about to say something very un-Prescott, but then I see her. Alone, in the corner near the door. She must've just gotten here.

"See you later, Jordan."

Pen is standing in that same green dress that she wore last month, the one from our pairing, and she's beautiful. Others walk around her, careful not to go near. I am amazed that she'd even show up here, after the news about her status, but Pen's never really cared about what they think of her. She's mad at me, but that's not really her. It's the magic. It's whatever the demon is telling her, and the stress. Penelope loves me, and that doesn't go away. Not just like that.

Suddenly, she looks up. Right at me across the room of people. It's strange and cliché to feel, in that moment, that I knew exactly what she was thinking, but I did. I could see it on her face, and in her eyes. Even with hundreds of people standing between us, some whispering, some pointing. She looks away from me, toward the large clock above my head, and her eyes darken. Nearly midnight.

I move quicker toward her, hoping that she won't decide to run away again. Or worse.

I vaguely notice the Triad standing off to the side of the room, and my father's glance in my direction. I don't give a shit about what he thinks. Or anyone else. Not right now. Not when this is the last chance I have. Let them say whatever they want. I want to be the one there for her when no one else thinks it's right—she'd do that for me.

"Hey," I say with a smile.

Pen blinks, focuses her gaze on me. She leans in closer, so near that I can almost feel her breath on my skin. "You shouldn't be talking to me."

"I don't care."

"Your dad," she starts, nodding across the room. I don't look anywhere but at her.

"I don't care," I repeat. I tilt my head toward the exit. "Come with me."

She shifts on her feet. "You won't change my mind about anything."

Good. That means my Pen is still in there somewhere. "Then you have nothing to worry about."

With a quick glance at the clock, she nods in agreement. "Five minutes."

Five minutes is all I need.

I hope.

We find a quiet corner outside the Nucleus House and away from the people. The cold air is a reminder of all the pieces I've put together that Pen doesn't know about. Of all the things that are happening. Things that have yet to come.

Pen crosses her arms. "What do you need to talk about? I think I've made myself clear on all of this."

I shake my head. "I know you love me, Penelope, but you're scared."

"And you're in denial," she snorts.

I smile the Prescott smile, charm and smolder, and if she notices the difference between my real one and this one, then she doesn't comment on it. "I think that's you."

"You don't know what you're talking about."

I lower my voice and step closer to her. "Let me help you."

"I'm not in trouble." But she doesn't look at me when she says it. She's trying to hide. I won't let her hide. If she's going to kick my ass and serve it up on a platter, then I'll at least get words in this time. I push some of her hair behind her ear, but she flinches and backs away.

"It's probably better if you don't touch me," she says. "I can't control it when I'm touched."

Finally, some information. "Can't control the void?"

"I hurt people…"

"Like who?" She looks at me, and I notice that her eyes are strange again. Darker than usual, glassy, completely empty of any emotion. It gives me the chills. "You can tell me."

She shakes her head. "I can't. I'm sorry."

I move in closer until I'm only an inch away and her breath hitches. "Don't touch me," she whispers. But even as she says it her body leans into mine. Like that's exactly where it wants to be.

"Why can't I touch you?"

Her lip quivers and she's not making eye contact. "I'll break you, worse than before. When people touch me, I ruin them: Connie, Gran, Pop. Everyone."

"You won't ruin me," I say with force.

Finally, she looks in my eyes. "I will. I already have."

"You didn't and you won't," I repeat. I need to show her that she can trust me. That we can touch each other. That I'm here. She closes her eyes as I let my fingertips graze her cheek. She opens her eyes again after a moment, almost surprised. "See? It's fine." I run my fingers down her neck and slide my other hand around her waist.

"Don't push it," she whispers. "It's unpredictable."

I kiss her neck. "Control it."

Again and again I kiss her, up her jaw, her cheek, and run my hand down her neck.

"You won't do anything to me."

Her hands finally move from her side and down my shoulders to rest on my back. My heart is racing from her touch. If I can let her forget all of the other things, let her think about us, then, maybe we can stop this. If she thinks she can be strong, if she trusts me again, then we can undo this damage.

Pen stares at me, and I refuse to look away, refuse to let go of her. Her usual cool blue eyes flash a deep green, and that should worry me, but it's not too late. It's not too late yet.

Then she closes the space between us. Her tongue finds mine, and her hips press into me, trapping herself between the wall and me. It's me and her, like it was before, like it should be. No magic or demons or Statics or lies.

And being like that, with her, I will never let those things keep us apart. I can say I'll fight for her, but I'm going to do more. I'm going to show her.

When we part for air, I press my forehead against hers and breathe her name. It's like a spell on my lips. She inhales the mingled air between us. "It's not too late."

She sniffles, her voice low. "I wanted to protect Connie."

"We can find a way, Pen. We always find a way. The Restitution, the demons aren't the answer." I'm saying it all too quickly, expecting too much, but I want her to say yes. I want her to find her way back. To this side, to us, to me, to herself.

Pen buries her face into my shoulder. Wetness spreads on my suit, and I hold her tighter as she starts to cry. I run my hand over her hair. "The void is part of me now. It's claimed me."

I hold her tighter against me until her body melds into mine. The void is part of her. If she wasn't marked, she would be able to harness both magics. But since she is, there's still time.

"I was trying to do the right thing, but now…" She doesn't finish the thought. "I'm so angry, and I don't know who—" The rest of her sentence is lost in my jacket. "I'm a monster."

I pull away from her so I can see her face. "You're not a monster."

"I am," she says. She looks at me again with that emotionless stare, the one that means she's gone again. "We'll do the Restitution and then everything will be better. You'll see."

I need her to fight this magic, to stay here. "Are you trying to convince me or yourself?"

She pauses, and shakes her head, hair falling from the fancy knot on her head. "The demons are the only ones who are willing to help me be a witch again. And the void is the only way to fix everything."

"They're lying to you."

She shakes her head, but her eyes are focused on me again. Focused and bright with anger or determination. "It's not a lie. No one else understands except her. Everything Lia said has happened."

I toss my hands into the air, and take a step back. "This is what she's wanted all along. She wants you to have no one left so you need the demons because they need you. They're using you." Pen looks confused, face all scrunched up. I reach for her hand and inhale. "There was a prophecy that one witch would come who could harness the power to destroy one side of magic forever—so afterward there's only void or essence. And that person is you. They are doing all of this to get you."

Her breath hitches, and I can see her hands shake, even though she's not moving. "What?"

"I've looked into this with Poncho. You still trust him, right? And Vassago. It's real—and this is what they want. They want to get rid of witches forever."

"They want me to destroy the other side?"

"You have to have an essence and the void, a halfling. This is what I've been trying to stop."

"Wait—what do you mean? You've been trying to stop what?"

"The Restitution. There has to be a balance, and that balance is way more than you choosing a side and becoming a demon. If you do this, then you'll destroy the essence and everything associated with it."

There's silence as she looks toward the ground. "I would destroy everyone?"

I reach out for her hand. "If the void is part of you, then you have the power to do that. It's a good thing you're marked—it will be harder for the demons to work the Restitution around that."

She looks down at her hand, anger and horror on her face. Her fingers trace along her arm, but there's nothing there. How is there nothing there? What happened to the blackness?

"How long?" she asks, her eyes wide with disbelief and anger. Her jaw is taut, her eyebrows set in arches.

"What?"

"How long have you known about this?" She yells it, her chest rising and falling heavily.

I sigh. "Since right after you were marked."

"Weeks," she says, she shouts. "Weeks and you didn't think to tell me?"

"I wanted to make sure I knew what we were getting into. Every time I tried, the demon thwarted me because she knew what I learned, she had to. Then, you wouldn't even talk to me about it. I was trying to do it on my own, but that obviously didn't work."

She pushes me, and I stumble backward. "You should've told me." She pushes me again. Her skin starts to glow white as she pushes me again.

"Pen, stop."

"How could you?" The words seem to rip from her throat.

I grab her arms and stop her from moving. Force her to

look at me. The light of the void pulses through her skin like a strobe light. "It's not too late."

Then the clocks strikes. Midnight. It's officially the Observance. The day has begun. Her eyes are wide and her face pale.

"Yes, it is," she says.

I blink, shaking my head. I start to ask what she means, but then she flickers out of my arms. I didn't even know she could do that. Or how. But it's not good.

Chapter Forty-One

It's too late for second thoughts. When I re-enter the party, the Triad is onstage in the center of the room. All the witches and Statics stand around in their best dresses, listening and smiling. I'm supposed to meet Lia in the center of the room at 12:05. Even though part of me says to trust her, the other part wonders about what Carter has said. Will this really wipe out the witches?

"Tonight we have gathered to remember," Victor Prescott says from his spot on the stage. Sabrina Stone and Rafe Ezrati stand beside him. "This day marks the year of our creation, the fall of Lucifer and the betrayers, and the beginning of our quest to protect Nons. Today is a celebration," Victor adds. He speaks with such authority that it's hard not to listen to him. "Today we honor the gifts we've been given, even in a time of uncertainty and danger."

I move toward the exit that doesn't lead to anything except the Triad offices. Carter's words play in my head. If I do this, then they're all dead. My family. Everyone.

"Without the gift of the angels, we would not exist. And therefore, every one hundred years we celebrate life, remember the lost, and prepare for the future," Victor says.

The dagger is safe at my thigh, and I focus on the steel against my skin. Lia has everything else set up, but I couldn't turn this over to her. I kept it close.

Maybe deep down I never trusted her as much as I'd wanted to.

I can't do this.

"Today, on this the day of the Observance, of new beginnings," Victor continues.

I can't do this if it kills all these people.

"We give thanks to the angels who created and—"

A scream resounds through the room. I look over my shoulder and the crowd is parting. I expect to see something else, but there's nothing.

Then I realize the crowds are stepping away from me. I'm in the center—and I'm glowing.

The void.

All eyes are on me, and the Triad is frozen on the stage. I glance up at Victor, who's looking over me toward Carter. Rafe looks confused.

"Seize her," Sabrina yells.

Hands grab at me, pull me in other directions. The magic clutches me, ready and willing to fight on my behalf. I can't harm these people. These are my people, witches like me.

But they push me toward the ground, and I have no choice anymore as the void takes over. I try to contain the emotions so the power doesn't go crazy, but it's too strong. I'm too confused, too stunned, betrayed, and I have lost everything.

Don't feel. Don't feel. But I can't this time. I can't turn it off. Everyone touching me flies across the room, others run, and it's chaos. I try not to look so I don't have to see what happens. I don't want to see what I've caused.

I hear Lia's voice above the others—when did she get here? How did she get inside past the wards? But I run toward her. No one stops me, and those who touch me get thrown back by the void. I'm almost to Lia when I hear Carter, calling my name.

In the commotion, I feel him looking at me, waiting for me. He yells my name again across the room, somehow louder than the other things around me. For a second, I think about going with him. I take a step toward him, and Lia calls my name. But no. She's going to kill all the witches, and she somehow brought all those demons inside. How could she even do that? How could I allow this to happen?

It's not too late until I'm lost, that's what Poncho said. I see my direction now. Carter. I should've stayed with him and his plans all along.

Then, an Enforcer shoots me with magic. Carter lurches in my direction, but Victor holds him back. My arm is bleeding, and I try to run but more Enforcers encircle me, and the void builds up. I know the protocol for Enforcers and what will happen next. They'll take me down.

Carter pulls away from his dad and tries to work his way through the crowd toward me. He's moving against the current as witches flock toward the exits. He shouts my name, but the void shoots out. Witches fall to the ground, screams echoing like dominoes.

Lia grabs my bleeding arm, and I cry out.

"Blood oath," she says, "and it's not finished yet."

I start to yell, but Lia flickers me out. The last thing I hear is Carter calling my name in the distance.

Chapter Forty-Two

I yell Pen's name in the chaos, but the hallway is empty. She's gone. The mauve demon took her. I have to find them before it's too late. Screams fill the air from a few feet away. I head into the fighting as my dad steps toward me. He looks exhausted, and his shirt is ripped. There's blood, but I don't know if it's his or someone else's.

"Carter," Dad calls.

I step toward him. My skin feels like its screaming with the urge to kill some demons, to fight next to the witches. But I'm here with him, and Pen is gone. "I should've told you," I admit, reluctantly.

"If she's partnered with demons, then we need to stop her," he says.

"She's been confused."

"How long?"

I pause and look at my dad. This is the first time I've seen him without the mask in a long time. "Since you marked her," I say finally.

Dad moves toward me in huge steps. "This is why I didn't want you to see her."

"All this is going on and that's what you're worried about?"

He shakes his head, and when he looks at me again remorse is written all over his face. "You should've come to me with this."

"You're so blind about halflings, and I didn't think…"

Behind him, I see a demon explode into guts, but it's only one demon. There are at least fifty out there, somehow. A chair flies into the corner of the hallway, and I glance out into the room beyond to see a body slide across the floor. "They think she's a thing called the sole witch."

Dad's eyes widen. "The gift for Lucifer. That's a myth."

"She can harness both sides."

He shakes his head in disbelief. "She's marked."

"She was driven into their hand because she was marked. You took her essence, so she turned to the void—and they were there for her. You *gave* her to them. All of this is happening because of that mark," I say. I need him to see what's really happening. That there's a reason the demons are here and she, conveniently, isn't.

Dad's face constricts. For the first time, maybe in forever, I see the guilt there. The realization that he did something wrong. If the whole world as we knew it wasn't about to implode, I'd enjoy the moment more. "If the demons have the sole witch, then they will destroy us. We must stop her," Dad says, his face switching into Prescott-leader mode. "I'll grab a team."

"No team. Please. Let me go to her."

He shakes his head, but I don't let him protest this. Not this. "Go to them. Worry about them."

I point to the people in the ballroom beyond us in the hallway. We can't really see from here, but the sounds force their way in. Crying, grunts, and objects hitting the ground. Sounds of fighting and death. Dad looks over his shoulder toward the others. "I'll go alone and bring her back."

I see the flickering of emotions on his face. To let me go. To make me stay. To send someone else instead. "I can do this, and I work better alone," I say. "She'll listen to me, not anyone else."

Dad stares at me, considering, and his eyes get that Prescott businessman glare. "This is a big task. If you fail…"

"I won't," I say. "Let me do this. Trust me to do what you've taught me."

Dad looks over my shoulder, and holds his head back after a nod. "Don't fail us." Then he moves without another word toward the crowd. A kid runs past the hallway, some demon that looks like a fat guy behind him. Dad yanks the kid from the ground and lunges a knife into the demon's heart. In a blink, the demon explodes and my dad disappears from my sight into the fighting.

Then the chanting starts, sounds trailing back to me. They're expelling the demons, finally. My money says they're making them extra salty, too.

He's got this now, and I've got to get Pen.

But how the hell do I find her?

I see Poncho standing against the wall in the corner. His eyes are focused on me, and when he sees me looking, he points outside. He wants me to go outside. I run down the hallway toward the exit.

Vassago is standing outside the Nucleus House when I get out there, waiting for me. "Where is Penelope?"

Without a word, he takes my arm, and we disappear.

Chapter Forty-Three

"Let me go," I shout as we materialize into darkness. It takes my eyes a few seconds to readjust, then I realize this is De'Intero. It's completely changed from the last time I was here. It's darker now, almost more desperate.

Lia pushes me against a wall. "Look. We had a deal. You can't back out of it now."

"I didn't know your part of the deal was using me to kill all the witches."

She blinks. "It's not like that."

"Then what's it like?"

Lia's eyes flicker green instead of blue. Those eyes, the humanness in them, is part of what had me so fooled. I am an idiot. I should've known more was going on.

Across from me is a glass wall, and behind the glass, there's a swirling pearly white fog that looks like smoke, but it's not. It's almost solid, based on the way it presses up into the glass. I can't look away from the mass. It's calling to me, my heart beating in tune with its movements as it ebbs and flows against the glass wall. It wants me to join it. To connect.

"You promised," Lia says, her voice pulling me away from the draw of the magic. "I swore to teach you and to save your sister. You swore to help me. A blood oath is unbreakable."

"I won't help you destroy everyone I love."

"Everyone you love?" a voice asks. It's not Lia. It's a man, deep-voiced and achingly familiar. My throat constricts and suddenly I'm nine again, when my parents died. It's a voice I haven't heard in years, and my legs won't respond. Won't turn. But the footsteps move toward me, a scream builds up in my throat, and then I see the orange eyes.

I face of the demon who killed my parents, who stole my powers. "Azsis," I say, breathlessly.

The demon moves toward me and takes my hand, presses his lips on it. I want to hate him and to let that hatred spew, but my feelings fade away. I feel nothing. "Penelope Grey, we finally meet."

I don't know what to say. All my life I've spent looking for this demon, and here he stands in front of me and I'm speechless. The only thing I can think is why, but I won't ask that.

I look from Azsis to Lia. I squeeze my hands into fists and hold them tight as anger twists through me. She was working for him all along. Azsis follows my gaze toward her, and steps in my view of her.

"She was merely doing her job. I wanted to see you." Azsis stuffs his hands into his pockets. He's well dressed, for a demon, in a black suit and silver tie. His Non body is shorter, dark hair, orange eyes shining through, and a slight accent that I can't place exactly. It's hard to focus with the void beating against my body and my thoughts on all the witches at risk, on my sister, on my hands wanting to kill him. To take back what's mine.

"Her job was to bring me here?"

"Yes," he says, "I have been looking forward to our meeting for years."

I scoff. "You mean since you killed my parents and stole my essence."

"Guilty," he says, holding his hands up in the air. "I'd apologize, but I doubt you'd accept it."

The anger bubbles up, and I try to contain it. The last thing I want to do is lose control this close to all that magic. It would kill him, maybe, but I don't know what else it would do. "Why am I here? Why would you want to meet me?"

Azsis walks around the room, arms crossed. "You are important."

"Important?" I ask.

He picks some lint off Lia's shoulder, and sends her a small smile. She looks at him like he's bacon ice cream and she's starving. "There's an old tale from our long history. Some demons were created, some magic was created and blah, blah, blah. We'll skip the boring details," Azsis says, stepping toward me. "In summary, an ancestor declared that one day there would be someone who could harness the power of both sides, the void and the essence."

Carter's words from earlier come back to me. *There was*

a prophecy that one witch would harness the power to destroy one side of magic forever—so in the end there's only void or essence. And that person is you. They are doing all of this to get you. And here I am. I let them use me. I got played. I cross my arms, trying to look fierce and to contain the magic swirling inside. "And you think out of all the halflings in existence that I am that person? I'm awesome, but that's pretty ambitious."

Azsis smirks. "I like a little sass in my allies."

"I'm not your ally."

"Yet," he says, smoothly. His accent gives him this way of talking that almost makes me comfortable. Maybe that's how he does it—he charms everyone into forgetting that he's more psychotic than the average demon.

I should gut him.

He tilts his head with a shrug. "There's much you have to learn, Miss Grey. I more than think you're that person—I know you are." His voice is full of certainty, but his eyes never leave me as he paces the room.

I look around for an escape route as he walks. The only exit is the door we entered through, and Lia is blocking it. I can blast through a wall. How far could I go before someone tried to stop me?

"And how are you sure?" I ask him, buying time.

"Because I created you to be that person. I set it in motion centuries ago with a girl like you who felt she had no one."

Centuries ago… "Emmaline Spencer."

Azsis smiles. "You've heard of her? My best work." The smile fades, and he stuffs his hands back into his pockets. "Pity it didn't work out as planned. I chose a lot of witches who I felt showed potential."

"What kind of potential?"

"The gift of sole witch can only be filled by a certain being. Someone lonely, desperate, wanting of a purpose. I carved out the qualities centuries ago, and on the brink of every Observance, I searched for them in witches, waiting to cultivate a few for my purpose. Emmaline was one of my chosen. She ended up not working out, but I kept searching, molding, waiting. Patience is key, you see. You, however, were only partially of my doing. Destiny made you the one I needed."

Destiny. There's that word again. Maybe she really is a b—. "Destiny needs a hobby, and a better punch line."

Azsis shakes a finger at me, smirking again. It's nothing like Carter's adorable know-it-all smirk. His is a mocking one. "Your parents knew the potential in you, Penelope, from the moment you were conceived."

My eyes search for his. My parents knew? Poncho said they were doing researching after they found out they were pregnant with me. That they were upset. It wasn't about the demon part of me, it was this. "They knew…"

"What you could become," Azsis pauses.

"How?"

Azsis smiles. "They knew of your history, and that you would turn eighteen the year of the Observance."

He doesn't say anything else, just stops, but he doesn't have to. My parents knew that this could happen? It's why they were upset. I can't begin to process all of this right now. My parent's secret was this moment, was me. "I can leave," I snap.

"Try, dear, I'd enjoy seeing it." Then, he throws out his

hands with a shrug. "But what would you go back to? You need me, and we need you." Azsis takes a step toward me. "Your people have a target on your head." Another step. "The Triad plotted your destruction. Your family has abandoned you, and you turned on them, in return. Can you go back to that? The whole society knows you're a halfling, and tonight you've betrayed them all. Your friends are injured or dead." Each time he speaks, he moves toward me, and soon he's close to me. Too close. "The boy you love chose himself. We," he points to him and Lia, "are the only ones who remain on your side. We have always been on your side."

Everyone did turn their backs on me. But I let them do that, didn't I? By turning to Lia instead of them. I caused the problems that made them turn away, and they tried. Gran tried. Pop, Carter. Everyone. I was too weak, too trusting and I didn't think. Because I failed them anyway.

Azsis runs a hand across my cheek, and I look up at him. "The key to ultimate power lies in you. Choose us and we will not fail you or abandon you. We will fight for you."

Wait a second... I step back. "That speech—it's the same one you gave Emmaline Spencer. I read it in her journal."

He smiles widely. "No need to let a good speech go to waste. They really are a pain in the arse to write fresh on the spot."

I shake my head. "Emmaline gave up everyone she loved for you. Where is she now? She failed to do what you'd hoped and you killed her."

"No, I'm right here," Lia says. She takes a step forward toward me. Her voice is low and soft. "I've been with you all along."

"You're Emmaline?"

Her blue eyes, human eyes, shine back at me. Eyes that look like Gran's, like Mom's, like mine. I'd never seen it before. Or maybe I hadn't wanted to see it.

"I felt it was best if I got to meet you, since you were so curious about me. I wanted to guide you on your path," she says.

Emmaline Spencer is Lia. I should've known there was a reason she was always there, grooming me, pulling me toward this side. Carter knew. He never thought she was sincere. "How?"

Azsis wraps an arm around her. "Emmaline has been with me for centuries. We call her Lia now, less connection to her forgotten life."

"A nickname," she adds.

Emmaline Spencer. My great-great-great-whatever-grandmother who gave up her power to run off with her demon lover. She's the reason our family has demon blood, the reason I was a target. She's also the only person I've ever felt understood me as the outcast and the weak witch trying to prove her worth. She died centuries ago as a witch, but she's here as a demon with my mortal enemy, her original lover. The demon that killed my parents and wants me to join him now. She used me, and it was all for this.

"Look at me, Penelope." I glance up and she wraps her hand in mine. For a second, I let myself wonder if she looked like Gran in her human form. "This is where you are meant to be. Here, you are accepted and embraced without judgment. You only need to be what you are and it's respected here. Find a home with us. Your old life is gone now. They all know what you are, and reject you, but here, you can be everything you've always wanted."

I could walk away from that. I could stay here. Trade being a witch for being a demon. Pick them over my family. But she's my family too, in some way. No. That doesn't change anything.

"But at the cost of killing all the witches. I won't do it."

Lia smiles. Emmaline, rather. "Close your eyes."

"I ca—"

She puts her hands over my eyes, and steers my body forward. My hand presses against the chill of the glass. Against it, a wave, a rush like the waves I feel when I use magic vibrates under me. I can feel every turn, every twist, and every tremor. Like this part of me has never been awakened before. "Do you feel it?"

"Yes," I reply.

Her breath is warm against my ear. It tingles, but the tingle is like a breeze against a storm. It barely matters under the pressure of the void. "The magic wants you. Embrace it, accept your role, and that feeling will never leave you. It will become part of you. Forever."

Forever. "How?"

"Embrace your demon hood and become ours," Lia says. Her voice is soothing, a lullaby. "End this battle that was never meant to exist. Witch and demon, Nons. The Statics, the people you love, millions you don't even know, we are all in your hands."

I pause. The magic still pulses under me, and I don't know how to deny it. I don't want to deny it. "How is this going to save the witches? It will kill them all."

"They die daily. This would rid them all of magic. It would end their fight. They could simply live."

"The hour is upon us." Azsis turns me to look at him,

away from the power of the void. Even though I'm not touching the glass, I can still feel it. "It's time for you to play your part."

I exhale, but the void makes it too hard to think clearly. I've been led here under false pretenses. I was wrong, and now everyone could die. "You're asking me to betray everyone and everything."

"This is a war, there are always casualties in war."

I shake my head. This isn't what I want. "I don't want to pick a side. I don't want any of this. I won't live knowing that I've ended the witches."

"You don't have a choice. Destiny," he says.

I stare at Azsis. His Non form doesn't hide who he really is to me anymore. What he is underneath. A demon. A murderer. A trickster.

A lie.

Destiny can go to hell. "I won't do it. I can fight you."

"Fight me?" He practically laughs it.

"I can use the void and I can leave right now."

I understand the void more now, and it's part of me. Being this close to it confirms how much it wants me. That means I could use it to get out.

"You could, but I still have some tricks up my sleeve. After all we have done to secure your place here," he says, moving closer toward me until he's inches from my face.

"What have you done?"

"Even if you go back, it will not be the same for you. Not for a girl with friends, no boyfriend, no status, no job—a *known* halfling."

The words sink in and the dots connect. "You did that? You told them all what I was?"

A smirk again, and it eats at me. "I had to. Lia warned you that you had too many relationships. It was our job to break them all, one by one," he says. "You know what they do to your kind. Do you think they'll allow a halfling traitor rejoin their world with no complaints? Your whole family will be ruined for harboring you."

I shake my head. He really did set me up. Lia set me up. He wanted me to be separate from my family, and he succeeded.

Azsis's eyes flash red, then green, and then returned to orange. "It's do or die time—no pun intended—so allow me to lay the rest of my cards on the table. Don't think of it as a betrayal or ending the witches. Think of it as saving one you love desperately."

He snaps his fingers, and three demons appear. The demons hold down Connie's arms, and she fights to get away from them.

"Connie!"

She's still in her hospital gown. Even from the distance in the room, I can see the circles under her eyes and how pale she is. They woke her up. They had the ability all along—and now I'm furious, because lying to me is one thing, but messing with my sister is a whole other story.

"Penelope," she yells back, her eyes wide and the demons keeping her back. She looks from me to Lia to Azsis and back. "Where are we? What's going on?"

"Poor dear," Azsis says, his breath next to my ear. "It must be a shock to wake up here after all these weeks. I wonder if she'd have the strength to survive me taking her essence, performing the ritual, and direct contact with the void. Or would it consume her entirely? Even I am not certain of that answer. Shall we try?"

"You said it was me," I snap, whipping around to face him.

"It is you, but I will use her if I need to. That's the bonus of having two halflings in one generation on the same bloodline—they're replaceable."

"What's happening?" Connie yells. Tears fall down her cheek, and I can't think. One of the demon's claws presses into my sister's throat, and she cries out as a single drop of blood falls.

"I can't kill them all for her. I can't."

Azsis snaps his fingers, then Gran and Pop appear instantly held down by more demons. He has my whole family. I can't do this. I can't think. I can't...

"Tick tock, Miss Grey," Azsis calls over Connie's screams.

"Fine, whatever you want," I shout.

Azsis's hand freezes in the air toward the demons, and the one with its claw on my sister's neck drops its hand. I close my eyes and inhale. I've traded everyone for my family.

"I knew you'd come around, love."

I stare into the void, and my entire body responds to the power of it. Azsis stands a breath away, and we both stare into the void. "The ability to harness both sides is only a portion of the deal. The willingness to do it is another, and someone who has done it before, that's the winner. It's why you're perfect," Azsis says, and he turns me toward the glass room.

The magic beyond the wall is crazy, like someone set

it into overdrive. I can almost feel it coursing through me with the reckless abandon. Lia looks intently at me, so much that I can almost feel her eye, but I refuse to acknowledge her. She was using me too, for this. All of it was for this. The destruction of the other side. My friends, my family. Witches everywhere.

"Let my family go," I say.

"They're insurance, love," he says, shaking his head. "Once you enter the void, you will perform the ceremony the same way Lia taught you. You enter alone, do the Restitution, and then it's over."

I stare into the void. If I don't do the Restitution, then they can't try this again for a century.

"Now, my dear," Lia whispers.

Azsis's eyes are a surprisingly dark shade of orange. His hand presses into my back, and he pushes me through the glass. I don't fall, or get cut, or bleed. There's no wall for me anymore. It's only air and my body beats against it into the void. I feel like I'm standing perfectly still, but I'm not.

Then, I feel it. This burning sensation that's lava in my veins, way more intensely than when the void was trying to make a connection with me. It's eating at me, peeling me apart, hollowing me out, and replacing it with cotton, with silk, with bubbles. I'm brimming over and I can't explain the feeling. It's painful and exotic and powerful and exhilarating all at once.

When I open my eyes, Azsis is staring at me from behind the glass. "Radiant," he says. I try to see what he's seeing, but everything around me is white and bright, foggy and clear, nothing and everything.

"Do it now," he says.

I look past him toward my sister and my grandparents. Their eyes are wide. Gran looks worried, Connie's jaw is dropped, and Pop's face is hard to read. I wonder what they're seeing. What are they thinking? There's some awe in Connie's eyes and remorse, but not betrayal. She doesn't hate me for this, and she should.

Panic fills my chest and my eyes dart between my family and Azsis. *I can't do this. I can't have their blood on my hands, every single witch. I have to stop this. I'm not ready to sacrifice myself or Carter or my family for demons to thrive.* But I'm standing in the middle of the void, and I've let it come too far. I'm lost. I can't turn around anymore.

"Now, Penelope," Azsis shouts, pounding on the wall.

I take a deep breath and try to push away all my feelings of uncertainty. I am bigger than this. I can figure a way out. Mind racing, I start the ritual with the Dragooni as Lia showed me. The ritual starts out with a scattering of the Dragooni ashes in a circle around me. As I move, I think. The void is mine, and now that I'm not marked I can harness both sides. What happens if I use them both inside the void? That's it. Azsis has basically given me a power boost. I can use it to my advantage.

The circle now complete, I lower the Dragooni to the ground. After the spell, I'm supposed to use the dagger to join my blood with the herbs. A completion of the cycle. I can feel Azsis watching me, even though I'm not looking at his face. Good. Watch me.

"*Renascentia redivivus, restituere, non est corpus,*" I start. Rebirth, recycle, restore, release. The words from the dagger. I glance toward the window, where Azsis and Lia watch excitedly. I fight down the feeling in my gut. It's now or never. "*Vita duo unum finem. Quid perditio haec verba factum invocábo.*"

The void seems to respond around me, the speed and power of it increasing. It's ready for the end. I'm not ready to end it. I'm just getting starting.

Azsis pounds on the glass. "The blood," he yells.

I meet his gaze this time and the void swirls around me like a vortex. I kick the herbs away from me and break the circle I made on the ground. If there's not a cycle, then there's not a ritual. With no blood to tie it together, this is simply dust on the floor. "No," I shout.

His eyes grow darker. Even through the magic of the void I can see that clearly. "No?"

"I won't do it."

There's a flash from the other side, and then a scream as he appears next to me. The magic flows freely through me, so much that I can literally see it dancing in and out of my pores as if I'm fog and not solid. But it bounces off Azsis. Each time he moves, the direct contact with the magic makes his skin seem to change colors and peel away the Non-flesh. This is why they needed me, someone who could handle the purity of the void because for whatever reason, none of the demons could stand it in here. All the more reason my new plan could work.

I take the moment to conjure up the essence. Hopefully my family is close enough that I can pull from them. Be stronger. It takes a moment to remember how to do it—it's been so long since I've used it—but then the power comes. I feel it tunneling into me, even though the void meets it with resistance. They're playing tug-of-war with my body.

Azsis knocks me to the floor, and breaks both my

concentration and hold on the essence. His talons are at my neck. "Say the words, girl. Finish this."

"Make me," I say.

"With pleasure," he says. Then my feet are off the ground and he tosses me across the room. I'm on my feet again quickly, trying to pull in the essence again. Azsis rushes toward me, swinging at me with nails extended. I duck under the movement and kick, taking his legs out. He's fast too and he's up, barreling toward me. I block it in time to avoid his knuckles meeting my mouth.

I'm stronger than him, he's said that. I close my eyes and let the magics pour through me. The void is more powerful, but I can feel the essence, too. They still fight with each other, but both want out. A tangle of good and evil. I focus all my energy, all the hatred toward this demon, the loss of my parents, of my power, the last few weeks of lies, of all this stuff with Carter toward the magic. Lia was wrong. Emotions aren't a liability—when I can channel them correctly, emotions make it better. They're another tool that I can use to make the magic stronger. The magic pours from me, straight toward Azsis.

The magic meets his form with a clash of light so bright I hide my eyes. His screams fill the air and I look up to see the magic levitate him into the air. He gurgles, spitting. A sound like a laugh squeezes through his half destroyed, melted, burned off face. The thing in front of me doesn't look like Non or demon. The magic is practically eating him, peeling his skin away from his bones, as it courses through his body like he's not solid. In one side and out the other. He's a melted toy, half of two things and not fully anything.

"You've lost. You've ruined yourself," he says, spitting

black demon blood. "You've destroyed your people even if you do nothing. The magic needs a sacrifice—it can't be stopped once it's started. If you don't release the void, then you destroy yourself and everyone here. You need me now, love."

Is he right? My plan was to stop the ritual, but the magic is still in the Statics. I try to think back on the things I read about the Restitution. I can't remember reading that anywhere…but the only solution kills the witches, and I can't do that.

"I don't need you," I say. I think I say it. It doesn't sound much like myself. How is he still bargaining when he's about to die?

"Do this and I can give you the one thing you've always desired—magic. I have your essence, intact." He says the words slowly and then smiles. I look at him as his skin literally melts off onto the floor. The orange demon skin underneath turns black. "That's right. I kept it. I've been saving it for you as a souvenir. A token of good will."

"It's a part of you. That's how it works." I yell.

He releases a crackling, breathy laugh. "I'm an old demon, and I have control that others don't. Your essence is in a jar on my shelf with all of my most prized possessions."

That's when I hear another bang from the other side of the wall. From the corner of my eye, I see Carter.

Chapter Forty-Four

Pen is standing in a ring of fire with a demon. Her eyes find mine for a second, and then I see she's not standing in fire, she is the fire. It's beautiful. I almost can't be sure where I should look. Staring at her is bright, but she's too commanding to look anywhere else.

"Behind you!" Someone shouts and I roll out of the way and then slash my blade through a demon's neck. Guts everywhere. My eyes search the room for the voice and find Connie with her grandparents, Frank and Deborah Warren, being held by some demons.

Three demons leave Connie's side and head toward me. Only Lia stands next to Connie now, but I'm getting her after I finish with them.

I pull up my shirt where four iron knives laced with salt are shoved into my belt. Before the first demon reaches me, I toss one of the salted knives straight at its heart. Bullseye. The demon explodes on impact.

The second demon, hazel colored, and the third demon, in Non form, don't give me much time to act after that. I pull a salt pellet gun from my boot, but the hazel one kicks it away from me. It slides across the room, and I don't have time to search for it before the Non-wearing demon jumps me. I grab a second knife and slice through its arm, leaving it screaming in pain as the salt burns. The other tackles me.

Stupid move.

I plunge the knife into its heart. The hazel-colored demon dies.

All that's left is Lia, the Non-demon, and me. I pull the final two knives from my belt and smile. Demons are weaker in a Non form, and there's no way it could shed its skin faster than I could kill it. I throw some magic toward the demon's feet and it tumbles to the ground. It hisses, and I throw another knife. The demon jumps out of the way to miss it and charges toward me. Before it's about to hit me, I toss some salt from my pocket on it, right in the eyes.

The demon stumbles backward so I run, knife ready, and stab it.

I win.

Lia claps her hands slowly. "Good job, halfling. You have a knack for killing demons."

"Demons have a knack for pissing me off."

Lia smirks. "Kriegen may have been right about you. It's not too late to join us," she says. She points toward the window. "Penelope has signed on."

"One problem with that," I start and pull out the salt gun in my pocket. "You're going to be dead."

Lia hisses and charges me. The gun shoots out of my hand, landing across the room, and now it's the demon and me. I really hate her.

Lia charges toward me, throwing magic at me as she runs. It finds my body at full force, and sends me back into the wall. She's stronger than I expected. Lia swings her leg at my face, but I block the kick and grab her by the arm. She ducks my counterattack and lands on one leg as the other sweeps me off my feet. I roll as she moves toward me, her fist coming toward my face. A shot of magic zooms against my shoulder.

She sends some magic toward me, and I roll across the floor, trying to stay out of the line of fire. She growls, then hurls her body toward me and flattens me. I struggle but the magic keeps me down. She sits on my stomach. I really hate this demon.

Lia has me pinned down, her nails pressing into my temple. I try to maneuver around her, but I can't. She bares her teeth and leans in toward me before I can process the chance to scream or fight anymore.

Then there's a gunshot and she freezes, her teeth inches from my neck. She rises slowly, and blood bubbles from her mouth. A second later, she explodes, guts flying across the room. I scamper backward in order to sit up, and then I see it.

Deborah is pointing the gun I'd lost in our direction, hands shaking. She saved my life.

There's a scream, and we both look over to the glass window.

Chapter Forty-Five

Azsis falls to the ground. His Non-form is completely gone, and his scales separate from his skin. They fall to the ground like corn flakes, dry and brittle, and shatter into dust when they land. What's left of his body is paper-thin and discolored. Parts of him are burnt away, leaving holes in his what used-to-be solid form. His eyes are tinged in black, wide, and bug-eyed from his skull. But it's the scream, the way he wails, that's the most jarring.

A green trail of fog rushes in the void, mingling with the gray that already exists. Azsis tries to reach out for it, but after a few seconds, the green changes into the same gray. Beyond the glass, Lia's body is a crumpled heap next to Carter and Gran. The magic was hers.

This is my chance.

I pull the black dagger from my boot, and use the void to prop up Azsis. His eyes are wide, staring at me.

"We can still do this," he says, but his voice lacks the same confidence. It's barely a whisper. "You and I are one, Penelope. We are cut from the same. I wanted to be loved, but God chose his humans. You want to be loved, but they all chose others. Not you. Never you."

I shake my head. "You're wrong. All those people out there, they chose me. And I choose them."

His eyes widen when he sees the black dagger. He mutters incoherent words, but what he has to say isn't relevant. Not anymore. Without my lifting a finger, the dagger tunnels into his chest. He falls to the ground and a high-pitched whistle fills the room. His body lights up in flames and the smell of burning eggs fills the void. I see his magic rejoin the void, and then he's ash and the dagger clatters against the floor.

I stand there and the void takes over my body. Where's the essence? I try to pull it back, but there's nothing that comes. Even with my family outside the window, I can't connect to it. I'm too late. It thinks I've chosen the void. A cry bubbles in my throat, but like a switch my worry fades. The void calms me. I could stand here in its center source and let it flow from me forever. In and out. The magic is a seduction, and as much as I shouldn't, I want it. I want the magic to be part of me. To never let go or leave.

"Penelope," Pop yells, pounding on the barrier between the void and that room.

I find Carter's gaze next to him. "Pen, stop. It's nearly dawn."

Dawn. I only have until dawn to make the sacrifice, to

choose one side of magic to survive.

I push the void away so I can be in control, but it doesn't work. I can't make it stop. The void gets stronger. Burns hotter. Blows faster. Then, I don't want to stop, even though I should. This isn't what I want to happen, but the magic coaxes me. It tries to make me forget the stakes. To bask in being this powerful. To being the sole witch who can stand in its presence.

"Come out here," Gran yells through the glass. Gran, Pop, Connie, and Carter are all staring at me. For them, I try to push the void out, but it refuses to leave. To let me move through it. I can't do anything. It's too powerful.

I didn't perform the ceremony, so the witch world is safe. My family will live, but I won't be with them. I've made my choice, even if I didn't mean to, and my fate is here. Sealed. The void won't leave me and the essence won't come to me. I can't stop this. Not now. I'm not a witch anymore. The void has claimed me, forever.

"I can't go out. Just leave."

"We're not leaving you," Carter calls.

"Go! I'm sorry. I'm so sorry." I look at Carter. "I love you. Go."

A new feeling rushes into me, knocking the breath from me. The essence. I try to reach for as much of it as I can access, and it flows in. The void and the essence pull at my insides, both trying to reclaim me. They twist together my stomach, latch on to my nerves, fight inside me—and I scream.

Chapter Forty-Six

I stare at Pen through the glass and hear those words. Somehow they're an anchor in the noise and chaos. When she screams, I can't leave her, not like this. I want to be here for her. I turn to Connie and her grandparents.

"You have to go," I say.

Connie grabs my arm. "What are you doing?"

I look toward Penelope, giving her sister my answer. I can't leave her here to deal with this alone. I move toward the glass and Penelope calls my name. Somehow, maybe because I'm a halfling, I push through the glass and straddle the line between both sides. One foot in the void and one out of it. Immediately the void pushes through my skin and it stings. It burns and lingers, like getting punched in the gut, stabbed in the eye, choking on popcorn all at once.

"Get out of here, Carter," Penelope yells through the foggy void.

But I can't. Not without her. I open my eyes. It's hard to see in all the swirling mist, but she's clear and bright like stars. The girl draped in fire and smoke. The sole witch, marked with magic on both sides. Without thinking, I move toward her. The magic burns at my skin, like a windburn and a sunburn, like the times my father and I used to go sailing near Annapolis. Tears sting at my eyes. It feels like the skin is peeling off my muscles, but it's a good pain. A purposeful one.

I find her hand somehow, and I am walking on clouds. It's the sun up here. The void is stronger than any drug could be. My brain is mush. If this is what it feels like for her, then it's no wonder that Pen couldn't stop using the void. No wonder my mom chose this over me. No wonder that Pen chose this, even to the point of it destroying her. She let it fill her up until it poisoned her, until she became something else. Until she popped.

The image of the red balloon flashes in my head. Then the blue balloon. My father popping it.

That's not how we use magic. This is not how Prescott men act.

I'm snapped back into the moment as the pain comes rushing to the surface of my head. I can't handle it. The void grows stronger around me, and everything is fuzzy. I fall to my knees. I still see the memory. The red-turned-blue balloon popping. My dad's face.

Popping.

My hand touches a pile of dust and then hard, cold

metal. I look down and the symbols of the dagger shimmer up at me. I pick it up. The dagger releases, but it also severs a connection. It's the one thing I needed to stop this. To stop her. And here it is, in my hand.

Pop.

I can stop this.

Somehow, I make it to my feet, and Penelope is screaming, crying out, glowing and shining like the sun, fire and heat. The void is burning my face, but all I see is her. Each step closer toward her is needles in my skin, movement against the wind, but finally, she's in my arms. I don't need to see the clock to know we're almost out of time. I need to sever this before the time is up. When it's up, she's gone from me forever

"Get away from me. Get out," she yells through tears.

"I won't leave you."

"Then we'll both die."

I pull her closer to me. "I love you," I say. I press her lips to mine and I want to kiss her. I want to kiss her while the world we live in goes to hell. Literally. Forget it all here with her. So, I do. I enjoy the moment with the girl, the feel of her lips on mine.

And then I slide the dagger into her side.

She falls into me, and I stand with her body bleeding into my shirt. She glances up, tears in her eyes. "I love you," I repeat. I say it over and over, hoping she understands what I did. The dagger severs a connection. It was the only way. To make it stop, I had to sever her connection to the magic.

Lightening flashes and the fire fades away, seeps out of her skin and into the room, and she starts to look like herself again.

Then she turns white, and I swoop her into my arms. The void thrashes against us as I carry her out. It almost feels angry. It's lost the thing it wanted. Each step I take with her makes it push against me. My legs are stiff in the wind of the void, like walking through quicksand during a snowstorm. I hold Penelope as tightly as I can in my arms, even as the void pulls at her, at me.

When I finally reach the other end, the glass lets me through, and I fall to my knees. My skin is still burning, and when I look I can see that I'm bleeding everywhere. Little marks stitched across my skin. Pen's blood on my shirt. Her head in the crook of my arm. Her family gathers around us, and then there's a cracking sound.

"Get down," Frank shouts out a protection spell as there's an explosion and the glass shatters around us, pulverizing everything like an unexpected downpour.

Chapter Forty-Seven

I wake up in my bed still sore. I'm not sure how long it's been, but I force myself up, and a dull ache forms in my gut. Everything that happened is fuzzy. I remember pieces, images. I remember everything clearly before I stepped into the void. The attack on the Observance, that Lia was really Emmaline, that Azsis brought in my family to motivate me. I sort of remember this feeling, that I had all this power at my fingertips, but I can't place what it felt like to be there.

I can see flashes of Azsis' body as he walked to me in the void, his skin falling apart, and I remember Carter's face with the fog swirling around him. Then I woke up here with doctors and medicine. What happened to everyone?

There is something gone. It is not so tangible,

unexplainable really. Just gone.

I anchor myself on the dresser as I try to move. I only take a couple of steps before my door opens and Carter rushes to my side. He looks the same, except for the small red cuts that cover his skin.

"You're awake," he says. I look up at him and he freezes, his face changing slightly.

"What is it?"

He shakes his head. "Your eyes."

I look past him at the mirror on my wall. Even in the distance, I can see it. My once blue eyes are now an emerald green, bright, and deep. "Holy cow," I say, taking a step toward the mirror. My eyes are green now. Green like a demon. This is because of the void? "I have green eyes." I have to repeat it to be sure.

Carter rests a hand on my shoulder. "I like it," he says with a smile. His eyes reflect back at me, a little lighter than mine. Not green like a demon's, green like Carter's. But having these eyes, after all the things I've done, the witches will never accept me. Not once the news spreads.

What I've done. I've caused so much damage. I grasp onto Carter's arm. "What happened? Are the demons still causing trouble? I didn't know they were going to attack the Observance. How many people were injured?" The words keep tumbling out, like the weight of the guilt I'm feeling is pushing them all to the surface. Tears force out of my eyes. "And the Statics? Carter, what happened to everyone? I did this. I caused all of this. How many people died because of me? How could I do this?"

Carter pulls me into him, and I gasp for air. He's trying to calm me down but I want answers. "Tell me, please," I manage.

He strokes my hair and lowers me to sit on the edge of my bed. With a sigh, he sits next to me. "The Statics—it all went away. The witches still have magic, but the Statics don't. It disappeared while we were…there, I guess. The demons are still here. The balance is in check."

I exhale. "How many died?"

"I don't have a number."

I close my eyes, trying to block the tears. Carter's hand rests on mine. "The Triad and the council are trying to clean up and recover. They want to have a meeting with us. I'm going tomorrow to answer questions, and they'll want to talk to you when you're better."

"What will they do to me?"

Carter exhales. "I have no idea."

I look back at the mirror, and the feeling returns, the emptiness. I focus on the magic that I usually pull from Carter, the intensity of the void trying to get out of me. I picture using the magic, making what I want a reality. Nothing happens. Gran, Pop, and Connie are downstairs, and I could focus on them. Focus on using the essence that I can pull from in their presence. But looking at my eyes and feeling the nothingness, I know. "I don't have magic anymore."

Carter meets my gaze in the mirror. "What?"

"It's gone." He looks surprised, but he's resigned. I replay the moments in my mind. I only had the void, then the essence came out of nowhere.

"The dagger severs a connection," I whisper. I was using them both when Carter stabbed me. "It severed both connections." The only reason everyone is safe again is because I don't have magic. I can't be the sole witch or a halfling or a demon queen. Without magic, I'm not a threat to anything.

"We can figure out a way to get it back. I promise, I'll figure it out," Carter says.

I stare at myself, at the green eyes, and suddenly, I don't want magic. Magic got me into this mess—I never felt like I was enough without it. Everything I did was to get it back. I've spent years working toward that goal, toward finding Azsis. But he's gone. It's gone. Maybe I'm not meant to have magic.

"I don't need it," I say. Carter looks surprised, but also a little relieved. Happy, almost. "I'm a Static now." As I say it, the weight of that rushes over me. I don't have magic, and if I'm Static then I can't be part of this world. I'll have to leave everything behind.

Carter wraps his arms around my neck and kisses my cheek. "I love Statics."

• • •

Gran, Pop, and Connie all stare at me in silence when I finish telling them everything. "I'm sorry for all the things I did," I say. And I am. I wanted to protect them all from what I did, and I broke my family more than anyone else.

"Please tell me that you'll all forgive me. Whatever happens with the Triad, I need you."

Gran nods in my direction. "We love you, Penelope, but it's going to take some time for us to forget all of this. We have a lot of repairing to do in our family." Gran looks between us. "No more secrets. We have to trust one another."

Pop takes her hand, and looks at me. "And that you're grounded until further notice probably goes without saying."

"That's all?" I say.

"For now. Let's wait until we hear from the Triad."

Gran moves first across the living room and pulls me into a hug. She wraps her arms around me so tightly that it hurts to breathe. I don't complain, though. I like this moment. I needed it. Wrapped in her arms, I cry. Gran doesn't let go. If anything, the tears make her hold me tighter.

She presses a kiss against my forehead, and whispers in my ear that it will be all right. I stay in her arms like that until the crying stops. I don't deserve them.

"You don't have magic at all?" Connie asks.

I shake my head. "It's probably better this way. I think I've had enough of magic forever."

Pop raises an eyebrow. "It will certainly make things less interesting around here. We could all be well-served with that."

Connie smiles at me, her eyes soft. "I love you."

Considering she was asleep for nearly a month of her life, she's taking all of this extremely well. My sister, ladies and gentlemen, classier than I can ever be.

"Maybe this means I will always win at rock, paper, scissors," she adds.

I shake my head with a smile. "I'm still your big sister. I know how you think."

She holds out her fist. I do the same. We move our hands three times and Connie holds out paper, which I knew she would do. I pick scissors.

I could let her win this one, but I don't want her to think I've gone too soft.

• • •

Later, I step outside to call Ric. He talked with Connie

while I was sleeping, but that was before anyone knew what happened with me. I owe him an apology and explanation. Nerves creep up in my stomach. He has every right to completely deny me forgiveness, to make me beg. I'm prepared for that. I'm prepared for worse, I realize, as I pull up his number. For flat out rejection, for him to ignore me, for...he answers on the second ring.

"I am the worst friend and if you never forgive me then I totally understand," I say in a breath.

He laugh-sighs into the phone. A sound of relief, almost. "I wondered when I'd hear your voice."

I gulp back tears. I guess once you cry, it's harder to turn off the emotions that brew under the surface. "The things I said were horrible. I have not been supportive of you at all through your loss and the rest of everything. I know you were trying to help."

"I was so worried when Connie told me you were conked out too," he starts. Ric doesn't sound angry, which is good. Angry Ric isn't someone I've ever been able to reason with. "I texted every hour. Like, for real, you Grey girls are such drama queens."

I laugh, and the tears squeeze out of my eyes. "Maybe we like to steal the spotlight."

"To steal it and dance in it for three encores."

I laugh, which was what he was going for. The tension seems to slip away, at least for this moment. It does give me strength to face whatever happens next. "I'm so sorry."

"I forgive you. You're my family," he says. He is my family, too. His voice gets louder and seems to drift at once, and I turn the volume up on my phone. "I'm not complete without you—you're the queen of stupid."

His voice has a weird echo. "Are you in a tunnel or something?"

"No, why?"

"I hear two of you."

"Oh! That's because I'm behind you," he says. I turn around on the porch and he's already on the bottom step. He slides his phone into his pocket and smiles at me. His eyes are big, rimmed in red from a lack of sleep or crying and his jaw has the thin scruff of a red beard. That's new for him. His hair is darker, a light brown now, and it's been shaved. I like this look on him. He looks thinner than he did when he left, but still strong. Still able to kick someone's ass, at least with some sleep.

He holds his arms out for me. Wordlessly, we hug each other. It feels right here. He squeezes me so tight I think he may snap me in half. I don't complain, though. "I thought I'd lost you, too," he whispers.

"You're stuck with me," I say back. "Unless you squeeze me to death."

He laughs and loosens his grip a little. We stay that way a few more seconds, and when we part, Ric keeps his hands on my forearms. "Girl, you better believe you are going to tell me every single detail. I'm going to call you stupid, over and over, and then I'm going to make you sit through every detail of my recoveration."

I smile. "I can't wait."

His hands fall away from my arms and he's staring at me. I know why before he says, "Wow, your eyes. You can definitely make green work."

I let the words stick with me. Stick to me. Become me. "I sure hope so."

Epilogue

Three Months Later

It's the perfect day for a run. Plus, I'm going to eat so much birthday cake tonight that I'll need it. The wind has a fall chill in the air, but there's still a glimpse of summer that is remarkable. I switch channels on my radio app and stop when I hear Victor's name on the WNN station.

"Change has come — and it's not the leaves. Tell us, Mr. Prescott, about the new Triad," the announcer says.

Victor's voice fills my ears. "We're growing a new leadership and life for our people. Statics, halflings, and witches, united in a common cause. It's an exciting time, and also a challenging one. This change in leadership will unite all in our community. The Triad, over the next year, will enlist an advisory committee run by a halfling, a witch, and a Static—equal representation for all parts. This is to build a pathway for the entire Triad to be run by a representative from each."

"And the Enforcers can expect a change as well?"

"Yes, Bob. The new task team will specialize in integrating Statics into witch society. We'll be training Enforcers to track demons before they attack, equipping all witches with tools in defense, and we'll continue safeguarding Nons, all in effect this month," he answers.

"Remarkable, really. What inspired all this change?"

I smile as I turn down a path. Obviously, he can't say everything that inspired this change, but he can certainly spin a story. He is still Victor Prescott, after all. I can imagine him there with that smile. The token Prescott smile.

"When the Statics got magic, it really made us think and revealed some negativity in our role as a community. As you are aware, after Miss Penelope Grey's outing as a halfling, and the incident at the Observance, others came forward. Pillars in our community—and my son was among them. It is due to his leadership that we have a real plan for change."

"And what of the challenges ahead for the change you're talking about? Old habits die hard," the radio anchor says. Indeed they do. The last three months of restructuring haven't been met with simplicity. Just determining how to do it was a nightmare for everyone.

Victor doesn't even hesitate. "We're talking about changing a stigma that has been around since our creation. Good and evil is black and white in our beliefs, but we're learning that there are also gray areas. It's the gray we've been afraid of. It will take time before a complete removal of prejudice against halflings or Statics occurs in our community. Acceptance is slow in coming, but we are making strides. Under new leadership, at the brink of a new era, they will be achieved someday."

I couldn't have said it better myself, Mr. Prescott.

"I am a supporter of this change myself with a personal stake in its success."

"Me as well," Victor says.

"Speaking of personal, your son Carter Prescott will be serving on the committee as the halfling representative?"

"Yes, and he's an excellent tracker. Remarkable young man, but I'm biased."

"And who else can we expect to see step up?"

"Ric Norris is representing the witches, and he offers a new perspective to change in the Enforcer pairings. Kelsey Arthur, granddaughter of the late Lindley Arthur, will be representing the Statics."

I flick the volume off with a smile. I always knew that Carter was meant for bigger things. At least, in all of this, good has happened. Victor asked me to represent the Statics on the committee, but I turned him down. I'm not really a good representative for Statics, even if am one now. I'm still trying to make it through a day without people asking me to tell the story of what happened during the Observance or if I knew about Carter.

Speaking of Carter, I'm supposed to meet him. I have only seen him at supervised visits to my house, thanks to my three-month grounding. But it's my birthday weekend, so I'm finally allowed some freedom.

I turn on the path and start back to my car. The wind

rustles the leaves as I run, pounding my feet against the ground. Not having magic, and being grounded, has provided the extra time my life has. More time to run with Connie, to kiss my boyfriend, to be with my family, to hang out with Ric whenever he's not busy working with the committee. The absolute best part is that I haven't had to deal with demons.

It's sort of nice.

The bridge back to my car is only feet away when I sense it, inhale the air, and stop running. Sulfur.

That isn't my duty anymore.

I can ignore this.

I keep running, grasping on to the salt necklace around my neck. I may not be a witch, but I'm never going to stay unprotected again. I've only moved a few feet when someone steps out in front of me. I gasp and freeze on the path, heart pounding.

"Poncho," I say. I've never seen him out of the library, and it's jarring. He seems so free now. It must be nice to be out in his real form. I pull my earbuds out, and glance past him toward the sun that reflects off the water. His being here can't be good.

"Miss Grey, I didn't mean to startle you."

I wave him off without words and look at him. I haven't seen or heard from him in three months, not since Carter and I took him the black dagger for him to destroy. I also gave him back my relay, since I had no use for it. "It's been a while."

"Yes," he says. "And I must say it shall be even longer before we ever meet again. If we ever do."

"What's going on?"

Poncho takes a step forward. "I wanted to thank you for

your actions. It's lovely to be home, where I belong, again."

Home. Not sure exactly if that's hell or De'Intero. "Why did they let you back in after all this time?"

A smile spreads across his face. "You killed Azsis, the demon who banned me from hell. With him gone, I was able to return."

Of course it was Azsis. All those times I looked for information about him, I had the answers in front of me. Poncho knew, but he wasn't allowed to tell me. "Glad I could be of service," I say.

"I wanted to give you a present." I watch as he pulls a small jar from thin air. Inside the jar, a gold fog floats slowly. It's a mist and a liquid and not quite anything, but it is beautiful. "Your essence," he says.

I stare at him. I must be going deaf because he didn't say that. "My what?"

He holds it out toward me. "It was found among Azsis's belongings, and I wanted to return it you."

I stare at the magic in a jar. Magic in a jar. My magic. The thing I've always wanted is practically being handed to me on a silver platter. And even crazier? Azsis really did keep it as a souvenir. "I can't take that. It will kill me."

After what happened with the Statics, I learned when magic's been mixed with another it is a poison. That may be my essence, but if Azsis used it, then it's tainted.

"No," Poncho says. "It's been in this containment since he took it. It's not tainted. It's pure and it's yours."

The gold magic dances in the jar. My magic. Magic I thought I'd never have again. I've been getting used to living my own way. I kind of like the possibilities that lay ahead now, more than the limitations. "Magic has possibilities," he says suddenly. "If you use it well."

Someone pinch me.

There's no way a demon is standing here offering me back magic and I'm having a brain fart. Poncho steps toward me, and places it in my hands. "Consider it a birthday gift." The magic is warm in my hands, and I can feel it stirring in the jar.

"I don't know if I want it."

"Either way, it belongs to you. You may use it, or not use it, however you please. Your destiny is yours now."

"Thank you," I say, pressing my palms against the jar.

Poncho nods, and then, without another word, he's gone.

Carter is waiting for me when I get to the top of the hill. The sun has already set and the stars are bright around us. When I see him there, my heart races. That boy is perfection. I don't deserve him. When he sees me, he smiles that drop-dead smile. Not the Prescott smile, the Carter smile. The one that's just for me. The one that's always been for me.

He holds his hand out to me and pulls me the rest of the way up the hill. "Hey, birthday girl," he says. I love the way he says hey. I glance beyond him, and see the spread on the ground of blanket and cookies.

"Cookies?" I ask.

Carter whispers in my ear. "Baked for you. Sorry it took so long. My girlfriend keeps me pretty busy."

I entwine my fingers with his, and they fit there with his. And he bakes cookies for me. I'm lucky. The luckiest.

We sit on the blanket, and he passes me a cookie. "I

heard the news. Victor is really supporting you."

"Yeah," Carter says. "He's a changed man."

"Aren't we all?"

"You're a man? We should talk about that," Carter says.

I elbow his side and he laughs. I look down at the cookies and my mind drifts to the magic in my car, my magic, preserved in a jar. Do I want that? To be magical again? The last few months have been really nice.

"What's up?" he asks.

I sigh and look into his eyes. "Would you love me if I was a demon?"

"You were a demon, and I did love you."

I wave him off. "Technicalities."

Carter leans in and kisses my cheek. "I'd love you if you were a demon," my other cheek, "or a witch," my forehead, "or a Static." I snort, totally ruining the moment. I've been both. "I'd even love you as a Non."

He presses his lips against mine. I have butterflies. And not because of magic. These are all because of him. I pull away from the kiss with a smile. "You only say that because I'm not boring yet."

"That is one thing I'm never going to be worried about," he says. "Why are you asking?"

I shrug. "Would you love me if I was three-headed dragon?"

"No," he says. "Two heads are my limit."

He laughs and I press a quick kiss against his lips again.

"Try the salted caramel chip," he says, passing me a cookie. I curl up in his arms and we lie back on the blanket and study the stars. They're golden and shimmering, dancing in the sky, magic all on their own. And right now, I'm content.

Acknowledgments

Right now, I am content as well. That's only because of the many people who guided me through this book and made it a reality. Writing a sequel really does take a village. Even though we writers hear that we don't really know it's our turn to face the challenge. Consider me a believer—and I'm so grateful for all the support and encouragement I received during this process.

Firstly, a huge thank you to my agent Nicole Resciniti, who has held my hand, fought ferociously, and been there with me each step of the way. She is more amazing (and I am luckier) than anyone knows.

To Traci, without whom this book would not exist, because she read every draft and helped me make my ideas work. She's the Best. Cheerleader. Ever. Even dedicating this book to her can't express how much she did, or my gratitude for her friendship.

To my editor, Laura Anne Gilman, for helping this

book turn into what I was trying so hard to make it be—and having it make sense! All the readers thank you, too. And my subsequent editor, Stacy Abrams, for everything you've done to give Pen and Carter's story a grand finale. I'm very grateful to have had this chance to work with you. Subsequently, but equally, to many hugs to Alycia Tornetta and everyone in the Entangled team.

To Patricia, Asja, Ashley, Lelia, Tim, Jenn, and the phenomenal ladies of the HB&K, who listened to me complain (a lot) for months and cry (a lot) for months and never ever let me give up. Thank you for reminding me I could do this, of why I do this, for listening, and for believing in me more than I believe in myself.

And to Jenny P., who not only gave this book a name, but also a face. Thank you for connecting the story and characters in my head to a cover.

To all the readers who love Pen and Carter like I do—you are golden. Thank you for your kindness, for your excitement, and for your Carter-swoon tweets and posts (he loves you, too, but his girlfriend may kick your butt if you try anything). This one is for you.

About the Author

Danielle Ellison is from West Virginia, where she spent her childhood pretending to fly, talking to imaginary friends, and telling stories. She hasn't changed much since then. When she's not writing, Danielle is probably drinking coffee while fighting her nomadic urges, watching too much TV, or dreaming of the day when she can be British. You can find her on twitter @DanielleEWrites.

Made in the USA
Charleston, SC
12 July 2015